I0579807

LUNAR CYCLE BOOK 1

DEBRIS DREAMS

残骸梦幻

DAVID COLBY

THINKING INK PRESS
CAMPBELL, CALIFORNIA

© Copyright David Colby.

Debris Dreams was previously published by Candlemark and Gleam in 2012.

All rights reserved. No part of this publication may be reproduced or transmitted in any form or by any means, electronic or mechanical, including photocopying and recording, or introduced into any information storage and retrieval system without the written permission of the copyright owner and the publisher of this book. Brief quotations may be used in reviews prepared for inclusion in a magazine, newspaper, or for broadcast. For more information, contact: editorial@thinkinginkpress.com.

This book is a work of fiction. Names, characters, businesses, organizations, places, events and incidents either are the product of the author's imagination or are used fictitiously. Any resemblance to actual persons, living or dead, events, or locales is entirely coincidental.

Published by Thinking Ink Press
P.O. Box 1411, Campbell, California, 95009
First printing, 2016

ISBN 978-1-942480-13-6

Printed in the United States of America.

Project Credits

Cover art: Sandi Billingsley

Cover layout: Streetlight Graphics

Lunar Cycle branding and Orbital Map: Nathan Vargas

Proofreader: Gayle Schultz

Chinese Language Editor: Roger Que

Interior layout: Betsy Miller

DEDICATION

To the random musers.

The Earth is the only world known so far to harbor life.
There is nowhere else.
Like it or not, for the moment,
the Earth is where we make our stand.

Carl Sagan (1934-1996)

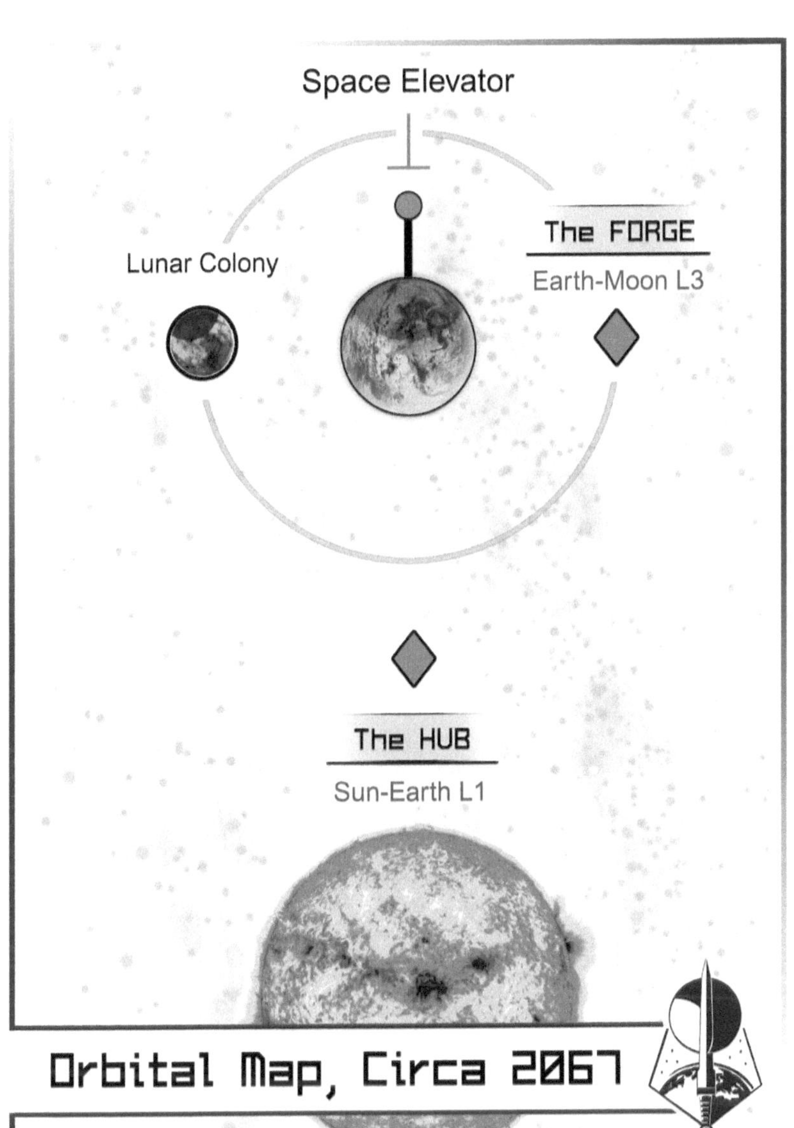

Orbital Map, Circa 2067

CHAPTER 1
THE DISASTER

12/22/2067

Sun-Earth L1, The Hub

1,500,000 kilometers above the surface of the Earth

I saw the flash out of the corner of my eye.

I didn't know it then, but two seconds earlier, my parents had died. They had been at ground zero, so at least it had been quick. I was in my bed at the time, looking at my wallpaper. I'd set it to my favorites—a few websites were above me and to the right, and I could switch between them by waving my hand. My vidchat with Sarah was right in front of me, and to my left, dominating the closer wall, was a spincorrected view of the Earth.

That was where I saw the flash.

"Did you see that?" I cut Sarah off mid-sentence, forgetting my light-lag etiquette for a moment.

"And then I heard that there were plans to actually restore the..." Sarah stopped, my interruption coming through. "No, what is it, Dru? Did something happen?" She sat before her camera, waiting for my return signal.

"*Qián kūn bǎo yòu!*" I sat up and turned to face my left wall full on. Despite my prayer, Buddha, the gods, and Jesus weren't particularly merciful or protective that day. See, the view of the Earth on my wall always had a little indicator on it so I'd know where my parents were, at the Elevator. The indicator should have been at geostationary orbit, thirty-five thousand clicks over the equator.

The indicator was gone. Was it a software glitch? An optical error in the telescope piping me the view? The worst option, the horrifying option—the true option—came to me last. My wallpaper shifted from my favorites to a series of emergency response drills, my lights dimming to low-power red. Mandarin flashed over the door: 好整以暇. *Haò zhěng yǐ xiá.* Don't Panic. Take Care of Pressing Matters.

I didn't think; I reacted. I rolled off the bed, and sailed through the air in the naturally graceful parabolic arc of any born Spacer. I hit the decking and bounced up before the gentle push of centrifugal force glued me back to the floor. My hands moved automatically, grabbing the wall and opening a hatch that revealed the clear-faced emergency breather. I jammed it onto my face and cycled the air, curling up against the corner of the room in the standard depressurization drill posture. I closed my eyes and tried to think around the instinct thundering through my brain. There'd be some actual situation reports coming out soon, with real information. I tried to stay calm, to not leap to any conclusions. But my gut said that something was wrong. Very, very wrong. Emergency drills were a fact of life in space. And like all facts of life, they had a time and a place.

The last drill had been two days ago.

"This is Daniel Lau speaking."

I opened my eyes and saw that my wallpaper had a vidchat open, showing Lau's face. He was the governor of the Hub, and he looked like someone had just whacked him on the side of the head.

"I...we're getting reports that there has been an accident at the Elevator. We're...our optics are doing preliminary scans, but we want everyone to remain calm."

The vid-chat vanished and I buried my face in my hands, rocking slightly on the floor. An accident? My heart felt like it was trying to punch its way out of my ribcage, but it had nothing on my stomach. I clenched my jaw and tried to keep the bile from rushing out of my throat. I hated vomiting. I hated it so much that it almost distracted me from the fear, the terror growing in my mind.

The Elevator had been my ticket out of this place. My ticket to Sarah. It's simple physics: moving anything anywhere in space costs reaction mass—remass—and propellant. That takes credits, which is simple economics. Governments have credits. Kenyan Aerospace corporations have credits. A sixteen-year-old pre-app does not have credits, end of story. Even with my weekly allowance and extra money from pushing my own mass in my various pre-app jobs, it would cost me a whole year's pay just to move one kilo from the Hub to the Earth.

Despite what they say about Spacer girls, we weigh a lot more than a kilo. But all those calculations, that kind of economics— it's all about pushing weight around with chemical rockets, fighting against the gravitational pull of the Earth. The Elevator was just that: an elevator from the top of Mt. Kilimanjaro to geostationary orbit. Thirty-five thousand kilometers of diamond cable, with cars running up and down it non-stop, no remass required. The cable was all that we had left to finish, after nine years of having my parents stolen away to work on it.

My parents had come to the Hub to build it, back in the '40s, and they had had me here when the place was still just half a wheel and some life support. I remember crying endlessly when they had been taken away on a shuttle, taken away to work on an Elevator they said would take a decade to finish. I'd learned to live with it, to see it as something to hope for and hate in equal measures.

I had help. No, better to say I had company. First, in the Crèche, I had all the flight techs and engineers and agri-experts who had pulled Crèche time to raise toddlers between their real jobs. It was like having a new mom or dad every few hours. Then, as a pre-app, I'd had the Lag-Net and tutor AIs to keep me occupied, as I learned about everything from basic math to current events. All of that had taught me about the Elevator, about how it worked and what my parents were doing so far away. It made me understand, even if I still didn't want to accept it sometimes.

And now it was...what? Damaged? Destroyed? I realized that the lights through my closed eyes had gone from red to white. I opened my eyes and looked around at my wallpaper.

Someone had hacked into our feeds. It was low-res and fuzzy, and lacked any contextual information or hypertext or even basic subtitling. It was just a simple vid stream showing the inside of a cavern. Gray rocks and compacted dirt made it look Lunar. The way the people moved confirmed it. There were six of them, in yellow and black jumpsuits, masks around their faces and harnesses on their chests that held all sorts of odds and ends. Their jumpsuits—their uniforms—looked familiar.

Their *toú zi*, their leader, let his last bounce settle and then reached up. He tapped a button on his mask and it became transparent. I immediately recognized his face from countless vids.

Omar Kaufman, the head of the Lunar Separatist Movement. His comrades bounced one last time, flanking him. Their masks became transparent now and I recognized them, too: Liesel Fong, Thomas Nau, Lakishma Gallagher, Doe Patil, Jax Vega.

Their names were the most common ones thrown out to scare people about Loonie terrorists, and with good reason. They were a load of *bùyàoliǎn de dōngxi*. The whole LSM was. The LSM had tried to nuke the New Mumbai dome. The LSM had tried to sabotage the Elevator; they'd raided troop transports on the Moon; they'd been behind every single major Loonie terrorist attack since the Singularity Scare. And there'd been more than a few.

They were crazy. And dangerous. But as scary as the boogiemen were—as scary as the whole LSM was—it was Kaufman who drew my attention. His eyes blazed and I could see anger in there, a smoldering rage that was infectious. Seeing those eyes made you want to get angry yourself. He lifted his hands up and began to speak.

"People of Earth and Space," he intoned, his voice strong and proud. "The long oppression by the Chinese and the Americans has come to an end. For too long, Luna has been at the mercy of the Alliance and their greed. For too long, the boot of Earth and her Earthers has been on our throats. For too long, taxes have bled us dry. For too long, we have been without representation within the Alliance. For *too* long!"

His hand chopped knifelike through the air. "The first generation of Lunar citizens were prisoners and convicts, sent here to mine deuterium for an energy-starved Earth. We saved the First World nations from peak oil. We saved the Third World nations from a new dark age. *We* saved the *world*. And our reward? We've been mocked, marginalized, ignored, and murdered in 'police actions.' All our attempts at a peaceful secession...rebuffed by silence! The world has ignored us, and in that darkness, we have suffered direct attacks to all of our innate rights as sentient beings, as human beings.

"We say, no more. We say that we will not stand for it. And so, we, the citizens of Luna, the ignored Seventy-Fourth State of the Alliance, declare our secession from this unjust and coercive union. And to keep your guns from our heads, we have removed the one chance you had to stop us."

His eyes grew sad. "We only wish—"

The video cut. My wallpaper was dead, completely black.

Removed. My parents...

Later, it was really obvious what would happen next. But the thing is, at the time, I didn't think about the political repercussions or the historical importance of Kaufman's speech, or the secession, or anything else that would happen. All I could do was curl up on the fake floor, in my fake room, with fake gravity and fake air and fake light and listen...

To the silence.

CHAPTER 2
THE AFTERMATH

12/26/2067

Sun-Earth L1, The Hub

1,500,000 kilometers above the surface of the Earth

The Disaster got worse just in time for me to be numb. You can only get whacked with so many horrible things at once, and once you hit that saturation point, it just becomes something you can't even absorb. Though, thinking about it, my feelings of distance and detachment might also have had something to do with how we Hub kids had been rounded up, and where. It's hard to feel any connection to the outside world when you're in the Storm Cellar.

The Cellar was actually the biggest part of the Hub, since it made up the axis of the station. Along that axis, the two wheels that made up the top and bottom neighborhoods of the Hub spun, providing the "I can't believe it's not gravity!" effect of centrifugal force. That axis was also the toughest part, being hardened against radiation in case our sun belched up a solar flare, something it managed with irritating frequency. It had enough room for all the kids and was nice and out of the way, which suited the adults. And, best of all, the kids and toddlers yanked out of the Crèche could amuse themselves, playing in the microgravity that comes from staying in the center of the axis.

However, among the pre-app and apprentice-aged group, there was less amusement. Not only were we too old to admit to enjoying microgravity, but we were all old enough to realize the difference between drills and not-drills. I remembered how it was, back before I was a pre-app. Drills were always serious, and you got used to being serious when you had to be, and to grabbing fun with both hands and riding the burn hard until you had to let go. I envied those kids and toddlers, laughing and spinning and jumping from wall to wall and chasing holo-bugs. I envied them and I faked everything being okay for them.

Those of us who were old enough to know worse when we saw it, despite the phony smiles, had spun into two groups. The kids whose parents had been vacuum engineers and micro-gravity construction specialists—the exact kinds of people who had been sucked down to the Elevator—clustered thickly, as if grief had become gravity. The lucky sons of godsdamned bitches whose parents were botanists or flight control techs or astronomers were floating at the edges of the Cellar, as if we were all contagious.

Get too close to us, you might catch orphan, too.

One of the adults had set the wallpaper to a forest sim, and the speakers played soothing music, layered with the sounds of a forest and wildlife. The illusion felt like a waste to me. Without gravity, it's pretty hard to believe you're in the Chi-cago Reforestation Zone. Still, the effect was so good that it was almost hard to tell where the walls were—and knowing where the walls were was important for moving around without grav-ity. Someone had thoughtfully put little cues here and there, but

I still moved carefully. Smacking into wallpaper was the fastest way to get labeled an Orange Peel, short of getting stranded in open space without anything to push off.

Thinking of Orange Peels hurt. Our tags were coded with different colors, and orange was the color for "dangerously untrained guest." An orange tag got clipped to the collar of everyone from the Earth who hadn't gone through training. We wouldn't be seeing many of those now. And it wasn't because of the expense anymore.

The Disaster had smashed up hundreds of stations and those stations had all turned into debris. Debris orbits like anything else, and it trapped us here. Anything going up would get torn apart by a thousand flecks of metal, while anything going down would have the same problem. Even minor damage could and would kill: crack a heat shield, shatter a window, damage life support.

The only upside I could see was that the Hub had gotten off easy in the Disaster. None of the debris had even gotten close to her. Now she was trying to put together enough food and supplies to ship to the stations that had been damaged. That meant that we Hubbers got to eat algae for the next few however-long-this-all-lasted.

But around all this, there were rumors that even worse things had gone down during the Disaster. I was too numb to worry about it—and the idea of something worse than this was almost laughable.

I got roused from my brooding by Chuck, who pushed off the wall near one group of orphans. He stopped himself beside me and checked to make sure no pre-apps could hear.

"I hear President Chang is going to present a plan," he whispered. "She's going to get us down and kick those Loonies in the butt."

"So…how exactly is a shuttle going to get off Earth?" My eyes flicked to his collar, a little insult. Pre-apps were more obvious. They just pointed and jeered: "Orange Peel! Orange Peel!" I liked to pretend I was a bit more subtle than that.

Chuck flushed and ran his finger ran along his neck, then jerked it away as if his tag was red-hot.

"Hey, the railgun in Qinghai could…"

I snorted. The railgun shipped heavy, tough things. Things that could survive the immense acceleration it put out. Humans tended to get smeared into a red paste. Intricate machinery fared about as well, but it tended to have fewer lawyers ready to sue your pants off.

Chuck glared at me.

"You know what happens the *instant* the Qinghai railgun goes off?" I asked, my heart starting to race. Chuck had cracked the shell holding in every scream, every whimper, every urge to pound my fists bloody against the walls just to try and escape this metal coffin we were floating in. I waited for him to open his mouth, then let some of those fist-pounding feelings out in a single, vicious hiss. "The Loonies drop a ten-ton tungsten rod on it, courtesy of the Shi-Armstrong railgun, signed and *ime-shuka mbali* by Omar Kaufman."

Chuck did the math. His face twisted and he spat the words out: "Fine. Brace here and be miserable."

He turned around, muttering something that sounded dangerously close to *chòu sān bā*. Oh, no, he didn't…

I pushed out, hand clenched, ready to beat Chuck's face in. He pushed off to face me, bringing his hands up. Before we could get into it, a sudden chime played, freezing us in place. We both looked at the wallpaper, which had snapped to the symbol of the Lag-Net: the Moon, Earth, and L1-L5 stabilization points, all connected by a green wire mesh. The Lagrange Network threw that symbol up every time it was trying to connect to Earth, to cover for any light-lag.

The logo vanished. In its place came a crystal-clear picture of the Alliance Senate hall, subdivided into two-dimensional views, like we were surrounded by televisions. There were people taking pictures, cameras clicking softly like a flood of correction jets, tapping away at the hull. President Chang walked up to the podium where the speaker usually stood. The screen flicked to the view of her face, angled up, so that the flag of the Alliance stretched out behind her: a threesided triangle, each side dedicated to red for China, blue for America, and white for the Alliance.

She started to speak. English subtitles for the Peels who didn't speak Mandarin popped up beneath her. It was a bit weird, though, to hear nothing but Mandarin without any Cantonese or English in there. No matter what the old folks said, English had too firm a stranglehold on too many technical concepts to be thrown aside. And where Earthers might grumble about us "corrupting the mother tongue" or something, we just went with what sounded right, even if that meant mixing Cantonese, Mandarin, English, and even bits of Swahili now that so many aeronautical advances were coming out of Kenya.

"Earlier this week, the world was shocked by an act of barbarism unparalleled in human history. The Space Elevator, the key to the future of our solar system, was destroyed by terrorists calling themselves the Lunar Separatist Movement. This act killed millions of our Kenyan allies. This act destroyed Nairobi, erasing one of the largest, most culturally and economically significant cities in the entirety of United Africa. This act killed thousands of our space-born cousins. This act has stranded those still in space, dooming thousands more. Beyond that, these terrorists have thrown our entire world's energy future into jeopardy."

She paused, letting this sink in. Looking around at the pre-apps and toddlers, I wanted to punch whoever had piped us this feed so hard they wouldn't eat for a week. The toddlers were still young enough to be confused, but they were getting the sense that something was wrong. The poor pre-apps looked like their hulls were spinning apart around them.

Chang continued: "These crimes deserve no response less than total war. As of today, I have signed an executive order conscripting every eligible Alliance citizen in space, pending ratification in the Senate and the House of Provinces. The fight will be long and hard, but the citizens of the Alliance will not give up. We will not surrender. We will not retreat. We will not stop until our colony is once more under lawful governance...until every last member of the Lunar Separatist Movement faces the justice they so richly deserve."

Her eyes hardened. "There is nowhere you can hide, Kaufman. Nowhere."

The screens went off.

"W-what does 'eligible' mean?" a boy asked. A little girl out of the Crèche started to cry. A chain reaction set the rest of them wailing, too.

"What happened to Nairobi?" a girl I never talked to asked. A debate kicked off, and so did I, using my momentum to sail down to the edge of the Storm Cellar, past the kids who stayed out of the debate to try and calm the toddlers down. I would've known more people here if I had spent more time hanging out and not so much time in my quarters, fiddling with my wallpaper and chatting with Sarah. Well, we all make sacrifices. This one paid off when I started futzing with the Cellar's wallpaper controls. I was locked out of most admin privileges, but the people who had piped in the President's video had left an exception for Chinese Central News Network's feed. I tapped it on, trying to pipe it to just a small, personal section of the wall. No sense traumatizing the kids even more.

Then the walls around us filled with tessellated Kibera Tower, the image surrounding us. Every single person in the room shut up faster than if we'd heard the bang-hiss of a blowout. Even the toddlers. Everyone looked around, eyes wide and faces numb. The tower had been smashed to the side and crumpled like an empty drinking bulb. Two lonely support struts thrust into the air; the surrounding high-rises were flattened. The city around it looked like it had been leveled by a nuke. There were fires burning here and there, and then the view changed, snapping to an interview with aid workers.

"The compression wave blinded so many." The doctor sounded bone-tired and was slurring his mix of English and Swahili so badly that subtitles popped up under him. "We're doing everything we can, but there just aren't enough optical implants to go around, or facilities to treat all the injured. The major challenge is feeding and clothing them. This is worse than anything I've seen in my life."

A shot of the Mau Mau Colonial History Museum, smashed to bits. A shot of what was left of the superstructure of the Elevator, bits of carbon composite embedded in the ground and buildings alike. It had dragged a two-kilometer-long furrow in the ground, since it had come in at a shallow angle when it was knocked out of orbit. My protective, numbing shell cracked and shattered, too, destroyed like the Elevator, like Nairobi. I stuffed my knuckles in my mouth to hold back the sobs. The news commentator said something, but I had no idea what it was; his words just slid through my head without registering.

"Turn it off," Chuck whispered. He pushed off the wall, facing me. "*Bǎ tā guāndiào!*"

I snapped out of my stupefied horror and slammed my hand on the wallpaper reset; it snapped to flat gray. I closed the control panel. Now I just wanted to punch *myself* as hard as I could.

The post-apps were silent, but I was at the center of attention. A big part of me wanted to curl up and cry and let my tears float away, let my problems float away. Let someone else deal with the world that had surrounded us. But something kept me straight. Something kept my eyes dry as people started trying to distract the pre-apps and toddlers again. I turned my back to the room, to the sounds of people comforting the kids.

In space, the only thing holding us up was hard work and the machines we tended—and, more than anything else, the people around us. That's why orange tags existed. Someone with an orange tag was an accident waiting to happen, because they didn't know how to move, how to act, how to think. Curling up wouldn't just get *me* killed. It would kill everyone around me, even if we didn't have any orange tags around. No orange tags—no actual ones, at least, no Peels—would be here for years. Maybe even decades. I shuddered at the thought.

The next thought was worse.

The President had talked about "conscripting every eligible Alliance citizen in space." Conscription. I felt a cold, creeping terror run down my spine. Dad had told me stories about the Second American Civil War, the one Granddad had fought in. The Centralists had conscripted everyone they could, mostly from the western and eastern megalopolises. My memories of Granddad were faded and thin, of a frail, haunted-looking man, the cyber-implant still obvious on his temple. He had died a few miles away from the crater of the nuke that had blinded him, died scarred by war-pox and augmentations, died haunted by what he'd seen and done.

Conscription. War. That was what was going to happen to *me*. I felt something like orbital vertigo, the feeling you get when you realize you are falling a thousand times faster than anyone has any right to. And just like orbital vertigo, the feeling racing through me wasn't an illogical phobia. Orbiting really is falling. Conscription really meant that I was going to die.

I pushed off the wall.

"Where are you going?" Chuck asked. "We have to stay here!"

I didn't answer him. Instead, I sailed to the Storm Cellar door and opened it, then ducked out. I focused on the pure physicality of the acts: I grabbed onto the ladder and pushed myself feet-first toward the floor of the Hub. The pseudogravity caught me and pinned my feet to the deck. I let go of the ladder and slid to the side of the central corridor. People hurried—practically leaped—past me. I made a break for my room, my heart thudding.

You could tell which adults were doing what by their tags. Green Tags, who managed the agriculture domes, were running around like out-gassing comets. They had to rip out all the best wine grape strains in the agri-domes, up on the sunside of the Hub, scrap anything that wasn't growing carbohydrates or vitamins, and start planting lots and lots of algae.

I got to my room and felt like I had an eggshell of control around the panic and the screaming and the crying. I leaned against the door, squeezing my eyes shut. After a moment, I heard an apologetic chirp. I opened my eyes and saw that my wallpaper hadn't gone back to its standard settings. Instead, it was showing error messages: "Computer Allocation Limits Reached. Bandwidth Limits: 1 kps."

My eyes widened. One kilobit per second? What was this, the freaking dark ages? But it made sense. Every computer in the Hub was crunching orbital numbers and beaming the information to the other surviving stations over the Lag-Net. It was a navigational nightmare up here, and dealing with that ate up our entire surplus, all our non-essential coms. I threw myself onto the bed and started running through my options. VR and vid-chat were obviously out, but at these speeds, even the humble instant message was denied.

I frowned, then called up a local word processor. I flexed my hands in front of me and the wallpaper did a quick scan of them. Once it figured out where my fingers were, it created a virtual keyboard around them. I lay back on my bed and looked up at the ceiling. There were my hands, projected as wire-frames, with my fingertips highlighted so I had some idea of what buttons I was "pushing." Yes, it was crude and primitive, but it was also cheap on computing power and bandwidth.

I typed.

Hello Fwordlil.

Dang. I waved my hand to send the words flying off the page, deleting them. I tried again.

Hello World.

I smiled, feeling a faint flare of triumph. The world might have gone down the C-chute, but at the very least, I could type.

Dear Sarah Cayer, I typed. *I'm okay. I'm coping. Or at least I'm trying.*

I stalled. Come on, Drusilla. Think of something, something good to say.

I can't waste a load of bandwidth doing a constant IM communication, so we're going to have to use emails for a while. Just pretend it's like we're in the 19th century, sending letters to each other. We can be pen pals ☺

I flexed my fingers. That created a jumble of nonsense syllables that I had to highlight and chuck away.

I'm pretty sure I'm going to be conscripted. Don't worry, the Loonies won't put up much of a fight, I bet. I mean, how much could they have prepared?

Okay, the jingoism was being laid on a bit thick there. I waved my hand.

I'm pretty sure I'm going to be conscripted. Don't worry about me. I'll keep my head down and stay ān haǒ.

Would Sarah remember there was no horizon in space and, thus, very little to put your head behind?

I waved my hand again.

I'm pretty sure I'm going to be conscripted. I left it at that for a long while, staring at the ceiling. What else could I say?

I miss you, I typed. *I miss talking with you in real time.*

I clenched my fists and my eyes shut.

I'm so scared.

I had to turn my ☺ into a :) and convert the whole stupid thing to plain text. I sent it, and then set my wallpaper to the Hub's public channels. I watched reports and orders flow past me and waited...waited for the funerals. Unlike external communications, there wasn't any bottleneck for these signals, so I got to see it all in high res. Wonderful.

Services were held that evening for every Hubber who had died. Our casualties had been down at the Elevator. I watched the proceedings stream around me, curled up there on my bed. Christian, Islamic, Jewish, Confucian, Buddhist, and Foundation ceremonies were held in that order, with a priest for each. Of course, each priest had a different tag for their actual job, a rainbow of professions. In space, there just wasn't enough time to tend to souls full watch. Hells, there wasn't enough time to raise children full watch. When Sarah first told me about having to deal with having full watch parents, every day, I wasn't sure if I should be insanely jealous or relieved. Now that I'd never have parents for any watch, any day, ever again, for my entire life, I knew that I'd be jealous until the day they launched me.

In concert with my thoughts, the symbolic ashes were reverently placed into the C-chute. The feed switched to an external camera and the chute opened just as the sun shone, brighter than bright. The light caught the clouds, which glittered like the tears of the gods. We were using runoff from the synth-diamonds. It was all carbon, in the end.

The feed cut back inside as I watched. The ritual words were said for the agnostics and atheists and the "unlisted," who had their own little paragraphs, to make sure their nonexistence was at least as respectful as, say, Jimmy Diem's heaven. There were too many names I knew for me to watch the funerals without feeling guilty. I was alive. I was alive because I was a stupid, untrained, useless pre-app. I should be dead. Then I felt more guilty when I realized how little I meant that, when I realized how glad part of me was that *they* had been the ones who died instead of me. Part of me—a sick, sad, twisted little monster in the back of my head—was *glad* that my parents had died instead of me.

I turned off the wallpaper.

I don't know how long I laid in the darkness, how long I just listened to the hum of life support. It was long enough for guilt to turn to disgust, and for fear to turn into acceptance, or maybe even eagerness. My mind started turning over ideas to end it on my terms, without pain. All I needed to do was let the oxygen out and just suck nitrogen for a while. There's no suffocation reflex, just...nothing.

Then my wallpaper dinged, a happy little noise. Words flashed up: 新邮件. You've Got Mail!

"Open." My voice sounded alien.

It was from Sarah. The words wrote themselves onto my wall.

I love you, she wrote without preamble. *Be strong. Be that brave Dru that we all know. You are so smart and so strong and so brave. More than me. You know more about math. You know more about physics. You know more about pretty much everything and I realized that if I listed all the good stuff about you this email would take for-freaking-ever. Well, okay, I suppose I could mention you're an awesome gamer and look awesome in a swimsuit on top of your sexy brain.*

You can survive, I know you can survive. I'm praying for you. And I'm sending my love. My super concentrated love beams.

CARE BEAR STARE!

I laughed a snot-filled laugh. Ugh. I needed tissues badly. I had no idea what a "care bear" was, but it sounded like the kind of insane thing that Sarah would reference.

Kill a Loonie for me.

My smile lessened, but didn't vanish. I didn't want to kill anyone. I just wanted to hold her.

xoxoxooxoxoxox

I tried to imagine each of those hugs and kisses.

PS: Print this out, if you can, and think of me.

There was a fragment of a file attached. The com laser let up just a tiny bit of it at a time. One kilobyte, then another one, and another, until finally, almost an hour later, when I was teetering on the edge of sleep, Sarah's picture appeared in all its mid-res glory.

I looked at it.

I blushed.

Looking at that picture, every thought of nitrogen and darkness faded. They didn't vanish. The darkness would never vanish. But I decided as I took in every curve, every shape, every color of that picture, that I would live.

I had to. For Sarah. As insane as it sounds...

Sarah kept me alive.

CHAPTER 3
CONSCRIPTION

12/27/2067

Sun-Earth L1, The Hub

1,500,000 kilometers above the surface of the Earth

The conscription notice appeared in the form of a red tag to replace my purple one and an email. I read it. It said I was to report to the Storm Cellar, 1000 hours. Sharp.

And so: 1000 sharp. Storm Cellar. As if I hadn't spent enough time there. I left my room later than I should have and made it up running down the gently sloping corridors of the Hub. It was kind of like jogging inside of a big wheel, possibly because that was exactly what I was doing. The Hub had originally been called the Hubcap by the workers who had built it, because its half-finished habitation sections had looked a bit like wheels on a ground-car. The name had stuck a hell of a lot better than Central Communication and Navigation Assistance E/S-L1 Station One.

I got to one of the six Cellar entrances mostly on time. The door opened and I slipped into the corridor, which was maybe two meters wide in both directions and had roughly textured walls, with handholds every few feet. They weren't really necessary at first, but as I moved further away from the inside of the torus, the pseudo-gravity of the Hub got weaker and weaker, until finally I could just push myself through the air.

Inside the Storm Cellar, I found a hundred-plus pre-apps and apprentices clustered around, maybe even two hundred. All of us with shiny new red tags clipped to our necks, as if we had had our throats slit in advance. The wallpaper was set to matte gray. No comforting forest landscapes for us today.

"Attention!"

The voice snapped like a gunshot in a vid. We didn't know how to come to attention, so we all did our own thing. I figured the standard microgravity position would do it: arms tight to the side, legs together and cocked back slightly, back straight. Just float there, and don't move any of your limbs or else you could whack a control panel or send your wallpaper the wrong signal and blow up your home. It was natural, too, 'cause if you didn't learn to do it without thinking, you'd get everyone killed.

Most of the other kids went into the same pose. Some tried to mount themselves on the wall, so they could salute at the man who was sliding along the wall, moving "down" from the door that led to the sunside torus of the Hub, where most of the command and control and agriculture wings were placed. Kids didn't tend to go up there unless they were mucking out algae vats.

"I said *attention! Bái mù!*" the man shouted again, his hand grabbing the wall, stopping himself. "That looks like this, you *ruǎn ruò wú néng xiǎotùzǎizi!*"

He snapped into a position that should not have been possible in microgravity. He looked like he was on an Earther parade field. How he stopped himself from slewing to the side, I had no idea.

I copied that position as best as I could. Out of the corner of my eye, I saw movement. I looked. A man and woman, both in similar uniforms, were floating along the walls, correcting postures with a combination of shouts and measured physical violence.

"Eyes front!"

We were in microgravity, so "eyes front" really meant any direction you wanted it to. But since the angry guy who had shouted this—a burly, half-Anglo-looking man with a red tag on his collar and three chevrons and a star underneath on his shoulder—looked ready to murder anyone who didn't do exactly what he said, I figured looking his way would do well enough.

"I am Staff Sergeant Antwiler, your senior drill instructor." He looked us up and down, his eyes sweeping like a scanning laser. "And from here on out, the first and last thing out of your mouths is going to be 'sir.' Do you get me?"

"Sir, yes, sir!" I shouted. Everyone else said about the same thing, but ragged and half together. It was almost as though we weren't exactly enthusiastic. Imagine that.

"*Hă? Wŏ méi tīngjiàn!* Sound off like you mean it, or else I might have to start getting nasty!"

"Sir, yes sir!" This time, we were more together. I wasn't sure if I managed to fake enthusiasm. Antwiler shook his head and started to move, cold-gas jets hissing around his ankles. It let him move unimpeded, unlike us. We had to kick and brace against walls. I wondered if that was the point.

"Right now, I need to make something preeminently clear to you slack-jawed *wōnang fèi*: This is your only chance. This is not a boot camp you can drum out of. This isn't a scholastic program that you can just half-ass. This is *life* or *death*, because if any of you flunk out, you will not be given a free ride to Earth where Mommy can wipe your backside for you. You will *die*.

But if you survive basic training, then you will no longer be the quivering *dǎnxiǎoguǐ* that you are. You will instead be Space Marines, and you will personally escort Omar Kaufman to the Ten Courts of Hell and make him sign in with his own blood!"

I was scared of how appealing that idea was.

"Now, normally, you'd have already learned the basics and gone through the Initial Physical Aptitude Course…so consider handling that a little vacation to take before you have to hack actual Basic. You will be administrated by Sergeant Wilcox." He nodded at the woman. "And by Sergeant Cao Cao." He nodded at the man. "You will follow their orders exactly, because they are fully within their rights to administer any punishment they deem necessary. Now…*dismissed*!"

If this was a vacation, it didn't feel like one. Instead, it felt a bit like getting beaten viciously about the head with a hammer. Sergeant Wilcox filled our heads with the various codes of military conduct—including the twelve standing orders of Space Corps Members, the Uniform Code of Military Justice, and a vow to abide by the Geneva Conventions and the Ratified Articles of War—and she had our skinclothes reset to the uniform colors of the Alliance Space Marines. Blue and black. Even though the actual cut of my clothes hadn't changed, I swore they itched and felt unnatural.

Then I met Sergeant Cao Cao. Cao Cao—the historical one—was one of the more enduring tyrant figures of Chinese history. Meeting someone named after him was kind of like meeting someone who decided to pick up the name Mao Zedong or Berzelius Windrip. But at first, he seemed like the nicest of the sergeants, just standing beside the track in the gym with a smile on his face. The gym running track was coated with a sticky substance that made running through it feel so awful and hard that it had to be healthy.

"All right, maggots," he shouted, ruining any hope that we'd get through this without being insulted. "Get on the track...and *go!*"

We ran.

I've never exactly been the fittest girl ever. Most of my time off had been spent playing MUDs or watching vids put up on the Lag-Net. But I still took my bone supplements and hit the gym every week to make sure my muscles didn't atrophy in the lighter gravity on the Hub. That didn't mean I was ready for this run. It was long and hard, and instead of jogging by myself with my favorite tunes piped through my collar, I ran with Sergant Cao Cao's voice in my ears.

"My grandmother runs faster than you and she's been dead for twenty years! Come on, legs up, get them out of the gunk. After me! *Kuài cuì, kuài cuì!*"

A few people collapsed to the side, gasping. I was one of them. I hit the inside floor of the gym and lay there, wheezing. I almost threw up, but I forced that down through sheer force of will. I was *not* going to throw up. Cao Cao didn't pay me any mind until I got up; he had already put the kids who made it to the end of the run to work on the next part of the IPAC.

"I've got my eye on you, cadet," he snapped. "You'll be running this every day until you can do it without passing out. Get on the pull-up bars and give me fifty. If you can't manage fifty, then we'll have you doing a hundred every day...and that's even before we get you into the PCP."

Before, I had wondered if they had just been trying to scare us with talk of killing us. Now I knew for sure—they were really, actually trying to kill us. But even that wasn't quite true. As I started to do my pull-ups, Chuck made a break for it. I don't know how he was able to run that fast after slogging through the track for three kilometers, but he managed it.

Cao Cao was faster. He had Chuck on his back with one knee on the poor guy's throat before I'd even blinked. "Listen, you *fàntǒng*," Cao Cao hissed into his ear, but it was quiet enough in the gym that we could all hear it. "Did you think we were kidding? This space station has enough fuel and water to support only eighty percent of its population. Do the math. You are either shipping off to fight...or you are going to Earth through the casualty chute, *without a suit*. So *get up* and give me fifty!"

Cao Cao stood and Chuck gasped, running back to the pull-up bars with tears streaming down his face.

The pull-ups were hell. The push-ups were hell. The manual dexterity trials were hell—though more of a "frustrating" hell than an "oh gods, why is this happening to me?" hell like the others. The single lowest point for me, though, was when I got pulled out of the manual dexterity trial by Cao Cao. He had me follow him to the corner of the gym, which reeked of vomit and had a few luckless cadets cleaning up. But it wasn't the smell that stopped me dead. It was what the smell hung around: my nightmare.

My nightmare was a gyroscope. I know Earther kids have nightmares about boogiemen and zombies and transies, but I had bed-wetting dreams about gyroscopes, ever since I was eight years old and a bully named Cho had strapped me into this exact one and left me spinning until the station AI heard my screams and reported them. Even so, they hadn't gotten me off it until after I had thrown up, and the rapid spinning had slammed my head into the hunks of vomit. The only thing that was even slightly good about that story was that Cho had been shipped to Shi-Armstrong, which was the only space colony large enough to have a juvenile detention facility.

And now, I stood before the gyroscope again, but this time was worse by several exponents of terrifying. I'd already failed to run three clicks, do fifty pull-ups, or manage fifty push-ups.

My manual dexterity ranked somewhere below that of a walrus. I was, in a word, screwed.

"Would the cadet like to explain why they're wasting our valuable time, or should I just administer corporal punishment now and save us the hassle?" Cao Cao broke me out of my terrified fugue.

I got into the gyroscope. It really was just that: a set of concentric rings built around a chair that had enough straps to keep anyone who rode the thing safely rooted. It was supposed to train you for intense changes in inertia and speed. It was great to test how well you could keep your head after spinning out. I stifled a sob as Cao Cao grabbed the rungs and hauled on them hard.

My head whipped around and around and I started screaming.

When the chair stopped, the straps released and Cao Cao barked an order—I think he was trying to give me a laser pointer and telling me to hit a target. I ignored him, hurled myself to the deck, and vomited everywhere.

When I got finished cleaning, my arms felt like the bones had been removed and replaced by rubber. Not even smartrubber, just regular dumb rubber that did nothing but flop uselessly. My nose was filled with the smell of vomit, and I felt like if I never had to eat anything again, I'd be grateful. Instead, Cao Cao had us all rounded up and started telling us who'd be assigned to the PCP, which turned out to mean Physical Conditioning Platoon. He stopped next to me.

"Report for PCP tomorrow." He didn't show a single hint of pity.

I had a premonition: I was going to ride the gyroscope a lot.

Cao Cao turned and led us out of the gym.

We followed him and I tried my best to explode Cao Cao's head with my mind. It didn't work, and soon we emerged into the barracks. The space had once been our private rooms, but the walls had been knocked down while Cao Cao was busy trying to murder us. The circuits that had once run through the walls were now taped to the floor, and instead of a series of separate beds, there were a dozen or so bunk beds, each with two footlockers at the front.

"You and you. Stand here." Cao Cao pointed out beds for cadets, and soon we all stood in lines beside our beds. Then Cao Cao went to the door and he and Sergeant Wilcox, who had come in while he was assigning us our bunks, started passing out plastic rifles to each of us. As they did, Sergeant Antwiler stormed in. And, shock of shocks, he had a lot to say.

"These are mock-ups of the Phased Pulse Rifle, which will be arriving from the Forge as soon as possible. Until then, you are to keep these mock-ups at your side at all times. You will have them with you while you run. You will have them with you while you ride the gyro." I flinched. "And you will have them with you while you shit, while you eat, while you shack up. If you ever have your rifle further from you than a breathing unit, we will personally tear out your throat and shove it up your asshole! Do you get me?"

"Sir, yes sir!"

"Thus ends your vacation!" He grinned, as if relishing our obvious physical pain. "Now, I'm going to say dismissed and you are going to enjoy your liberty, because tomorrow gets a hell of a lot worse."

He glared at us.

"*Dismissed!*"

It kind of looked like a load of ragdolls had their physics routines deleted—or more like a load of marionettes getting their strings cut at once.

He laughed, and then left the room with a last call: "Lights out in ten minutes!"

Boys and girls and trans and unidentified around me groaned and rubbed at sore and bruised and tweaked muscles. My bunkmate was another girl, whose face was haunted and hollow, like someone had scooped her brains and emotions out.

"I'm Drusilla Zhao," I said.

She blinked, looking at me. "S-Susan Kolby."

"Well, Susan, you get top bunk. Need help?" I asked, feeling sorry for her, although not sorry enough to give up the bottom bunk. She looked like someone had just beaten her about the head. Then again, we all did. I noticed that the headboard of our bunkbed had screens set in it. It wasn't wallpaper, but gods, I had to get my hands on it. I looked at Susan, suddenly regretting offering any help.

"I...I'm okay," Susan stammered, crawling up into her bunk. Thank the gods! I dove into my bed and almost passed out immediately, despite desperately wanting to get at that screen.

I forced my eyes open. It felt like my own lungs were punching themselves, just to get revenge for me not sleeping. I rolled to my belly, propping myself up on my hands. I turned on the screen and pulled up the email service, struggling with the outdated interface. But, hey, at least they were actually letting us *use* email. Every other function on the screen seemed locked down tighter than a space suit.

It was all worth it when I checked my inbox. I had a message from Sarah.

Hey Dru, she started. Today has been a busy busy day. We're all getting stuff together to send toward Nairobi. There are a bunch of refugees, I hear, and we're all going to need to pull together if we're going to survive. They've put up an electricity ration, so I have to write my emails really fast. It's so quiet now. No more electric cars buzzing around, no more airplanes zipping overhead. But there are some upsides. I actually got to talk to my neighbors. One of them did a tour of duty down south, back when Mexico was called Aztlan, during the Slump.

He said that he was there when the Texans surrendered and the Mexican loyalists ran up their old flag and everyone was celebrating. Well, except for the losers. After he was done talking, we played Asteroids together and I won. Guess that fighting in an actual war does not make you super good at board games, not even if he claims he let me win :3

I smiled. "Go get 'em, Sarah," I whispered, drinking in her normal day. I tried to imagine standing under a sky. A real sky. I imagined crinkling my toes and feeling real dirt between them, against the soles of my feet, in my soul itself.

I opened my eyes and kept reading.

The sky looks amazing. It's like there are all sorts of lights in the sky that were never there before. But it always makes me sad, looking at it. Cause I remember...each of those lights is like someone's soul. I pray for them, and I pray that I won't have to pray for your soul. I'm so worried, please tell me that you're okay. Love, Sarah. Xoxoxoxoxoxoox.

I rolled onto my back and sighed, eyes closed. I wanted to write a response. My body had other plans.

CHAPTER 4
REVEILLE

12/28/2067

Sun-Earth L1, The Hub

1,500,000 kilometers above the surface of the Earth

The screen stabbed me in the back. It turned on while I was in the middle of the deepest, most complete and utter sleep of my life, where every atom of my being was focused on nothing but sleeping…and then it blared a trumpet in my ears at max volume. I rolled out of bed and almost got squashed by Kolby, who had done pretty much the same thing, which meant she fell in slow motion and hit the deck with a light thud. I helped her to her feet and she looked like she didn't know where she was or what was going on. She figured it out by the time we scrambled into the line of bodies forming along the rows of beds. Good thing, too—a few seconds after the trumpet started playing, Staff Sergeant Antwiler burst in and started shouting at us.

"The sun shines, maggots, so get on your feet. Line up and follow me! *Kuai!*"

We must have moved fast enough to suit him, because he didn't make us drop and give him twenty, or fifty, or something. Or maybe he didn't want to kill us. No, wait, that would imply that Antwiler had something approaching pity or remorse in the black, twisted thing he called a heart. We marched to the communal cleaning stalls. This, at least, was normal. At least, I thought it'd be normal. But instead of saying something like "get scrubbed off, you filthy maggots," Antwiler stood and shouted some more.

"All right, *rén zhā*! Today, you're going to start doing things by the number. Step one, remove your skinclothes. Step two, lather your face and neck and only your face and neck. Step three, vacuum the lather off with the handheld…"

He went through something like twenty steps, and if anyone got out of order, he yelled at them. Oddly, it still ended up being a comforting experience. Here was something we actually felt halfway familiar with. Yes, it was anal-retentive, but I just thought of it like donning a spacesuit. You have sets, procedures, numbered lists to follow. Once we were back in our skinclothes, we all got our rations and water, and then got split into groups. The people who made it through IPAC okay were put into the actual training platoon, while the rest of us got to see what happened when your best was the equivalent of the putrid stain after a bad batch of algae.

We poor, dumb slobs got to be entrusted to the tender mercies of Cao Cao, who was even more a *gǒuzǎizi* in the PCP than in the IPAC. We ran. We did push-ups. We did limbering workouts. We did cool-down maneuvers, and through it all, we "sounded off," reciting orders, regulations, and everything else that Cao Cao thought we were slow on. And worse, if we screwed up, he had us added to Scribe. Now, if I could ever one day punch a computer program in the face, I would gladly do that and more to Scribe. It was just a dumb namelisting program, but when your name got slipped onto its lists, it would juggle you around and spit you out a punishment, and it was a real *sǐ pì yǎn* about it.

I learned fast that the punishment was always worse than what you'd normally handle in training. Always. At first, I had this stupid idea in my head that there was nothing that could be worse than being strapped into a gyro chair and forced to shoot at targets—and, of course, getting push-ups and running assignments if you failed or screamed or vomited. Then I got my name shouted to Scribe and spent a night with only four hours of sleep. Two were spent on "blowout watch," where I had to stand around doing absolutely nothing but listening for the signs of an impending decompression.

This meant I got to stand there in the cold and the black, my body aching, my eyes begging to close, and my brain twitchy from being abused all day, just waiting for nothing to happen. Frankly, if a blowout happened, there was nothing much that a cadet on watch could do to help, other than suck vacuum and die.

Another thing I learned really fast was that the DIs—the drill instructors—expected a very specific set of vocabulary. Left became "port." Right became "starboard." Backwards became "aft" and forward became "fore." Up was "zenith" and down was "nadir," which was at least semi-familiar. More than that, I got to learn Mandarin and English all over again, because if you said the wrong words in the wrong way in the wrong language, then they would space you fast. You had to use English for "Sir," "Yes," "No," "Cadet," and so on. For actual questions, you prefaced your Mandarin with "The recruit wishes to know," in English. And yes, you always referred to yourself in the third person. It was like I had suddenly turned into The Recruit, a faceless hunk of putty that the DIs didn't mind grabbing and hurling against the wall a few times if I ever had an idea like being Drusilla Zhao without permission.

But there was an advantage to having your life run like a sick parody of a Spacer's daily watch. Unless you had pissed a DI off, you got free time. One hour of free time, to be exact. If you squinted and bashed your head against the wall and forgot that you had once had six, or even seven, hours of free time before conscription, you could almost be grateful for it. We had exactly three ways to spend this time. We could write emails, my preferred activity. We could watch instructional vids from the Khan Academy or other vetted sources. Or, last but far from least, we could shack up.

Antwiler hadn't been kidding when he had said that we had to keep our rifles at hand all the time, even when we were… relaxing. Two boys who managed to work up the energy to shack up were stupid enough to leave their rifles in their foot-locker instead of beside the bed, or even on it like most of us. Wilcox noticed and had them set to CAPE. Corrective Action, Physical Exercise, though sometimes we called it Corrective Action, Physical Extermination.

When I included that little story in an email to Sarah, I got slapped in the face by the staggering gulf between us. Not just the physical one—though every day, I could practically feel every single stinking kilometer of empty space between us— but the cultural one.

Wow, they let you have sex?! I thought that that kind of thing would be frowned on in the freaking military. Heck, it's frowned on down here. Before I met you, Mom wouldn't even let me near any of the farmboys. Then we figured out I was gay—and believe you me, the less said about that conversation the better (old people talking about sex is GROSSSSSS >:V)— and she…actually still would not let me near the boys, now that I think about it…

I shook my head. Part of me snickered at the mental image of Sarah and her mom having a "the sperm and the eggs" conversation, but I was more thinking of a tactful way of explaining the whole thing without sounding really snobby and stuck up. Peels—even lovely, wonderful, amazing Peels like Sarah— were so weird about shacking up sometimes. I started typing my response.

Sarah-Bear, they can't really stop us from having sex, not unless they want an actual mutiny on their hands. And we'd be in our rights, too: It's included in the Uniform Code of Military Conduct that recruits DO GET RIGHTS. I know, I was as shocked as you were. But one of those rights is to any form of recreation that they can squeeze into their free time, so long as it's not chemical in nature. And thanks to our hormone shots, sex isn't much more than a...handshake. Well, okay, a really sweaty handshake, but still!

Maybe it was because Sarah expected different things about sex that I didn't do it with anyone up here. I had just called it a handshake, but...I couldn't treat it like that with Sarah a jillion kilometers away. It'd kill her. Or at the very least, kill our relationship, and both thoughts filled me with almost as much terror as the idea of being shot at. And at least training simulations were getting me over being shot at. There wasn't any "breakup simulator," at least none I wanted to try. So I floated between what I wanted and what I feared, with the only thing to cuddle being my rifle.

And when my rifle wasn't acting as a really *nai yòng* replacement teddy bear, I studied it. The things they gave us were just crude mock-ups of the actual guns, so we actually studied manuals and got quizzed about them at the most random times. We used the fake rifles constantly. We practiced how to hold them at parade rest, in microgravity, in combat. We even visited the holodeck's augmented reality chambers and practiced on simulated firing ranges, to try and qualify for Rifleman, Marksman, Sharpshooter, or Expert training.

That's where everything changed.

I woke up that morning feeling like *shǐ dàn*. Sarah's latest email had described a rash of food shortages. She tried to make it sound chipper, but really, there's no way going hungry sounds like anything but a rehash of the Slump and all the terrors that entailed. On top of that, I felt like total crap. The night before, I'd drawn another blowout shift because I'd been a little too slow to get my rifle in order. And now, we were going to qualify for our official ranking. Sergeant Cao Cao—who still rode my ass pretty freaking hard in the PCP— had made no secret of it.

"Going to try for Marksman, or think you can manage to screw this up, too, maggot?"

"Sir, yes sir!"

I mean, what else could I have said? I *wanted* to say *cào nǐ zǔzōng shíbā dài*, but I didn't. As nice as it would have been, I don't think any DI in the history of the universe would like someone telling him to screw his ancestors back to the eighteenth generation.

So we were called to the holodeck in little groups. I got called third, which meant I arrived while still shaking from a ride in the gyro-chair. The holodeck was actually a few rooms and two closets, and none of them involved actual holograms. The closets were for VR nuts like me who could get past the vertigo and headaches that VR headsets trigger. The rooms were plastered with the most sophisticated, advanced wallpaper in the universe, which gave us the perfect illusion of being somewhere so long as you didn't mind not moving at all. If you moved, you'd walk into a wall. Fast way to kill the illusion.

Naturally, I had my faux-PPR with me when I stepped into the room. Sergeant Wilcox spoke to me through the wallpaper.

"Cadet, assume firing position."

I snapped my PPR up—Motion 1, Motion 2, Motion 3—the numbers ratcheting through my head.

"Cadet, targets will appear in five seconds. You will target and destroy them by the numbers and be graded on your performance. One...two...three...four..."

The wallpaper shifted to a pitch-black field, with me standing on a white circle, denoting where I could move, i.e., nowhere. Targets began to swoop up. The perspective made them look a hundred, two hundred, three hundred, and four hundred meters off. I sighted—1, 2—then fired. Sighted, fired. Sighted, fired. All my shaking and misery floated away as the targets exploded and the training guided me.

"Cadet, assume firing position two."

I knelt. I hit every target again.

"Cadet, assume firing position three."

I lay on my belly and propped the faux-PPR against my shoulder. I knew this was ridiculous. For one thing, we'd be fighting in microgravity. Why use these positions at all? But that thought vanished from my head faster than water in a vacuum as the targets popped up.

I hit every target again.

When I came out of the holodeck, Wilcox nodded. "Congratulations, Cadet Zhao, you've qualified for training on a live PPR. You've earned your Marksman badge."

She looked at me expectantly.

"Sir, this recruit humbly requests permission to qualify for Sharpshooter, sir!" The words sprang out of my mouth without hesitation. Wilcox nodded.

From then on, I used my free time to write emails to Sarah and to study up on proper energy weapon use, learning the tricks for hitting long-distance targets with a pulsed blast of laser light. I must have dry-fired my fake PPR more times than I breathed, but then the day came when I went to the virtual range and potted targets. We started off without enhancement, and then went to the targets that were two or three kilometers off in open space. Then we went to the extreme ranges: thirty, forty, and fifty kilometers, using a simulated enhanced sniper scope. After I had bull's-eyed my fifth target at fifty clicks, Sergeant Wilcox smiled at me. She actually *smiled*.

"Congratulations, Cadet, you've qualified as a Sharpshooter with a fake rifle. Now all you have to do is manage it with a real one and you might actually deserve to call yourself a Marine one day."

From then on, I had a little badge on my collar next to my red tag. You'd think being a "fake" Sharpshooter wouldn't count for much. You'd be wrong. In training drills and simulations, Sharpshooters were given important positions, and they had only slightly less responsibility to make the platoon look good than the cadet squad leaders. If we missed, we let everyone down.

For a long time—an absurdly long time—I felt proud as hell to have that much responsibility, and I was eager to kick ass and take names. That eagerness got me through the PCP and into the actual training platoon. That eagerness got me made a squad leader, and even Cao Cao started saying things like, "You might just hack it after all."

But through it all, a niggling thought kept spinning in the back of my head.

What the hell was I proud for?

CHAPTER 5
THE THREE PS

I had just been finishing off an email to Sarah, detailing everything from the PCP to my Sharpshooter qualification to the fact that the Forge had finally made our real guns and they were being shipped off when I heard a voice behind me.

"Hey."

I rolled onto my back, thumbing the screen-off button.

It was one of the other cadets. He smiled. He had more pigment than I did, but he had the faint fold of the eyes that loads of people Post-Slump inherited, during the Amalgamation.

"What's up?"

Oh great. Forced conversation.

I shrugged in bed. "Just writing a letter to my *nǔ péng you.* On *Earth.*"

I added the inflection to let him know that this was a monogamous relationship.

He looked somber, sitting down across from me. "Sorry."

"Hey, I like writing her emails. *Méiguānxì.*" I smiled, trying to ignore the reason he had said "sorry": *Sorry, you're not going to see your girlfriend for a decade.* I wondered if he pitied me or thought that I was a real Peel. Sometimes I wondered the same thing. Was I just being stupid? Then the thought of breaking up with Sarah came, and with it came my lungs constricting and my heart trying to force itself up my throat so it could beat the snot out of my brain for even trying to think such things.

"So, anyhoo..." He tried to think of something to say. He had been looking to shack up, I could tell. The only rule (and, like all the other rules and regulations, it was beaten into our heads with a metal pipe) about shacking up was that you couldn't do it with someone above or below your rank. That was easy enough to follow, what with there being only two ranks right now: Cadet and Drill Sergeant. And the *thought* of kissing Wilcox made me feel like cutting off my lips, just in case.

As I silently considered facial mutilation, the dude floundered, trying to find something to talk about until he could think of a way to bow out of the conversation without looking like a real jerk.

"Do you have one?" I asked, trying to give him some remass. "Ya know, a *duì xiàng*?" I used the slang, making it a joke, something he could brush off if he wanted to.

"No." He sighed, sliding his hand along his face. "Never got around to finding a girl, and I'm not really into boys."

I smiled. "Maybe you should have eaten more." I patted my belly, which was flat and tight as hell thanks to all the drills in the PCP. "Put some mass on. Attract some girls the old-fashioned way: gravity!"

He snorted. "If I took your advice, the nutrient AIs would be after my scalp."

My grin got wider. "Hey, if you don't tell them, I won't." I winked. "I'm gonna finish this email, then catch some freefall."

"Right." He stood. "Tell your girlfriend I said hi." He winked back. "Hi from Dan Ts'ui."

"I will." I rolled back onto my stomach and started typing again.

At least today is a Saturday. So we get half the day off. I'm shocked, but I think it's more of an issue of not having the guns yet, and less a case of actually being merciful to us poor cadets. But we still had early morning PT and gyro-rides, all by the numbers. And here's the scary thing...I've almost started writing emails down by the numbers, like I've got a little Antwiler on my shoulder saying 'STEP ONE: POUR HEART AND SOUL INTO ELECTRONIC MEDIA! STEP TWO'...lol. But anyhoo, as our wind-down, we got lectures in theory. Like, everything we've learned by watching war vids and playing VR games—you kinda need to chuck that out for fighting in space.

A small warning I had programmed into my screen popped up, bleeping at me. We were five minutes away from lights out. I banished it with a tap of the keyboard.

Anyhoo, lights out is soon. I love you and think of you when it feels like going is hard. Tell me if you beat your neighbor at Asteroids again. ;) xoxoxoxoxoxox

I hit send and the lights went out.

And now, now, I settled down in my bed, thinking. Once, I'd called CAPE an hour of hell. CAPE had nothing on lights out. That was when you had time to think, and despite all the shouting, training, molding, we were still just scared kids at heart. And maybe the nighttime was when we all felt it the worst.

People cried, see. There were more reasons to cry than there were lights in the night sky. You could have hurt yourself during training. One of the DIs could have berated you for talking back or not going fast enough or something. Or, more likely, that was just the surface pain; the throbbing hurt underneath was a parent. A brother. A cousin. A lover. Dead. Dead. Dead.

I wasn't crying. Instead, my eyes were open, looking up at the bunk above me, and I was trying to not go down the dark vectors that my brain wanted to. But those thoughts, they were like the Earth's gravity well, sucking you down, pulling you under.

I closed my eyes, trying to force out the thoughts of all the ways you could die in space, trying not to focus on the empty, infinitely cold and yet blazingly hot *nothing* that surrounded us all the time.

Instead, I thought of Sarah. I recreated her piece by piece in my mind. I imagined what her next email would be about, what she would tell me. How her day would have gone. Everything.

It worked. The same way it worked every night and every morning. Sarah was my numbers, my secret little set of instructions that I followed in my head, underneath the numbers I followed every day. That's why I kept on surviving the shouting and the molding and kept a piece of me, *me*.

>+<

The next day was Sunday. We didn't get Sunday off, not for military stuff. And in space, the concept of Sabbath or any other holy day of not working was deadly. If you took a day off—like, completely no work at all—people could and *would* die. Another joy of living in a tin can surrounded by nothing: You never stopped working except to sleep. And even that was ill-advised sometimes.

So, we did our morning PT; we did some basic micro-g hand-to-hand training in the Cellar. And then we were all taken to the machine shop, where a shipment had arrived from the Forge by rocket booster. There were five crates. One of them was open and full of plastic-looking pistols. The pistols were almost completely smooth and seamless, with no ejection slit for a bullet, nowhere for a magazine to go. The thing that really made them different from the slugthrowers we'd all seen in games and movies, though, was the gray dish around the barrel, which was inscribed with thin black circles. The barrel was shiny.

"This," Antwiler said, picking up one of the pistols and holding it up for us to see, "is the Phased Pulse Pistol, or the P3. It is a laser weapon that fires about a thousand joules in a half-second-long phased pulse of coherent light. The first quarter-second will boil away about a third of a centimeter of ablative armor. The next quarter-second, assuming you keep on target, will burn straight through organs, bones, brains. Effectiveness depends on not just hitting the target, but keeping the target."

I wondered if Antwiler cared that we all knew this already. Probably not.

His finger ran along the dish. "This is the radiator dish, which keeps the gun from burning your hand. The whole thing is capable of running and recharging from your spacesuit's backpack, but its batteries can be used for roughly thirty pulses before they need to be recharged. Forget everything you think you know about guns: The P3 has no recoil, and being shot by one is not pleasant."

He set it down and stepped over to the next crate. "The next item on our little shopping cart of destruction is the next step up from the P3, and someone you should all know very, very well."

The crate opened and he hauled out a rifle. It was sleek, too, with a folding stock, a strap to slide around your shoulders, and a dial on the side, near your thumb, so you could adjust it while holding the gun. It had radiator fins around the barrel, making it look almost comically like a ray gun from century-old movies that we sometimes watched to mock. And yes, it was as familiar to us as our left arms.

"This is the Phased Pulse Rifle, or PPR. It works on pretty much the same principles as the P3, but with a higher joule count. It also comes with a basic spectrograph, so you can feel out a target, and then change the pulse's strobe frequency to penetrate specific material better. Now, if you aim the spectrograph at a station or any target that we designate as non-combatant, your PPR and your P3 won't fire."

That wasn't in the tech manuals; they must have added it recently. I raised my hand. Antwiler nodded.

"This cadet respectfully asks," I said. "What if the Loonies trick our spectrographs? If our weapons won't fire, the cadet wishes to know how we would successfully engage the enemy, sir."

"Very carefully, Cadet." Antwiler's voice held that tone that said you weren't over the line, but you were getting close.

I felt a squirming fear in my guts. I didn't know that much about military tactics, beyond the basics, but it just seemed like a really dumb idea to make it possible for our guns to *not* shoot something. Because if I had a dozen Loonies with laser rifles shooting at me, I'd really want to shoot back.

Even if I could hit a station? part of me asked. A station stuffed full of people who had survived the Disaster and now had Loonie boots on their necks...

I felt a little sick, realizing that a big, big part of me would rather risk their lives than mine.

What was this war doing to me?

But Sergeant Antwiler was talking and I had to focus.

"The second setting on the PPR is a conical heat ray. This is more like the classic idea of the laser, thought up by old H. G. Wells almost three hundred years ago. It's useless in cover. Rocks and debris soak up the heat; dust disperses it into the vacuum. But if you catch five or ten Loonies out in open space, you hose them down with the heat ray and they'll cook faster than their radiators can bleed off the heat. Just like a spring turkey." He grinned.

Ugh.

Antwiler set down the PPR and headed to the next crate. From this one, he pulled out a helmet and what looked like chest, arm, and leg coverings. Thin armor, shiny and slightly flexible.

"This goes over your skinsuit and turns it into a G.I.S.S.S., aka, the Government Issue Space Survival Suit. A Giss." He pronounced it like "hiss" with a guh sound to kick it off. "It's got three layers of protection, designed to release puffs of gas when you get hit by a laser weapon, so that it diffuses the beam and makes it less effective. It's also got flexible Kevlar and impact-resistant gel packs throughout. Good for everything from micrometeorites to bullets, assuming they're not traveling too fast. Anything going too fast will kill you dead."

After that, we were split up into five groups of five. One group of five got to spend an hour getting fitted for their skinsuits. Their actual, real-to-gods skinsuits.

Okay, there are two kinds of skinsuits in space, and if you've never been, it can be confusing. There are the regular skintight clothes we wear all the time inside. It's just dumb fabric laced with a few electronics. Enough to let the station computer track you and make sure you're not urinating in the cistern or something. We usually call those skinclothes.

Then there are the actual, *zhēn pǐn de* skinsuits.

Those are something else entirely. They're made of specialized smart cloth, and they fit to your body nearly perfectly. The only places they don't fit are where you have little crevices, like your butt, armpits, or boobs. Thanks to the lowfat diet that Spacers eat, most girls are blessed with pretty small boobs. And it *is* a blessing, because imagine bouncing around with huge ones, like the ones you see in movies and vid-games from the '30s. That'd be hell and a half.

I was in the third group to get fitted, so I got to spend three hours practicing repair work on the actual PPR and P3 units. First in the workshop, with tools. Then in microgravity with tools. Then in microgravity without tools beyond what we'd always have on our Space Survival Suits—our Gisses.

That was frustrating, but also kinda fun. I worked methodically near a wall, setting the wallpaper to be just sticky enough to hold the parts still. As I needed them, I plucked them from the wall and imagined I was picking fruit off a part-tree. It was nice to finally put our book learning and simulation practice to physical work. I was already raring to try my PPR out at the range, to use the real hardware, to get an actual Sharpshooter badge.

Then came time for our skinsuits. My group of five—all girls—was taken to a place I had never been before on the station: the fitting rooms. Skinsuits were for adults cleared to work outside, so the computer had always kept this door locked for me. It opened now and I finally got to look around. Inside, there was a woman with a few measuring devices, who was sitting on a table covered with soft gray fabric. On the fabric was a collection of little bladders, plastic bags full of some fluid or another. The wallpaper was all set to the pastels that we were used to, with a few vids that were playing spin-corrected views of the Earth, ballooned up to fill them, like the Hub was a million kilometers closer than it should have been. That was just mean.

The woman slipped off the table, catching my eye and distracting me from staring longingly at the vids. "I'm Miss Stru. You can call me Stru." She smiled. "Get naked, girls."

I sighed and started to unzip my skinclothes. No one hesitated. We were used to cleaning up in the same communal cleaning stalls to say nothing of seeing each other shacking up and humping one bed over, so it wasn't that hard to get naked now.

Stru started measuring us, first with regular tape that snaked around our bellies and thighs and breasts.

"Sir, this—" one of the girls started, looking down at Stru's head as the woman looped and measured her ankle. She caught herself, realizing that Stru wasn't wearing a red tag. She wasn't military. "Miss Stru, this is a bit primitive, isn't it?"

"It also tests your skin's flexibility and various other important things, like strength, durability, etcetera. No good having something fit you perfectly and then try to squeeze you into jelly the instant you put it on." Stru whipped out a small penlight that she flashed over each of us in turn, slipping a band of light across our bodies. First horizontally, then vertically.

And then we got to actually get our skinsuits.

I went second, so I got to watch the whole thing. The first cadet lay on the table and Stru picked up what looked like an electric pen, then ran the pen along the fabric, which split as smooth as butter. She left a precisely measured length on either side, creating a rectangle of fabric around the girl, who was trying to stay perfectly still.

Then Stru attached cables to the square of gray fabric and plugged the cables into an exposed socket for power—both the electrical and computational variety. The fabric writhed and squirmed like it was alive. The girl on the table kept herself still through sheer force of will, teeth gritting all the while. The fabric flowed up and wrapped around her, then sealed itself into a perfectly fitting skintight glove.

The cadet stood, holding her arms out. "Feels loose in some places," she said.

Stru nodded. "It should. Arms up."

She used the electric pen to cut holes in the armpits, then put in those bladders we'd seen, trying out the biggest one first. Too big. She tried a few more, going smaller and smaller until she got the one that was just right. She sealed up the fabric again with the same device. The girl lowered her arms and rolled her shoulders. "Comfy."

"Okay, let's finish up." Stru repeated the song and dance, putting two small bladders underneath the girl's boobs, then sealed the fabric up. The next parts were easy. The girl got to put on big stompy boots that sealed up around her calves. Then she put on sleek gloves, which sealed up right below her elbows. The gloves had little screens on the back of each hand, which lit up.

Stru held out a square helmet, and the girl slipped it on. The fabric of the skinsuit and the helmet met, sealing together. On went a backpack, and a few tubes were attached to the helmet, plus wires to the gloves and boots. Finally, a pair of pouches was strapped to her thighs; she got a holster on her back, and the armor for the shoulders, calves, and chest was attached. The armor was set to a nice Alliance blue, and looked like a semi-flexible plate of foamy stuff. When you looked close, you could see that the foam had a latticework of lines, and over it all was a faintly rubbery sheen, like the whole thing had been laminated by something even thinner than plastic.

In the end, it looked like about fifteen kilos of added mass, but the girl held it well. We'd all run with heavier packs during CAPE and PT. She laughed.

"I feel ready to kill Loonies already."

"Yup," Stru muttered, pressing a penlike device into the cadet's hand. "This is your scanner. Check yourself every time you go out to the big empty, or you might miss a seal and get yourself killed."

"Right." The girl held out the pen at arm's length, then scanned herself. "Seems clear."

"Did you check your back?"

"Uh…"

"I'll do it," I said, taking the pen and sweeping her back.

"*Xiè xie*, uh…"

"Dru," I smiled, giving her the pen back.

She laughed. "Yolanda."

"All right, enough bonding." Stru stepped up and pushed a button on Yolanda's glove. "This is gonna pinch!"

"*Tā māde!*"

Yolanda jumped, but I could see a tube had moved under her skinsuit. She looked chagrined, rubbing at her backside. I figured she was kicking herself for not guessing that was going to happen.

Hey, it's not like you can just go to the bathroom in space. There was probably a recycler in the backpack. Better to not think about that too hard.

"Y-you could have warned me."

"It's *wèi nǐ zì jǐ*." Stru smiled. "Imagine if I had warned you. You'd have tensed up and it would've hurt worse. Now, get into one of the decompression chambers. It'll be a dirty vacuum, but it'll be enough to test."

Dirty vacuum: i.e., there would only be a few trillion molecules of air floating around. A clean vacuum was something like one atom every cubic meter. Yeah. I know. Huuuuuuuuuuge difference.

Yolanda climbed into one of the chambers in the back of the room, which I had thought were changing rooms or something. The door closed.

"You're going to feel an intense need to fart," Stru said. "You'd better do it, or else you'll rupture your intestines."

"What about the tube?"

"It's not pressurized, and for a good reason. You don't want that kind of differential, not in a skinsuit. Not unless you like internal organ failure!"

Yolanda grumbled.

There was a hissing noise, and the decompression chamber emptied of air. That meant we didn't hear Yolanda fart, but she laughed, audible over the microphone.

"How does it feel, Cadet?"

"Ya know what they say," Yolanda said, some of her good humor coming back. "Silent but deadly."

We all got fitted. The only thing I can add is that there is no feeling weirder than smart clothes wriggling onto you, fitting perfectly to everything except for under your boobs and your armpits. Okay, well, the bladders felt a little strange, too, all hard and supportive. Once that was all on, finally, came the extra weight of the armor, the big clunkiness of the boots. And the screens!

One of them showed my biometrics. Heart rate, breath rate, CO2 output, blood pressure: a bunch of stuff that might mean the difference between life and death, maybe, sometime in the future. The other one, though, was a multi-use screen. I could change the temperature in my suit, its color—though the color options were limited to different kinds of camouflage and the standard blue. I could send and receive messages over the radio. The screen also had readouts for any gun linked up to my suit to tell me about its internal components, its remaining energy, and any technical problems with it that I could fix.

And then tubes jammed into two holes I didn't want anyone to jam anything into. *Tā māde*, that hurt!

"Please, stop fiddling with the screen, Cadet," Stru said. "And get into the decompression chamber."

I glared at her, rubbing my backside. I walked, and the tubes squirmed, and that felt weirder still. But it wasn't that that made me pause outside the de-com room's door.

This was hard.

Living in space has me always on the edge. Sure, I've always been a Spacer. You'd think I'd have gotten used to it over sixteen years, but you really, really don't. Or at least I didn't. We spent our whole lives training for what to do if something went wrong, if there was a hull breach, if vacuum started ripping away our fragile, precious hold on life here in space. So the thought of being sucked at by a vacuum, even a dirty one, was petrifying. And doing it willingly? Not fun. But I stepped into the room and closed my eyes, back to the door. There was a hissing noise and the biometrics bleeped. I glanced and saw my heart was racing. Well, no shit. And then I felt the overwhelming urge to fart Stru had mentioned. So I did.

I was in silence so complete that I couldn't believe it. The only noises were my own faint breathing, the soft hiss of my Giss's life support system, and the thrumming I could feel through the soles of my boots, the humming of the station.

"How is it?"

"T*ài hǎo le*," I said, teeth clenched. Don't think about how there is a vacuum around you. Don't think about how a tiny little hole would suck out all the air and…

"All right, we're repressurizing. Report to the Storm Cellar and get into practice groups." Stru was grinning, I could tell. "I hear those sadistic bastards are going to work you guys silly, until you know the suits like your own skin."

She was right.

CHAPTER 6
TWO-DIMENSIONAL THINKING

1/28/2068

Sun-Earth L1, The Hub

1,500,000 kilometers above the surface of the Earth

"In wars of bygone eras, there was a concept called enfilade fire." Our instructor on space tactics, Dr. Yu, wasn't in the classroom, because the Alliance brass decided that a "real specialist" should teach us and not a Spacer. We had to settle for an image beamed up from Shanghai and squirted on the wallpaper of our classroom. That meant we got all the joys of light-lag, with none of the advantages that vid-lessons and AI instructors give you. We couldn't "pause" Yu, or rewind Yu, or query a local AI to find more information about what Yu was talking about. But some idiot with his head in a well thought having a "specialist" lecture at us like we were a load of Peels would be a totally necessary part of our educations.

Life sucks sometimes.

"It is a concept based around the idea of flanks. But in space, there is no gravity to force 'down.' There is no horizon to hide behind. By all rights, any attack should be seen coming from a great distance, meaning that defenses can be prepared before the attack arrives. This seems to make flanking impossible. Can someone tell me whether that is true?"

We all waited a few seconds, to make sure that was really the end of the transmission. Dan raised his hand. We waited another six seconds.

"Yes, Cadet Ts'ui?"

"It *is* true because we, uh, we do have a horizon, of sorts. The debris field is thick enough, and it orbits at different speeds depending on where you are. If you slip some men into a debris cloud with their suits powered as low as possible, they can surprise a target, once they orbit under or above them, of course. Also, if you outnumber the enemy, don't you by definition flank them? You can attack from two directions at once."

After all the training we'd had hammered into us by Sergeant Antwiler and the other DIs, it felt weird to not be prefacing everything with "the cadet wishes to know" or "the cadet humbly suggests," but Dr. Yu's class was very lax on military discipline. Maybe it was because he was a civilian. Still, we waited silently, Dr. Yu nodding in delayed reaction to Dan's comments.

"Ah, you raise good points, but do remember!" Yu brought up a projection on the screen he filled. "The Sandcaster."

We all shivered. I had been having nightmares about that ever since I heard about it.

Basically, you take a big tube. Stick an explosive in one end, then compact some scrap on top of it. Then you aim it at a possible attack vector and let loose. Poof. Scrap fills the area in an expanding cloud.

Because the original design, thought up way back in the 1980s, used sand as the payload, we called it a Sandcaster. Sort of like how we still use "port" and "starboard" (incorrectly— I actually went and looked up what they meant during a boring evening once) even though we're a few million kilometers away from an ocean. Since they were the first terms used for the thing, "Sandcaster" and "sand" stuck, despite the fact we'd actually be killed by junk, scrap metal and, if we were lucky, tiny rocks.

You wouldn't think that a tiny piece of junk could kill, but remember your basic physics:

$$K = \tfrac{1}{2}\, mv2$$

In other words: it doesn't matter how small something is. If it's going fast enough, it'll kill you deader than debris.

"Sandcasters are cheap, easily hidden, and with proper intelligence, one can face them toward any attacking force." Dr. Yu frowned. "They can even be automated. A single soldier can hold off a thousand with no more than six Sandcasters."

"W-would the Loonies use that?" Yolanda asked. "It's inhuman!"

We all waited.

"Inhuman, Cadet Hsing?" Dr. Yu was older than all of us, and in that pause, he looked every second of it. "As inhuman as the German machine guns that shot dead almost a million English-men in the First World War? As inhuman as the atomic bombs detonated over Hiroshima and Nagasaki by American pilots in the Second World War? As inhuman as the tanks that rolled on protesters at the Tiananmen Square massacre in the 1980s? As inhuman as the war-pox released by French ultranationalists during the Slump? As inhuman as the Transhuman Massacres in the Second American Civil War? The Lunar Separatist Move-ment has already committed the greatest act of terrorism in the history of the world; do you really think they would balk at this?"

Yolanda didn't meet his eyes. I wasn't sure if she was upset at having humanity's inherent inhumanity shoved in her face or upset that she'd been shown up in cynicism by an Earther, of all people. Yu barreled forward, squashing any questions or comments in the kind of tactless way that only someone who hadn't used the Lag-Net much could manage.

"Fortunately, the Sandcaster cannot accelerate its payload rapidly enough to penetrate a Reusable Orbital Vehicle's hull." No one called ROVers that. "Well, not one that has some DLV armor, that is, but tradeoffs in weight-to-fuel ratios is a conversation for a more advanced course. If any of you wish to try for officer training, though, you will cover that."

He looked distant, as though he had lost some of his train of thought, and we could tell the difference. He didn't look expectant, like he wanted us to start speaking up; he just kind of fuzzed out and stared past us. That happened depressingly often with Dr. Yu. Fortunately, he was surrounded by a doggedly persistent set of AIs that kept him somewhat on track. One must have popped up with a reminder of exactly what he was supposed to be teaching us.

"Oh. Right." Yu brought up a new picture. This was a three-dimensional grid, with a few floating pieces of debris in it. "This is going to be a common battlefield..."

"Dr. Yu?" I raised my hand as the grid started to appear, already realizing the problem with the simulation.

"...and you will need to...uh, yes, Cadet Zhao?"

He blinked at me.

"Wouldn't almost every battle be centered on something of importance?" I paused. "Battles normally *have* objectives, right?"

We waited, trying to hide smirks.

Dr. Yu nodded. "Good point, Cadet Zhao." He fiddled with something and in the center of the debris field popped up a reasonable simulacrum of a damaged but still livable hab, in the mode of a regular cylinder. It wasn't spinning, so it either did microgravity work, like growing crystals and other experiments, or it was an observational hab. Or it was about as accurate as a spaceship with wings, and you could always trust an Earther to forget about spinning a hab.

"So, let us say this habitat is wanted by the enemy. Let us say they are defending it like so..."

Several figures appeared around it. Two were behind metal shields, with Sandcasters mounted in the center. The others were doing light patrols outside, their backpacks poofing with air jets and brighter rocket jets. They were zipping around pretty fast.

"They are outside because they know an attack is coming. We have the following attack vectors open to us due to the time and fuel that a G.I.S.S.S. would have." He pronounced every letter instead of just letting "Gissssss" roll off his tongue. Orange Tag, Orange Tag.

We all watched as Dr. Yu outlined the possible attacks. They all seemed to be covered by the Sandcasters.

"Do we have a ROVer?" Yolanda asked.

"No. R.O.V. fuel is expensive, and most of them are dedicated to rapid supply transfers. High impulse, high thrust, and all that."

We glanced at one another.

"So we're going to just use our suits to approach?"

"Yes. Well, you most likely would have ridden along with a supply transfer to a closer station, and then shipped out 'on foot,' as it were."

We all exchanged glances again. That sounded dangerous. It sounded dangerous even without clouds of debris in orbit and a bunch of Loonies ready to shoot us with Sandcasters. Suits didn't have much margin for error in pilot calculations or accidents or anything like that.

"Now, there are many ways to attack a station, but they are all dependent on fuel-to-mass ratios and relative positioning. For now, I have done away with those strategic thoughts so we may focus on what you cadets will need to handle: the immediate, tactical situation." Dr. Yu started positioning us on the screen. We were little blue figures, with our rifles and suits.

"So," Dr. Yu said. "This is the theorized attack pattern. You want to cover every angle of attack as best as possible."

"Sir, why do we have anyone deployed in the way of a Sandcaster?" I asked, raising my hand after I spoke.

"Ah, but are those people?" Dr. Yu responded after a pause, tapping the figures on the screen. "Or are they decoys? It is remarkably hard to disguise a vehicle as anything but a vehicle, but a suit is small enough that it is relatively easy to make a decoy. These are such decoys, nothing but suits with some basic electronics to make them appear real."

The decoys moved in first. The Sandcaster fired and the simulation didn't deign to show us exactly what would happen when rapidly accelerated junk met soft, yielding smart fabric. Instead, the decoys just turned into floating gray blips.

"Now, you have the advantage. Your attack routes have opened up, as the Sandcasters take a few moments to reload. What you must worry about are laser weapons and kinetic weapons. And so, deploying diffusion grenades before you—"

The non-decoy blue figures moved forward, even as puffs of simulated vapor appeared around them, shrouding them. The Loonies fired back, but they only got a few of the blue figures before we were on them. And it was over pretty quickly after that. We outnumbered them. Two blue-suited figures blasted the Sandcasters while the rest shot the remaining Loonies dead.

It looked quite clean.

"We don't have diffusion grenades," Dan said, shifting in his seat. "The Forge has been going full-tilt making armor and guns and parts for broken habs."

"I'm sure your superiors will have some kind of smoke-screen cover for you before your first engagement," Dr. Yu said. His smile looked like those old pictures of Mao: great promises with lots of corpses buried under them.

I stole a look around the room and could tell that everyone else was thinking the same thing.

Fantastic.

>+<

After our class on space tactics, we had dinner.

I sat across from Yolanda, with Dan next to her. We had kinda fallen in together, if only because we were the only ones who regularly asked questions in class. Dan hadn't brought up his incredible failed pass on me, and I hadn't teased him about it. Instead, we all ate and talked about what we got on the news screens from the AllianceNN.

"The Loonies took Fresh Kills," Yolanda sighed, her chopsticks clicking.

I shook my head, sipping from my drinking bulb. "Took? That makes it sound like there was a battle. Fresh Kills still hasn't fixed their radiators. They're living out of suits and stored rations."

"Yeah. Well, Kaufman's been on the Loonie bands, talking about how he has brought security and safety to Fresh Kills. Do you know what they renamed it?" Dan shook his head in disbelief before answering his own question. "Friedman."

"Friedman? What is a Friedman?"

"Who. *Who* is a Friedman. He was some libertarian saint or something." Dan worked his synth-noodles around his chopsticks and slurped them into his mouth.

"Now, I'm no expert on libertarian philosophy," I said, trying to sound stuffy and serious like Dr. Yu or any other Orange Peel up from Earth. "But isn't a primary concept behind their entire ideology to *not* use *force* against people?"

Dan and Yolanda snickered.

We finished eating and started up evening PT. We ran. After we ran, we did our push-ups, crunches, lifted weights. That whole shebang. Then, mercifully, we got discharged for the night. Early by military standards, but then again, it was Saturday. Theory and light PT was all we got.

"*Dismissed*!" Antwiler shouted, standing at the doorway of our barracks, with us all standing at attention beside our bunks. We relaxed, but we didn't collapse immediately like we used to.

I plopped down on my bunk.

Susan Kolby stuck her head over the corner and looked down at me. She always seemed shell-shocked, but she managed well enough when the instructors weren't screaming at her. Right now, though, she looked like she was about to get a halo and become an Angel. Angels—people who couldn't hack their jobs, who lost it in the face of daily life in space—were sent up to Heaven, the hospital station. Before the Disaster, going to Heaven was the single best way to end any chance of a career. Now, with Heaven barely intact and the crew living hand to mouth, it sounded like it'd be easier to just shoot yourself in the head.

"D-did you hear about Fresh Kills?" Kolby asked, her voice wavering and drawing my thoughts back to the Hub.

"Yeah," I said.

"M-my parents were both there." She hung her head forward, loose and limp in the Hub's lighter gravity. "D-do you think the Loonies will treat them all right?"

I nodded. "Sure they will. Fresh Kills is a...uh, fuel distillery. They need fuel distilleries or they're going to be stuck."

Kolby seemed to be mollified by that. She crawled back into place.

I sighed, then rolled onto my belly and checked to see if I had gotten any emails from Sarah. *You've Got Mail*, the screen flashed in Mandarin.

Yes!

Man, physical training sounds really miserable, but then again, I get so flabby sometimes, I wonder if maybe I should join the army just to lose some weight. (I kid, I kid J) Anyhoo, I did beat my neighbor again (it's 12/10 so far), but things are getting a little freaky down here. I know that you get all the space news up there, but do you get much Earth stuff?

We did get some, but, since Earth was effectively a no-go until I was almost thirty, I didn't think about it that much.

Well, in case you didn't, Tibet has risen up in full revolt again.

I gulped. Tibet was a long debate in the Senate and House of Provinces, chucked between politicians, party members, and talking heads like a hot potato. Technically, it was a state. Technically, it had its own representatives, but when had that ever stopped someone from getting screwed? Me, I'd never really thought about it. I mean, it was there, it existed, but it had never meant much to me.

But here's the scary thing, Sarah wrote. *Texas joined them.*

Now that was a lurch and a half. Why the hell hadn't we heard anything about that? Had I just missed it?

That said something real bad about me. I hadn't even noticed that the biggest sore thumb of North America had just sprung up again. They had more recent bad memories than Tibet. It had only been forty years...

So, we have Texas and Tibet going up in arms and actually saying that, while they deplore the loss of life, they do see that we "forced the Lunarians to take such drastic actions."

I felt sick. People were supporting the Loonies? After what they had done, all the people they had killed?

That means that we've got a load of boys and girls signing up to fight on the ground. People are calling it a police action, or a revolt, or a riot or something, but we all really know what's going on. It's World War Three. Or Space War One. Whatever you want to call it, I'm scared. No one's gone nuclear yet, but that's just 'cause Texas lost all their nukes after the Disarmament and Tibet never had them in the first place. But...I don't know. Things are getting ugly.

How had everything gone so wrong so fast?

The thought that answered that question was sickening: they'd always been wrong. They'd always been teetering on that edge. I mean, I lost count of how many times little news stories had popped up about little problems here and there. People used words like "police actions" and "minor shootouts" to hide what was actually happening, because we'd all gotten so sick of wars. The Golden Age had cracks in it, and I had had bigger things to worry about than noticing them.

My whole life before conscription tasted like ashes in my mouth. People were dying and all I was worried about was mooning over a girl I talked to every single day. How...petty. It didn't seem so bad now.

Love you. Stay safe. Xooxoxoxoxox.

I switched away from the email, frowning. I had five minutes until lights out. I'd write an email later. For now, I was sweeping the news feeds, trying to get the whole world in my head before I had to log off. I checked the public Alliance bands, but it was all about some celebrity getting killed, with a few minor notes about forces mobilizing to "police actions." I switched to the United African Broadcasting feed; Sarah always said they were a good place to check.

She had been just about right. Tibet and Texas were in open revolt. President Chang was condemning both of them, and the

Alliance's ground army was being readied to stomp them down. I shook my head, then actually started to spool the news stories backwards in time, trying to get a feel for life before Christmas, before the Disaster. The life I had apparently sleepwalked through, my mind focused only on eventually going to Earth.

I felt like a royal Orange Peel by the time lights out hit. Rumbling unrest in Luna, Tibet, Texas—it had been obvious as day, looking at them in retrospect. But the comments on those news stories, they'd always been by either profoundly bigoted trolls or people just shrugging their shoulders and saying: *they'd never do it.*

The lights clicked off, but my mind kept whirling.

I mean, think about it. The Slump got really bad in 2022. The only industry that hadn't screamed into the ground was local agriculture, and that was because so many people were starving and desperate enough to try and grow anything anywhere. The food they had been eating had become too difficult to grow, let alone ship to starving cities. There wasn't enough oil to push cars around. Weird climate stuff knocked over a few harvests. Civil wars popped up left and right, the worst being the nuclear firestorm in North America that had left two cities glowing in the dark, even now. The cherry on top came when everything seemed like it couldn't get any worse: an asteroid whizzing straight at us, ready to smash into Europe and turn billions of people into so much dust and memories, then send the rest of us packing into a new dark age, bread and circuses all over again.

The Alliance had stepped up, forming when the USA and the PRC signed a cooperation agreement. They built *Liberty and Unity*, one huge spaceship that flew up and attached rockets to the asteroid, slowing it down. It got parked in orbit, hollowed out, and crammed full of factories. And lo, we had a race for the sky. Shi-Armstrong was founded, turning our barren moon from a tourist attraction with an old, faded, out-of-date flag to the biggest energy exporter ever. The Hub and a hundred other stations, large and small, started to ring the planet, each of them with a different job.

Fuel distilleries caught interstellar hydrogen and turned it into usable fuels for our ROVers. The Hub watched the sun and grew plants. Microgravity wineries started to drop caskets of exotic wines. Microgravity crystal factories started to make new and faster computer components. The railgun at Qinghai launched the mineral wealth of South America and Africa—traded to us fairly by the United African Nations and the Confederation of South America—into space. Huge ingots of metal were caught by the Forge and turned into everything you could imagine.

The Slump had ended. The Alliance had formed officially, and the world had gone from two nervous superpowers to one, confident superpwoer looking toward the future.

It was all so good.

How much had it really changed us?

With those thoughts bouncing around in my brain, I fell asleep.

CHAPTER 7
PRACTICE MAKES PERFECT

1/30/2068

Sun-Earth L1, The Hub

1,500,000 kilometers above the surface of the Earth

I breathed slow and careful, my hands gripping my PPR. It had no heft, but it still gave me *something* to squeeze in a death grip. The strap felt like it was hugging me. I moved like I was turning, twitching my hips slightly, and the skinsuit felt that and translated it into my backpack. Jets of air puffed silently, and I spun around. And there was the Hub, or at least the entry point on the lower axis. I could see the sun, flickering as the solar panels rotated overhead like spokes in a wheel. Sun, darkness, sun, darkness, sun, darkness.

Another suited figure puffed around, coming between me and the sun.

"Have you tried lateral motion, Cadet?" It was Sergeant Cao Cao. He didn't have a specific grievance against me anymore. That, alone, was nice. Still, he had been the one watching us for the past week as we worked our way up to this. First, we practiced inside with cold gas thrusters. We learned the moves by the numbers, until...until today. We had gotten damned comfortable. It had felt nice to do something so easy. But that boost to morale had gone away real fast the instant I got outside.

"Sir, no sir." I tried to hide my fear. I closed my eyes and made like I was going to move to the side. It's kinda hard to explain. Basically, the skinsuit is made up of this smart fabric that takes electrical impulses and vibrations from the skin and uses it to tell the backpack and other thrusters that are all over my body how and when to fire. A light motion uses a puff of gas. A bigger motion turns on the thrusters.

So, if you wanted to "sneak," you had to use a light touch. Go too hard, and your thrusters would blaze bright as the sun behind you. Now, in some places, that wouldn't be so bad—like if you were coming in with the sun right behind you. But most of the time, you'd show up like a white flashing light in a pitch-black room.

My thrusters puffed and I started to sail to the left. I laughed, despite the vacuum surrounding me. It was nuts, but I was actually having fun in open space. The big empty. The void. Whatever dramatic name you wanted to slap on it (and trust me, we Spacers have a lot of dramatic names to choose from), space didn't just surround our homes and our bodies. It permeated every single nook and cranny of our brains, from the frontal lobes to the twitching lizard stem. The first lesson I had beaten into my head, from Crèche into pre-app-hood, an endless, relentless maxim: Space. Is. Death. Don't go outside, or you will die. Don't forget your breather, or you will die. Don't touch airlock controls, or you will die.

Well, now, we were outside and we weren't just surviving.

We were dancing. There was no bracing and pushing. No air resistance to slow down any soaring leap through microgravity.

No walls to contain us. There was just the suit and us and the empty, and for once in my life, I could forget the empty.

We got about ten more minutes of getting to play around, time to revel in our faux-freedom. Then we started getting marshaled into formation by Cao Cao. And I had a feeling I wouldn't be able to forget the vacuum outside for very long now.

"All right, this is our basic formation," he said, tapping his glove. An image of the formation appeared on the screen of my helmet.

Despite humanity's long affair with the bubble helmet, our helmets weren't the kind seen in classic spec-fics, or the even older golden-faced model of the early American astronauts. Those were elegant designs, for all their low-tech crappiness. But here's the thing: they don't let you talk. The old cliché is that if you want to talk privately to someone, you press helmets together and turn off your radios. Then the sound of you talking carries through the helmet. Muffled as hell, but it'd work.

Only problem is, a bubble helmet does not give you enough surface area to actually transmit sound. So our Gisses have helmets that are more like a flat front with a curved back. You can make out, so to speak, and talk fairly well, even if your entire suit is nothing more than skintight dead weight. Now, normally, if you want to talk privately, you just glance at someone and the little laser turret on your helmet will link up with their com-systems and lase at them. If that fails, you can link helmets directly with a tiny wire hidden behind where your earlobe would be if you weren't wearing the helmet. And if *that* fails, you fall back on making out.

Redundancy. It's a Spacer's middle name.

The second misconception I'm pretty sure everyone who's never been in space has is that our helmets have nice big glass faceplates. Yeah, vids love that, so you can tell the actors apart and stuff. Heck, some of them even have bright shiny lights that illuminate their faces. That always cracks me up. No, no, our helmets were covered with micrometeorite/ flare shields, with two bug-eyed cameras on the front with fancy optics that shunted us not just visual light, but a load of other things up and down the EM spectrum. IR, UV, T-tays, hard Gamma: you name it, we could sense it. And there was a slit of infrared-sensitive material across the front, too. The cameras piped to a wraparound screen inside, with a heads-up display that gave us various readouts.

Still, if your electrical systems died, you could flip the faceplate up and see with your normal eyes.

Redundancy. It's a Spacer's middle name.

So, we had our formations pop up on our HUDs. Two people designated fore. Four people in a kind of cross shape, facing four directions for zenith, nadir, port, and starboard, then one person aft. They all would link their camera feeds and information into their tactical local network. That way, everyone could look everywhere all the time for any telltale thruster flares. If the cameras noticed something we didn't—like, say, a burst of infrared from cloaked spacesuit—then they'd circle it and give us warning bleeps.

Audio simulations also played every time the suit cameras picked up on something they thought we needed to know about. If the suit saw a thruster flame, it'd made a "thruster flame noise." If it saw a distant thruster flame, it'd make a "distant thruster flame noise." And finally, if it wasn't quite sure *what* it saw, it'd make a "not quite sure what I'm seeing" noise.

And you thought that in space, no one can hear you scream.

We split into our formations. They looked kind of like little stars. Mine included Susan Kolby, Dan Ts'ui, Yolanda Hsing, and three other cadets I didn't know. But I learned their names quick, 'cause their feeds popped up in my HUD, with their names displayed underneath. Carlos Alvarez, Hung Cao, and Jason Mandalla.

"What kind of a name is Mandalla?" Dan cracked over our private network.

"Shut up." Jason was grinning, I could hear it.

"All right," I said. "Uh, let's get into formation."

It didn't work very well. Dan and Jason tried to take point in the same spot and ended up jouncing slightly. Dan swore and overcorrected and his thrusters burned in Jason's faceplate, splashed off by the metal. Jason swore and overcorrected and ended up flying backwards, zooming towards the Hub.

"Shit shit *shit* shit!" Jason cursed, spinning off, his thrusters puffing fitfully.

"Calm down, Cadet!" Sergeant Cao Cao's voice came over the line. "Stop twitching, you're confusing your suit."

"Right. Damn," Jason muttered. I found him, my suit's HUD circling him with a green symbol. I tapped my glove and the view zoomed in. He was floating out there, alone, but at least his thrusters weren't firing.

"Now, remember. Correct your spin, and then turn to us, then burn back."

"Right." Jason gulped. He sounded tense. I felt tense. Imagining him out there, floating with nothing around but more nothing—it made my skin crawl.

He puffed a few times with the gas nozzles, turning, then his back thrusters started to burn, illuminating him. He got a fairly good speed up, then coasted. He turned and decelerated until he was at rest relative to the rest of us.

"Very good. You only get three hours mucking out the algae vat instead of five," Cao Cao said.

"I hit him, sir, it's my fault," Dan spoke up.

"I know it is. You get the five hours."

That shut Dan up.

Working the algae vats comes in three flavors: Job, Work, and Punishment. Green Tags with high IQs and a degree in molecular chemistry and genengineering are the ones who do it as a job. They reconfigure strains of algae to better do whatever it is they want them to do, whether it's making explosives or food or purifying waste. They get to do their work with computers in labs attached to the vats, but completely sealed off from the stink. And there was always a stink, no matter what strain sat in the vat. Algae ate a slurry of human waste and biological goop that got dredged out of the recycling systems, and the biological process smelled like a sock fermented in urine stored in the stomach of a dead horse that was being digested by a rotting whale.

"Work" is when you're a poor Space Marine cadet and you draw the algae vat work card for your Monday afternoon. So instead of spending your day screwing your brains out with some of your best friends, writing letters to girlfriends or boyfriends or transfriends, or sitting in a corner sobbing until it hurts, you get to muck out the vats. Like, literally. You scrub the vats clean with a scrubber so that a new strain can be put in without cross-contamination. But you get nose plugs to filter out the worst of the stink.

And then there are the poor SOBs who draw algae as punishment. It's exactly like working the vats, except you don't get the plugs.

"*Saāng jai mou sí fāt*, Cao Cao is a freaking *júhuā*! May he come down with *gǎn rǎn xìng fù xiè* after someone superglues his suit. And he can *duàn zǐ jué sūn*!" Dan muttered as he worked the scrubber up and down the side of the vat we were cleaning. He turned to me. "*And* he's an asshole."

I grinned. "Sometimes, I think old-timers are right. English cussing really lacks the poetry of the Mother Tongue." Dan did not look amused. "Hey, you can borrow one of my plugs," I said, glancing over my shoulder at him. We were both in disposable skinclothes. When we were done, they'd be tossed into a vat and mulched for the biomatter that splattered them.

Dan shook his head. "I'd still smell through one nostril. And besides—" He grunted as he hit something encrusted on the side of the vat, his butt bumping mine as he tried to scrape it off. "Isn't self-sacrifice…grrr…stupid piece of shit, *come off*!"

"Spray it, and then let it sit for a bit," I suggested.

Dan sighed, then grabbed a little squirter he had clipped to his hip. He sprayed down the encrusted bit and coughed. "That smells even worse…ugh…"

The lights dimmed. The lights went out.

We looked up. "Oh, *wǒ de tiān aaaa*…" we whispered as one.

Then the lights came back up. Dan and I were already scrambling out of the vat, ripping off our clothes. We chucked them at the dumpchute and then turned to the wallpaper, which flicked on, revealing General Lau—not just a governor; this place was a military base now. He deserved the posting, too, being the only person in space with a command rank. He'd been a major wheel in Luna's garrison before retiring and becoming governor up here. I wondered how he felt about being dragged back in. If he felt anything like we did being dragged in the first time, he didn't show it.

"Congratulations," he said. "We've just won the first actual battle of the war."

His face was replaced by a graphic of the Earth's orbital system, a load of circles and ellipses and blurry probable rotation patterns for the larger debris clouds. "Fifteen seconds ago, two dozen missiles were launched from different points across the debris field. Each clocked in with a relative velocity of maybe five hundred meters per second, arcing towards us. If one had struck, we'd be so much glowing debris right now. However, the Loonies didn't count on Big Bertha."

The picture changed to the familiar sight of the microwave power transmitter at the bottom of the Hub, but it looked different. It had a new cover, as well as other bits I couldn't identify off the top of my head.

"Our power transmitter is now the solar system's largest maser weapon. We shot down each of the incoming projectiles before they were within half a million kilometers of the Hub."

"Wooo!" Dan shouted. I laughed, clapping him on the back. Suddenly, the punishingly low information speed for personal communications made a lot more sense. Our antennas had been repurposed to make a freaking maser cannon.

Other faint cheers were coming from the vat-labs that overlooked us. We could hear the celebration through our feet, thrumming through the station. It's not often you got a reprieve from death like this.

"Return to your duties," General Lau said, before the screens flicked back to standard status reports.

But as we headed back to the tank, getting new sets of disposable skinclothes from the dispenser, Dan started thinking out loud.

"There is no way the Loonies couldn't have noticed Big Bertha," he said. "Heck, they'd prolly know better about it than us. They can look at us with telescopes. We're cooped up in here when we're not bouncing around outside making ourselves look like asses for the Loonies."

I shook my head. "What gets me is that the first battle fought in this stupid war took twelve seconds and was won by a computer." I started scrubbing the algae tank again. "So, remind me please, why the flying *diǎo* do they need Space Marines?"

"To clean algae tanks." Dan scraped at the stubborn hunk he had sprayed down earlier. It came free. "Duh."

I got off two hours before Dan. Before I left, I patted him on the back. "Sorry *Dì-di.*" I climbed out of the tank just as my replacement came into the room, buck-naked. He waved at me, and I tugged out my noseplugs and handed them to him. He made a face, but I shrugged. "Listen, whatever's in that tank is worse."

"Mondays." My replacement turned it into a four-letter word, jamming the noseplugs in—and, to be frank, I was already missing them. The stench that filled the tank room made me want to gag. "Why couldn't we do the nice jobs?"

"'Cause if you *could* do the nice jobs," Dan chimed in, grunting as he scrubbed, "you wouldn't be in the Marines."

My replacement wriggled into some skinclothes, even as I ripped mine up, wadded the shreds into a ball, then chucked it down the chute. My actual clothes waited in the nearby changing room. I felt a bit sore, but not as much as after some PT, or heaven and gods forfend, CAPE. I put my hand on my arm and squeezed. Oh yeah. I had muscles now. That still surprised me.

I got to the locker where I had put my clothes and laid them out on the bench that ran through the middle of the locker room. Then I stepped into the cleaning stall, closed the door behind me, and braced myself as every bit of biomatter that splattered my face and hands got sucked off. Ow. Ow. Ow.

Once I was dressed, I headed out. While walking through the corridor, other people smiled and grinned at me. I grinned back. Yeah, first battle of the war won. If I could take some credit, just for having a red tag on my collar, well, go me. I arrived at the bunk and found a state of general revelry. There was some music thudding out of four linked screens and a few of the cadets were dancing to classical headbanger. Soft, of course, to keep people in the next room over from getting pissed off.

"Dru!" Chuck called to me. I still kinda didn't like Chuck. For someone who had been so sure he wouldn't fight, he had swapped sides awfully fast once Antwiler started screaming at him for being a *gāisǐ de* coward. Kolby, she had the dignity to be miserable.

I walked past him, glancing his way. "What?"

"Want to dance?"

"Screw you." I grinned, to make sure he didn't try and slug me. He snorted, shaking his head, then tried his bunkmate, a cadet named Chin.

I sat down on my bunk. Kolby stuck her head out from over the edge, looking down at me.

"We won the first battle," she said.

I nodded.

"Why can't Big Bertha shoot Loonies from here? I mean, any Loonies that show themselves on our hemisphere of the planet?"

"Well," I said, cracking my neck. "It probably can. But the Loonies can use the debris field to hide. It can target a ROVer, but we need ROVers as much as the other side, so Command probably wants to try and take them in one piece."

Kolby bit her lip. "They're throwing our lives away for a shuttle?"

I sighed. "Pretty much."

She thought. Kolby had a real expressive face, one that showed when she was thinking in every little dimple and pore.

"Assholes."

I blinked. That had to be the most vulgar thing I'd ever heard from her.

"I dunno," I smirked. "I prefer *dá bá gwaí* crapping *chaǔ baǎt* whose grandmother humped a goat."

Kolby made a sound halfway between a giggle and a snort, even as the dancers in the room traded partners with a "hey" and started to do some complex light-gravity dance that involved a lot of bouncing and laughing.

I sighed, then got to work on my next email.

CHAPTER 8
TAKE HOPE

2/1/2068

Sun-Earth L1, The Hub

1,500,000 kilometers above the surface of the Earth

We managed to make some coherent Stars and move around in them for the first time on Wednesday. It felt pretty good, even if we did drift and bobble a bit.

This was after almost two hours of exterior practice, not to mention the torturous test where they essentially chuck you out of an airlock, send you tumbling, and then make you correct and shoot at targets. It was a bit like riding the gyro—which I still hated, but was now able to bear with the stoicism of long-accustomed torment—but at the end, your involuntary movements would trigger maneuvering jets. That is, they did until I figured out the trick of how to cut and automate the jets using a little program that could help straighten you out.

I earned my Sharpshooter badge ten times over after that.

Still, all the groups—called Stars now, after our basic formation—worked and learned and we got better and better every day. Then it hit.

We were in a slightly-understaffed Star: me, Dan, Jason, Yolanda, Karl, and Carlos.

I checked my visor for anything odd or unusual, even as we started to head in another direction, our thrusters carefully bleeding off momentum to make a smooth right-angle turn. Everything looked fine...

"All cadets, report to the Cellar, now!" Antwiler's voice cut through the lines, startling all of us. Yolanda braked so hard that she almost slammed into me, correcting for her correction just in the nick of time.

"Did something go wrong?"

"Maybe the Loonies—"

"I think—"

"*Zhù zuǐ*!" I snapped over the coms. They shut up, for some ungodly reason. "Let's get back to the Cellar and find out why."

When we did finally get everyone back inside, we got to sling our backpacks off for remassing and refueling. Antwiler grabbed onto a support pillar to anchor himself and shouted, "*Attention!*"

We all snapped to attention.

The door opened and in came General Lau. He looked at the lot of us, sweeping his eyes back and forth. He came to a stop above Antwiler, who pushed gently away. Lau looked unflappable and calm, focused, like he had everything under control.

"A complete tally of what was lost during the Disaster was completed last month. For the past two weeks, Alliance Space Command and I have discussed, debated, and planned and have, unfortunately, come to the following conclusion: the stations that the Alliance still holds—the Forge, the Hub, minor agriculture stations and three fuel distilleries—are at a serious risk of running out of water and remass."

Remass. It's such a little thing, being the stuff you squirt out of a thruster when you want to fly. Only by chucking remass out can you go forward—thank you, Newton. It takes a *lot* of it to push around a ROVer packed with supplies for stations on the brink of collapse.

"As you are all aware, the primary source of remass…" General Lau paused for effect, even though we all knew what he was going to say. "…is the Moon."

Ice covered the moon. It was more abundant than people had thought, back before we colonized it. Trapped under dust, hidden in craters. Everywhere. Shi-Armstrong was built near a dense pocket of it; it has buried aqueducts running from the underground ice caps. Before the Disaster, Shi-Armstrong would slingshot hunks of ice all over the place with their railgun. Now, they kept it for themselves, letting us…

Letting us fly ourselves to death.

"I know your training is nowhere near complete. But the simple fact is, we have a narrowing window of opportunity to pull this off. So, I have picked twelve of the best cadets, based off the reports of Staff Sergeant Antwiler and the other drill instructors."

General Lau began to read off names. Didn't know them, didn't know them, didn't know them, Chuck, didn't know them…

Then.

"Drusilla Zhao."

I blinked. Then I blinked again. I clung to every inch of steel that Antwiler had beaten into me to keep from looking terrified. Once Lau was done, I knew that Jason and Chuck would be coming with me. No one else had been someone I knew.

"Those of you in the mission, report to my briefing room for details. The rest of you, Sergeant Antwiler will deal with you."

We doomed to die followed General Lau out of the Cellar. I saw Yolanda and Dan staring at me, like they'd never see me again. I tried to smile.

The general's briefing room was in the Red Tag area. I'd never been there before—it was another one of those places the computer would lock if you didn't have clearance. It was remarkably spacious. There was a hologram projector in the middle of the room, showing every known hunk of debris, every possible enemy, every station, and the Earth, and all the Earth's nuclear missile launch positions. And two bright golden spots: the railguns at Qinghai and Shi-Armstrong. One on the Earth, one on the Moon.

There were a bunch of big, heavy-hitting computers, making the room feel damned toasty, even with their optical chips. At the end of the day, computation still meant waste heat. They were calculating trajectories, possible attack vectors, everything you could imagine.

"So." General Lau gestured and the view expanded, zooming in on the orbital pathways around the Earth. "The Loonies have their own ways of transporting goods and supplies here and there and back again. This is one of them."

The view expanded to a fuzzy holo of a DOTtie. Dedicated Orbital Transport. I had never been on one, but it looked spindly compared to the good old ROVer—just a long thin tube, with cargo crates attached all around the sides, and two engines at the front and back. The thing was slower than molasses, unable to enter or leave the atmosphere, but it could carry bulk anything to any station. And then I felt something like weak-kneed relief and total idiocy. We were going to raid a transport, a freighter. I had been imagining landing on the Moon and trying to mine it for remass with a million Loonies bearing down on us.

I tried to keep the embarrassed blush off my face.

"The Loonies can manufacture one of these in about a week, but we don't have the material for it. The Forge can make small parts and rifles and armor just fine, but for anything bigger than a car, they need to assemble it in pieces outside. Which, frankly, gives the Loonies a big 'shoot this' target floating right outside the Forge, which can handle some schrapnel." He grimaced. "Taking this from the Loonies gets us supplies, most likely remass and some food we can redistribute, possibly even complex material and civil power."

Civil power. In other words, people we could either conscript to help run stations, if they were talented, or just plain conscript if they weren't talented. Like me.

"Sir, do the Loonies escort them?"

"Not according to our intel. And we have a lot of intel. Every Earth government has a telescope aimed skyward and they beam their feeds right to us." His lip curled; it was almost a smile. "They will after this raid, though, so this is the first and last time we'll have it so good."

I nodded slowly. The other cadets did the same. Maybe, just maybe, this wouldn't be a suicide mission.

"The DOTtie you will be acquiring is designated the *Hope*," General Lau said. "You'll take a ROVer straight down towards it, burning hard and then coasting. You should arrive in her path after ten days transit time."

"Ten days?" Jason asked, shocked. "That's...that's burning a lot of fuel, sir. Doesn't it normally take two weeks at least?"

"It's a tradeoff," General Lau sighed. "We don't have enough intel to predict Loonie ship movements two weeks or more in advance, so we're burning fuel to get into the timeframe of what we *do* know. Once you have the DOTtie, it'll be a three-week journey back with what you've got; then we can appropriate the DOTtie to our own ends."

"Right, sir." Jason frowned.

"I guess we should pack some books," I muttered. General Lau, instead of screaming at me like Antwiler would have, just nodded.

"Well, suit up and head to the ROVer." The general glanced back at the holo. "Sergeant Cao Cao will accompany you into battle and lead the takeover of the *Hope*."

We saluted. He saluted back. "Dismissed."

We walked along the corridors of the Hub, heading towards the ladder that would bring us up into the Cellar.

"So." One of the male cadets spoke up. "I know we have the next ten days cooped up together in a ROVer, but…might as well start getting acquainted now. Your name?" He pointed at me. "What was it again?"

"Drusilla. You?"

"Mack." He grinned. He looked pure Caucasian, making him stick out like a sore thumb.

"Jason," Jason said.

"Ping," The male cadet next to him said.

"Ping!" Jason grinned, making the name sound like an onomatopoeia.

Ping frowned. "Don't do that."

A series of "Pings" came from a few other cadets, each one of them enjoying the way it made Ping's face turn red. It was kinda funny; he did have a face that was made for looking mad, all pinched and focused.

"All right, shut it up, all of you," a girl snapped. She sounded hardass. "It was only funny the first fifteen times."

"Fine, fine," Jason said, laughing. The hardass girl grinned. Okay, I liked her.

Ping, though, remained unamused.

We climbed up the ladders and arrived in the Cellar. The other cadets had left and we got to suit up. Since we hadn't taken off our skinsuits, the hard part was done. We just needed to strap on the armor, the thrusters, and our pouches. Our old training guns were gone, though. Sergeant Cao Cao came in with PPRs and P3s. But they had one thing different about them: they were equipped with power packs that had a tiny green light on the side.

He handed them out and we strapped them on.

"These are live weapons," he cautioned us. "Leave the safeties on for now, or I'll gouge out your eyes."

"Sir, yes sir!" we chorused, snapping our helmets on, hooking up cables to our backpacks. This all felt unreal. We had done it before, often, *constantly* for the past week or so. But this time, we were doing it for real, which just made it feel less so. And if you think that sounds stupid, imagine trying to parse it while you were actually there. I put everything on like I was in a dream, in a scattershot of vague images and concepts and feelings that never quite came together into something coherent until later, much later.

"All right, good," Cao Cao said, even as he checked himself with a scanner and we did the same. I scanned his back, and the hardass girl scanned mine. I grinned at her.

"Dru," I offered.

"Jillian," she said, scanning my butt for slightly longer than necessary. "Is this taken?"

I snorted and blushed. "Yes, but thanks for the compliment."

And like that, we were done. We got into the airlock, let it cycle, and then we thrusted towards the ROVer, which hung outside of the Hub, ready to be ridden down, closer to the little blue marble that was the Earth.

The airlock door opened and we got into the ROVer, which looked kind of like a sleek, flying wing. It was black, too, matte black, because it's made of lightweight grapheme. Tough stuff, but thin and flexible. A ROVer's pretty basic inside, with just a cargo bay and a cockpit; the pilot was already there, a slender woman in a normal skinsuit. No armor. Which meant we got an astounding view as she squirmed from her seat, then turned to face us, taking off her helmet once the vehicle's inside was pressurized. And I had to admit, she had a real nice...view. I blushed and shook my head, remembering what I had just said. Taken.

"Hello, boys," she drawled. "And girls of the right persuasion. My name is Leah Jones and I'm going to be your pilot for this trip. The only rules are if you're going to shack up, use the curtains we have set up in the back, and use something for a gag." She smirked. "It's kinky and keeps the noise down for the rest of us."

We all laughed. It felt a bit refreshing to have some friendly sexual perversion thrown at us without a load of screaming. I got a bit wistful, thinking about how red Sarah's face would be if she were here. Then my wistful feeling just became glum.

Jones got into the cockpit and started up the engines as we settled in. She turned the ship around, and the engines began to burn, acceleration pushing us against our straps. I closed my eyes, counting down to when we'd stop burning. I had never been inside a ROVer accelerating before, so this was all real novel. It felt long. Longer than I'd have thought. The acceleration slowed, and stopped, and then we were in freefall, zooming towards the point in space where the *Hope*—mawkish Loonie name if ever there was one—would be.

"All right," Cao Cao said. "You can take your armor and thrusters off, but stow them like this." He showed us how, slipping them into straps. "Your helmet goes here." He put it on a hook, easily grabbed. "If we get decompressed, you get your helmet on first."

We resisted the urge to say something sarcastic. I say we, because I just knew everyone else wanted to do the same. We might have been new to combat, but we still knew how to keep breathing units close, just in case.

"For the rest of the trip, I will be leading us in combat workout, group discussions, and so on," Cao Cao continued. "We'll have a few hours of rest time between, but we're still on military discipline."

Anyone who groaned, I knew, would get shoved out the airlock.

So we all got to practice throws, holds, how to kick with a brace, how to kick without a brace—that only worked with thrusters, so we had to just learn the theory. We discussed possible scenarios and what to do. But we also started to slide out of boot camp. It was like stepping into a decompression chamber. Suddenly, we could use first person. Suddenly, Sergeant Cao Cao wasn't Sir. He was Sarge.

It was awesome.

"All right, what if they have an escort that pops hatches and engages us?"

"We, uh, we hose the ship down with setting-two lasers. Anyone inside will feel uncomfortable, but anyone outside gets microwaved."

Sarge nodded. "Good. What if they have a Sandcaster on the bow?"

"Scatter," we all said at once.

Cao Cao smiled. "Exactly."

Between discussions, we read. We slept. We talked. I got to know the others better: Jason, Mack, Jillian, Lou, Ulysses, Ping, Liam…

Liam. Oh, Liam. He was the friendliest member of the group, without a doubt. The first day of flight, when I was still settling in, he pushed over and grinned at me.

"Wanna shack up?" he asked.

"No."

He had been a bit taken aback. And, in a clinical sense, I could kinda see why. He had all those things that het girls went nuts over: abs and shiny teeth and stuff. It fit together right for them, but...ehh. He in specific, and boys in general, did about as much for me as the engine of the ROVer, and at least putting my hands all over the ROVer wouldn't be cheating on Sarah. I still felt guilty for ogling Jones and getting flirted at. Which was stupid, but the worst thing about stupid feelings is that you can't just *un*-feel them. They stick in your head and bug you.

"May I ask why?" he asked, the formality jarring after his blunt-as-a-club opening line.

"I'm gay?" I ventured.

"Ah, never mind, then. Sorry for disturbing you." He pushed off, heading to the hardass, Jillian, who accepted.

The pilot grinned at me. "I'm open," she offered.

Shit.

I wanted to do it with Jones, no questions asked. I mean, she had a killer body, a wicked sense of humor, and wasn't in the military chain of command, so...yeah. And it wasn't like I hadn't done it before. One fumbling, half-aborted attempt with a girl when I was fifteen. It had been the thirty-seventh anniversary of the End of the Slump, and we had been given a day off. Now, you take a load of fresh pre-apps, not used to actually having to work for a living, and you give them free time, then you have a party on your hands. We danced awkward teenage dances and listened to terr'r, which had been all the rage back when infrasonic music was big. And Erica, this girl I had made googly eyes at for the better part of a month, swooped over and danced with me. She'd dragged me into a closet and we started making out and...

And it hadn't been great. But talking about it with Sarah had sparked something amazing. I had just been friends with Sarah then, slinging good-natured insults between playing MUDs and

PBPRPGs with her. But then I mentioned I was gay. And she mentioned she was gay.

Even thinking about what happened next was getting me a little excited, and we had just been using text. And here I had a bombshell in skintight clothes flat-out offering to go behind the curtains for a bit of playing around.

And half a million kilometers away, Sarah was waiting.

You don't know what it's like to be offered something on a golden platter, with someone you love so far away that it hurts. It physically hurts. Guilt and desire sit at an emotional Lagrange point and the grinding of your mental gears rips into your heart like a chainsaw.

"I've g-got a girl," I stammered out. And the knife got yanked out just to stab back in.

"Where?" she asked, curious.

"Earth." It felt like chewing on carbon. And Jones got a look of intense pity on her face that was worse than any temptation could be.

I closed my eyes and tried to count to fifty or something. "Do we have email capacity in this tomb?" I asked, trying to smile. I'm pretty sure it ended up looking like a death grimace.

"We can lase them back to the Hub and they can shoot it back down," she said softly, reassuringly.

"All right." I opened my eyes and looked around, finding my gear netted above my head. I worried my right glove out, tapped the screen to turn it on, and started composing my email.

Sarah-Bear, I typed. *I'm going out on my first mission. I think I can tell you about it, but if half this email is blank, then just assume, well, whatever you can. You're a smart one, I just know it. :)*

I glanced around. The curtain was closed, because if you crammed a bunch of sixteen-, seventeen-, and eighteen-year-old Spacers in an enclosed space, the horny ones found a way to congregate and get down to what they do remarkably quickly. A few of the other cadets had set up a 3D chess board with magnetic pieces, with Ping and Lou playing, everyone else floating at random angles to watch. Sergeant Cao Cao was telling Mack and Jason—the two cadets who weren't interested in shacking up, writing emails, sleeping, or playing chess—about some kind of space tactic he called the "spin pop."

Basically, we're crammed into a ROVer, falling towards the Earth. The plan is to grab a Loonie DOTtie. That is, a Dedicated Orbital Transport. Yeah, we have such creative names up here :P. I know my training isn't really officially done, but they picked me and the rest of the mission 'cause we're the best of the best (apparently).

I mulled over that for a minute.

I'm not as scared as you'd think. It still feels kinda unreal. Like this is just a...what did they call it? A road trip. Or maybe a pleasure cruise. Anyhoo, the pilot is pretty cute. She's making eyes at me, I must admit ;).

Should I leave that in? I chewed on my lower lip, then decided to. Honesty first.

I miss you. Tell me one of your long rambling stories, bonus points for being salacious.

I stuck my tongue out of the corner of my mouth.

And...maybe another picture? >:3.

Love, Dru. Xoxoxoxoxoxoooxox.

I hit send and leaned back, sighing as I waited. There was nothing here to look at, other than Jones, who was working with her pilot switches and checking various gauges in between watching a muted episode of *Monkey: Most Honored and Potent Sage of Heaven.*

I shrugged, then grabbed my helmet, stuck it on my head, and tapped my glove until the HUD keyed into the shuttle's entertainment systems. With my helmet on, I didn't have to worry about annoying anyone with sound, so I leaned back and watched TV with Jones.

CHAPTER 9
FIRST BLOOD

2/11/2068

Elliptical Orbital Transition: L2/L4

400,000 kilometers from the surface of the Earth (approximately)

My ten days in space were an exercise in carefully controlled insanity. And that was on top of the normal carefully controlled insanity that made up life in this glorious corps.

It all started with the salivating dreams about Jones. Everything from peeling her skinsuit off to crawling onto her while she was in the pilot chair and...ahem. Anyway, to cope, I had started taking as close to a cold shower as you could in space, by turning my suit's temperature down. That kinda worked, until I got basic thermodynamics beaten into my head by Sergeant Cao Cao, who noticed that my suit's radiators were dumping my waste heat into the cabin for everyone else to enjoy.

"Is there a particular *reason* why you feel like making the rest of this place a hotbox?" he demanded, sarcasm dripping from his voice as I wriggled my upper body into the algae tank in the back of the ROVer and started scrubbing. No noseplugs, so I got the distinctive bouquet of shit, piss, and bile shoved right through into my brain. Plus, the awkward small size of the tank conspired to make the worst parts of cleaning an algae tank even worse. The splatter was worse, and any chunks I had to scrub were even nastier because I couldn't get a good brace against anything.

Wán meǐ wú quē.

And, to add to the enjoyment, the entire exercise was pointless. I was scrubbing without disinfectant or soap or anything else. Really, it was more like just pushing algae strains around for the sadistic enjoyment of my comrades, armed as they were with their own noseplugs. Well, okay, only two of them got a chuckle out of seeing me scrub like that. The rest were being polite and not ogling.

Oh, yeah, I got to scrub while naked to boot. We didn't have disposable skinclothes on the ship, and no disposal vat. So I had to be naked. Once I was done, one of my team—I picked Jason, because he was gay, too—sucked the algae off me with a little hose and squirted it back into the tanks.

Finally, I got to wriggle back into my suit, face beet-red.

"Don't worry," he muttered as he helped me brace. "Most of us aren't algae fetishists. Watch out for that evil Ping, though. He's like a mirror-universe version of me, I swear..."

I snorted, zipping up my skinclothes with a single tap.

There was one nice thing about all that scrubbing, though. It had eaten up most of the day, and when I went to sleep, I just dreamed of drowning in tanks of bile, rather than dragging Jones into a sleeping bag.

Big improvement.

The next few days, though, saw us all getting a bit twiggy. Close quarters meant everyone was getting a little on edge, even with military discipline and almost constant drills. Jillian kept ragging on Liam to stow his gear better, and snapped at me when I snapped at her to lay off. Then Ping snapped at us both to stop snapping. Sometimes, it seemed like we were getting a little too into the combat practices and debates. Mack nearly broke his arm on Monday, and spent the rest of the day sitting it out, rubbing a huge bruise.

On Tuesday, Cao Cao set us to doing little chores and tasks. He had us divvied up into shifting units, so no one would work close to any given other person for too long. That worked—if by "worked," you meant "kept us from murdering each other." It didn't make morale get any better, but I don't think that Cao Cao much cared. By the time we hit Friday, I had not just learned that war is long periods of boredom followed by longer periods of being dead, as my grandfather had once said; I had internalized it. I had felt it suffuse every bone of my body. I felt it in my *shen*, my soul, my very being. If you cut me in half, you'd see the word "boredom" crammed in there around my organs and bones. That was how boring it got.

Still, on Friday, I noticed—possibly thanks to my constant ogling—that Jones was hitting the same series of buttons every few minutes. As she did it again, Cao Cao shouted: "Come on, everyone, don suits! *Gǎn kuài!*"

"What is that?" I asked, tugging on my boots. I anchored myself on the wall with the magnetic clamps built into their soles, then started to pull on my gloves.

"Eh, the Loonies tag us with their standard warning every once in a while," Jones explained. "Saying that our trajectory crosses with theirs and they will open fire. They don't have any anti-ship guns on the *Hope*, and no radiators or energy systems that could support hidden ones. At least, nothing that can crack a ROVer's armor."

I smiled. "That's good." I slid my thrusters on—arms, then thighs, then calves, by the numbers—and then I locked my helmet into place and strapped on my backpack. I clicked my heels together and detached, finally slinging on my rifle and P3.

Jones scanned me, then leaned forward and kissed my helmet's camera. "For luck!" she said, grinning, but there was a hint of fear in her eyes. She wiped the lens clean with her sleeve. I glanced at my friends. Jason and Jillian were scanning each other. I wanted to give them a kiss for luck, but my helmet was already on. I wished I had thought of that earlier.

We were all suited up and floating. Sergeant Cao Cao turned to us and sighed. "All right, troopers," he said. "We're going to be suited up like this for the next day, in case the enemy hits us with a weapon on our final approach."

That sounded paranoid, but reasonable. In other words, a perfect Spacer plan.

So we spent the rest of the day in our suits. We watched movies. We played some primitive AR games. But most of all, we realized that we were going into battle. You'd think after a week of waiting around with nothing to do, that realization would have sunk in thoroughly. Nope. Jones, though, she got to do the real work, fiddling with our approach and what-have-you.

Finally, I got an email from Sarah. The date stamp said it was a few days old, so maybe the Hub had just not sent it until recently. *Tā māde!* I hoped she wasn't too worried by my silence.

I've been thinking about this for a while—sorry about not sending it back sooner. And, well, the truth is that we're not going to be seeing each other for a long time. Decades, even.

My heart beat faster.

I can't cut you off from other people by my absence. I can't let that be on my conscience, Dru. I love you. I've loved you for a long time, and I hope to keep loving you even longer. But I can't keep you from, well, loving. And being loved. Or, to be blunt, getting horny.

Sometimes, Sarah was so ignorant of everything from physics to mathematics to basic personal safety. Sometimes, she seemed to know pretty much everything. I closed my eyes, not reading any more until I could get my emotions under control. She wasn't dumping me, even if parts of the email *read* like that. Stay calm, Drusilla Zhao, stay calm.

I opened my eyes.

So, I hereby give you permission to fool around. :) I'll be jealous, but I won't hate you forever.

I gulped. Permission to fool around?

Part of me wanted to salute and say, "Yes, sir, thank you, sir" and immediately dive into the shacking game until I was number one in sex points. Another part of me wanted to slam my head against the wall. Monogamy was silly, stupid, old-fashioned and so very...Orange Peel-y. But it had sunk into my head. I had focused on being there for Sarah and just for Sarah for so long that simply stopping felt as painful as *not* stopping.

And I didn't have the time I needed to unwind that thought. So I sent back the shortest email I had written in a long while, but I had to get it out of my head before we went into battle. Because I might not...no. No thinking about that.

I typed out: *I need to think about it, okay? Thanks for trusting me. I love you so much right now, I can't even describe it.* I hit send, forgoing the loves and xs and os that we normally attached at the end.

"All right." Sergeant Cao Cao forced our HUDs to a graphic of the *Hope*. "This is the *Hope*. We're planning to scramble into space and immediately go here." An arrow drew down—from our perspective, at least—to a bundle of debris that the *Hope* was picking its way through. "The Loonies are using the debris to avoid Big Bertha. We're going to use it for cover. While we approach, I want four cadets to stay here and hose the ship down with setting-two lasers."

Hey, that had been my idea! I was mildly pleased to see it being used, and also sort of irritated that I wasn't getting credit. I squashed that thought under a boot.

"The rest of us are going to make for the debris. We're going to find cover, then advance in half-Star formations." He divided us. Jason, me, Jillian, and Mack would be in the first half-Star. He, Liam, Lou, Ulysses, and a quiet kid whose name I could never remember would make up the second.

Now my heart was jangling and my brain was chanting in the back of everything: *You're gonna die. You're gonna die. You're gonna die gasping.*

"All right." Sergeant Cao Cao looked at each of us, and then nodded. "Attack on three."

All those days in transit, that entire dreamlike nothing was honing in on the right-now. On the three. On the two. On the one.

The airlock blew open. The air had been quietly evacuated out of the main room, and Jones had a helmet on, too. I didn't know what she was doing. Maybe she was doing ECCM or observations or—

Then I was out, following the blue flare of Jillian's thrusters. My breathing was loud in my ears.

"Alliance troops!" a voice crackled over my headset. "You are in violation of Lunar space. Withdraw, or we will ope—"

And then the sound was cut off. A glance showed me that one of our covering cadets had blasted the antenna with a single well-aimed shot, the antenna now just a cherry-red stump and a floating rig that was spinning off into space. It provided some color: the ship was a study in starkness. The computer models we had seen were all based around a simulation with Earth-like light, because humans see best in that. But out in space, the black is blacker than black and the bright is really bright. Shadows blotted out pieces of the *Hope*, making it look like a checkerboard put together by a madman, and it was all in monochromes. There wasn't even a logo painted on the side of the ship to break it all up. I tapped the image enhancer on my suit and the entire thing bloomed into false color depictions, courtesy of a combination of my suit's LIDAR, infrared, and other visual inputs.

"Okay, we—" Sergeant Cao Cao started.

And then he and half his Star were dead, their suits turned into a fine mist of shredded fabric and blood that turned instantly to crystals, catching the light of the sun and scattering it into a red halo that was as beautiful as it was sickening, even in enhanced vision. It was all silent, my suit's sound systems unable to simulate what was going on, bombarded with too much happening, too little information.

"*Sandcaster*!" Jillian screamed, even as the survivors burned hard for cover, manuvering behind the hunks of debris that floated nearby. They were remarkably flimsy up close, just plating from a station that got scragged, surrounded by a cloud of smaller bits—screws, dust, dispersed metal fragments.

I whipped my mining pick out and jammed it into the hunk near me. Stupid. *Stupid*! The hunk started whirling with me, not nearly massive enough to slow my spin around. I corrected with jets, feeling like an absolute Peel. The rest of the cadets made similar mistakes, and if the Loonies had had a gun that could fire faster, we'd have been so much ground beef.

Our covering cadets shouted, panicking. Everyone was.

"What do we d—"

"Bug out!"

"Ohshitohshitohshit..."

"Everyone shut up!" I shouted, glancing around. My HUD showed me that we had lost Cao Cao, Ulysses, and Lou. Liam and the quiet kid had been lagging, and the cone of death had just missed them, but Liam's HUD indicator was flashing, indicating a suit breech of some kind. The quiet kid's name was David, according to the HUD. It felt like the name was burned into my head now.

"David, patch Liam's suit!" I snapped. "Covering Star, give us a sitrep, what is the *Hope* doing?"

"Uh...yes, sir," David stammered. Somehow, I had tapped into David's "follow the godsdamned orders" instinct, the one that had been beaten into him along with the rest of us. He reported back as he slapped a fix-patch on Liam's suit. "The Sandcaster spun out of a hidden compartment. They're reloading it!"

"Okay, we have a few seconds. Spread out and attack! Get into that ship!"

Not the best plan, no. But I kicked any fear in the head and thrusted up and out from behind cover. The *Hope* loomed before me, a giant spindly pencil with crates attached all around it. The Sandcaster had been on the "front" of the ship, hidden in a rotating turret. Everything focused onto the ship, the space around it, my body. Nothing else mattered. In the back—the distant back—of my mind, someone was screaming her head off.

The HUD showed everyone was doing the best they could, but some people were moving too slow, too cautiously. We were all spread out, though. That was something.

Then the Sandcaster spun around, going so fast, too fast. I hit the accelerator as hard as I could. Out came my pick. Wham. The pick slammed into the barrel and my momentum yanked it up and bent it. And I knew I'd die, but at least I had stopped the thing from...

From...

Doing nothing.

It didn't fire.

I didn't have long to wonder why before I heard a shout. "They're popping troops!"

I thrusted up, leaving my pick wedged into the Sandcaster. I unslung my PPR and stuck my head out from behind a storage crate. There were a few Loonies out there. Their suits were patched and they worked their thrusters with a single hand on a joystick. Their other hands held pistols with boxes around the barrels. They fired and their thrusters corrected for the recoil of the weapon. I ducked back down. "They've got slugthrowers!"

"Got one!"

Someone screamed. Their icon started flashing red and yellow. Whoever it was, their suit had a hole in it and they were wounded. Neither was good. "David, see to him!"

I bounded up and over, kicking my feet against the *Hope*'s decking to shoot up, then burning my thrusters hard to the starboard, giving myself a perfect angle for enfilade fire. Funny how I remembered all the terms our lecturers gave us in the middle of chaos, when I couldn't in class.

My PPR strobed, biting into the hull at a Loonie's feet with a gasp of boiling metal. He kicked off. And then my next strobe got him right in the chest plate. He didn't have armor. The spray of steam and flash-fried blood spread out before him and he went cartwheeling backwards into space.

And then it was over.

No more Loonies. No more Sandcaster.

I gulped. "E-everyone okay?"

"God, it hurts...*Mommy*!" A whimpering voice came over the coms. Jason. "Mommy! It hurts so much!"

Okay. Battle over. I didn't focus on anything until I got to Jason, who was floating out above the Loonie ship. David was beside him, indicated by the HUD and by his last name, painted onto his boots. The powers that be figured that boots and gloves would be most likely to survive an explosive death. Gloves had their computers, which could ping you with any information you needed. So boots had names.

"He's bleeding bad," David said over a private link. "The bullet got his thigh."

I swore. Blood was spurting out and freezing everywhere but where it should. His skinsuit fabric had been scrambled by the bullet, and did nothing to stop the blood flow. I put my hand over the wound, squeezing. "Okay, David, get the ROVer over; we'll get him inside, get this suit off, and wrap him up."

"Roger."

"Dru...Dru, tell Liam I love him, okay?" Jason was gasping. "I know he's straight, but tell him, okay? Give him a kiss from me."

"Jason!" I flipped his visor up, then flipped mine up, too, so he could see my face with his eyes, not just cameras. "You are *not* going to die!"

My suit made a rumbling noise, and I looked up to see the ROVer moving close with puffs of air and a few tiny squirts from its thrusters.

"Okay, David—"

"Dru!"

I glanced at my HUD. The other cadets were floating around the *Hope*, at a loss.

"Gonna enter this thing, see who's inside," Jillian said.

"Do it! Be careful," I warned, like I needed to remind anyone out here to be careful. I could have kissed Jillian right then, because if someone had asked me what to do next, I would have burst into tears. It was all just too much. "I'll stay here, keep pressure on his thigh. Move carefully."

Jason screamed when David and I used our suits to move, puffs of gas spurting from our thrusters. He screamed and writhed, which made his thrusters fire, which caused him to scream even more. "Godsdamn it!" I shouted, letting go of him as he started to spin slowly off. I pulled out my P3 and aimed it at Jason. "Sorry, Jace."

I fired the P3 at his thruster pack, severing the power cable. The thrusters on his suit cut out. He kept writhing and screaming in pain. "Mommy!" But his movements were getting weaker.

I gritted my teeth, near tears myself. It almost hurt worse to hear him. Almost.

David and I grabbed him again, with me trying to staunch the blood. It was flowing slower now, which was bad, if I remembered my emergency medical training right. Still, we got him inside the ROVer. The airlock door closed and we got his armor off, revealing his wound. Jones came out, carrying a medical bag. She got to work, wrapping up his leg, injecting Jason with some chemicals.

"No-Shock, clotting agent," she named them. "And bone marrow stimulation. He'll be a bouncy boy for the next few hours."

"Will he be okay?"

"Sure." She grinned. "If you're not dead when you get in here, you'll prolly live. Now, uh..." Her face became somber. "Cao Cao is dead."

He was dead. The adrenaline was also starting to wear off and my hands were shaking. I should...I should go outside and...and...

I closed my eyes. "J-Ji...Jillian, sitrep."

"Some crew, I got their hands on their heads," she said, her voice a little fuzzy.

I took off my helmet. David was looking at me. "Don't we need to go out?"

My hands kept shaking. I...beyond that airlock door was... no. I couldn't face it. Not after surviving it and coming back inside, where there was a skin of metal against the darkness and the cold and the death.

"I...c-can't do it." I whispered, softly, just for David and Jones to hear.

Jones put her hand on my shoulder, even as my vision blurred.

"She needs to look after Jason. David, head out and police the *Hope* with Jillian. The Loonies can wait." Jones said, her voice gentle. "I've sent the sitrep back to General Lau."

David said something, but I didn't hear it. I was too busy crying. I'd shot someone. I shot someone without a second thought. He kept spinning off inside of my head. Spinning and spinning and spinning, trailing blood and air and memories. I put my hands over my face and couldn't breathe.

When I was done shaking, crying, and rubbing my shoulders, it was almost an hour later. We were still getting reports from the other cadets, and Jones was overseeing it all from the cockpit.

Jason grinned at me as I sniffled and wiped away whatever was on my hand to my hip.

"We're alive," he whispered.

"Not all of us."

"No, but *we* are alive." He closed his eyes, seeming so happy. Content enough to just float there in a haze of drugs and fading adrenaline.

It took less than two hours to secure the *Hope*. Jillian—with advice from Jones—went through the place bit by bit, finding that there were only two crewmen who were just pilots and loader/unloader. I could hear them over the radios.

"Thank you, thank you," one of them was saying.

"We've had to keep real quiet on Luna; everyone who isn't with the LSM is a traitor and gets either forced labor or a bullet to the back of the neck. So half the people are keeping quiet— the other half are giddy as clams to be working with mass murderers."

"Thank you, thank you, thank you..." The other just kept repeating it.

"Milo!" his friend hissed, shutting him up.

"Sorry, I just...t-they shot Cypress."

"Yeah, our third crew member was trying to send packages to a couple of Alliance stations, where his sisters lived. They shot him. Just flat-up shot him and dumped him into the recycling vats."

I sniffled and had my first coherent thought in a while. I wondered if our side would shoot someone who tried that. Because, really, it was a betrayal on four levels. You were essentially throwing away a valuable piece of equipment—rocket boosters were cheap, but not plentiful anymore—to aid the enemy by giving them supplies they could use against you. Somehow, I thought our side might just do it. After all, they had threatened us with death if we didn't hack through basic training.

"Can you fly her to the Hub?" That was Jillian.

"No," the talkative guy said. "*Hope* can only manage orbits that are within the magnetosphere. That's the big problem with—"

"Yeah, whatever." Jillian's husky voice switched to private channels. "We've got a full manifest. Sending."

"Got it."

The shakes were still there, but curiosity pulled me forward. I grabbed onto the ceiling straps and dragged myself to float over the cockpit. There, I could see a scrolling list of what was on the ship.

Jones grinned. "Water, food, and fuel. The three things we need."

"What's that?" I asked, pointing at something that jumped out at me as being odd. I recognized the rest of the cargo—since, well, it was just fuel and water and food. Not much else to be gotten from that. But, what the hell was AM Storage, Salvaged from L2 Fragments?

The salvaged bit was easy enough to figure out, but the rest of it?

"General Lau—" Jones was saying, breaking into my musing. I realized she had a com link open to the Hub. "What's at the L2 point?"

"Not much anymore. Why?"

"Well, 'cause," she pointed at the screen, her finger tapping the word to highlight it for Lau, who was probably observing our data feed. "The Loonies salvaged something from there. AM Storage."

There was a long silence, longer than light lag would account for.

"You are to load as much water and fuel onto the ROVer as possible. You are then to take the AM Storage straight back to the Hub, hardest burn. You are authorized to leave behind the cadets to cut down on your mass and increase your storage space."

"W-wait, what?!" I blurted. "S-sir, with respect, we have wounded!"

"If Cadet Mandalla is not in immediate need of replacement limbs, you can treat him there." General Lau's voice was hard. I was suddenly reminded that he had been watching the whole fight from the Hub. Heck, he probably had feeds from our suit cameras and gun cameras and everything, watching everything we did. "His suit readout indicated it could still hold air with a patch."

I gritted my teeth. I wanted to tell him to go screw himself, but...

But godsdamn it, the discipline kicked in. It was all I had keeping me from going completely nuts, and discipline is hard to just let go, especially after something like that. Letting go of discipline was the first step on the slippery slope, heading straight to freaking out. So I bit back my response.

"Yes, sir." I tried to inject weapons-grade venom into my voice.

"Cadet Zhao, I am promoting you to Field Corporal. You've shown some command abilities. If you keep this up, you might make Sergeant. Consider this your first test." General Lau paused. "I want you to take the captured DOTtie to the Forge. From there, you will oversee the defense of the Forge until we can scramble a ROVer to provide support. You and your troops will also be called on to perform raids on nearby Loonie-held stations. Do you understand?"

Sucker punch one: Field Corporal. Sucker punch two: Me? In command? Sucker punch three: taking the DOTtie to the Forge. That was—shit, I'd need a calculator and some wallpaper to figure it, but the back of my head said it was about three days travel from where we were.

Sucker punch four: perform raids on Loonie stations. Stations studded with Sandcasters and full of pissed-off Loonies.

With just a couple of cadets.

Miaò jì! We were going to *zhōng liè*.

"Do you understand?" General Lau's voice came through again, hard and flat.

I nodded, firming up. "Y-yes sir."

Jones was looking at me with wide eyes.

The linkup closed.

"Good luck," Jones whispered. "You know, I mean, don't...I..." She tried to find some words. "Lau will be on your ass and in your ear the whole time, even with the light lag."

Somehow, that didn't help me feel any better.

CHAPTER 10
REAL SHOWER

2/14/2068

Earth-Moon L3, The Forge

500,000 kilometers above the surface of the Earth

The trip from where we took the DOTtie to the Forge was really *fěi yí suǒ sī* boring. And I, foolishly, had thought that the worst of boring would be being forced to watch the same videos, listen to the same music, and hang out with the same people, day in, day out without any privacy or quiet. At least in the ROVer, you could switch off, or slip out of your suit and shack up. Or at the very *very* least, you could write an email or play a game on the ship's computers. All that let you escape the boredom, even if only temporarily.

No such luck out here. I figured that if the Loonies managed to scramble a ROVer after us, we'd get warned well in advance. So I just had us strap up to the side of the DOTtie, our magnetic clamps keeping us tethered. With my new command authority, I was able to turn off everyone's suit thrusters so no one would accidentally thrust hard and turn their tether into a pivot that would slam them into the ship. That tended to break bones and faceplates and radiators. Not recommended.

And thus, we remained stuck to the side of the DOTtie.

Unlike the ROVer, the DOTtie didn't have a good high-effiency chemical rocket. Instead, it had hall-effect thrusters: little electric gadgets that spat out ions and slowly—very, very slowly—pushed the DOTties around Earth orbit. But a DOTtie could never push hard enough to fight against the roaring monster of Earth's gravity well. Hall-effect thrusters were good for probes. They were good for expeditions to Mars, where a lonely Alliance flag flaps near the base of Olympus Mons. Hall-effect *wasn't* good for a multi-purpose ship, which would be heavy with gear and armor and weapons and what-have-you. It wasn't useful for getting somewhere quick. It wasn't useful for getting to and from a planet.

But DOTties, as per their name, stuck to orbit. They got the slow, stable, tortoise engines. On the upside, DOTties—and there had been a lot of them before the Disaster—didn't cost a lot to build, and they were built to make money shipping supplies all over the place. Being able to last on the cheap was more important than burning hot. So DOTties were stuck hauling freight between stations and Shi-Armstrong, and left everything glamorous and exciting to the ROVers. They got where they were going, but they took forever to do it.

The two pilots we rescued talked to us from time to time, and they let us slip in to use their cabin room when someone got real bad suit fever and needed to jerk off or something, and they shared their air, water, and rations with us. But for three whole days, most of us watched space drift past, or talked, or hacked our HUDs into doing text chat, which caused an impromptu PBPRPG to spring up. I was invited to play as a Half-Elf Cleric, but turned it down. I was more of an Exalted fan.

Me, I looked at the Earth as it orbited below me. I could see whorls of clouds. I could see a hurricane growing off the coast of Florida. I could see the pyramids at Giza—though it took me a few minutes to pick those out. I could see the Green Wall of Africa: a giant wall of forests that was expanding into the Sahara Desert, turning silt and sand into usable land again. Looking at it, I had to admit just a little bit of respect for the United African Nations. They might not have had a foothold in space—especially with Kenya smashed and the Elevator that they had partially funded destroyed—but they knew their geoengineering.

And I could see lights.

I had seen pictures of the Earth, back before the Slump. It always struck me as painfully wasteful, all those lights crammed into a single strip of land. Now, at night, it looked like fireflies covered the Earth, tiny specks everywhere, but the only major concentrations were in the places that still had major industry and city culture: China, bits of Mexico and the rest of the Confederation of South America, and most of Africa. Highest standard of living in the world, Africa. Highest concentration of billionaires, too. I wondered how badly all that suffered now.

And, of course, I could see Sarah's house.

Well, I couldn't see it with my naked eyes. I had to link up to a LEO sat and request a camera feed. It took a few seconds, but the computer saw my rank and patched the feed in—and there it was. A cottage a few kilometers out of what used to be Quebec City, which was rapidly being consumed by forest, near a few other cottages, with a communal agriplot where they raised fish, grew plants, even had a herd of genefixed cattle.

It was all fuzzy, though. I had to infer what was there from what I knew. That blurry shape had to be their fountain. That little whizz of motion that my suit HUD tried to identify as a potential enemy? A bicyclist or an electric car. And there, though I only saw it for a moment, was a smear of darkness in front of Sarah's cottage.

And though it could have been anything from a speck of dust on the camera lens to a bird at the right angle, I knew. I knew in my heart that it was Sarah. Looking up at the new stars in the sky, and praying for the souls lost.

>+<

The Forge itself was impressive. It swelled out of space, first a dot on the horizon, then a baseball, then a looming mini-moon in its own right. It was huge, easily more than a kilometer across, filling up my cameras with its bulk. The surface was plated with solar panels, but between them, you could see the rock that made up the sandwiched layers of the Forge. It went: solar panels, rock, metal plating on the inside. It orbited at a stable orbit, but went a bit faster than most stations, meaning it got chucked underneath the Moon's shadow every day or so. That made us nervous, but so far, the Loonies hadn't made any major play for it.

The airlock door that opened for us was big enough to let the entire front half of a ROVer slide in. The DOTtie had a different way of doing things. It detached its cargo crates, which were then flown into said airlock by the two pilots, managing the crates remotely. We watched, "sitting" on top of the DOTtie like a bunch of Marines on an old waterbound Navy ship.

"They're good," Jason said. His leg was wrapped up in some clear, hard stuff. A cast, basically, on the outside of his suit. It didn't hinder him much in microgravity.

"Heh. And you'd know," Liam teased. "The way you handle joysticks."

"Shaddup." Jason was blushing hard enough to see it through his faceplate.

"Hey, hey," Ping laughed, breaking in. "I think they're done."

They were. The last of the crates had slid in and the airlock was open for us. We floated inside.

"Why don't they spin this thing, anyway?" Jillian asked, even as the airlock door stayed open. The pilots were coming out, wearing Loonie suits they had hastily re-skinned with Alliance colors and insignias. Handy thing about smart fabrics, that.

They joined us in the airlock. The doors closed, and air hissed in.

I took off my helmet for the first time in three days and gasped, eyes closed. Gods, that felt good. I mean, helmets are made to not feel like they're on even when they're on, with little air vents and fans to keep air circulating, and the option to turn the visible HUD off and leave you with nothing but seemingly open space between you and the void. But at the end of the day, my hair kept growing like a *gǒu zǎizi* while I was on the DOT-tie and away from the injections that keep Spacers' hair short. Sometimes, I swear hair tried to take revenge for hormonal blockers by making up for the lost time and growing insanely fast when the shot wore off. That meant it itched and felt hot and pressed up against the helmet and reminded me that I was still trapped in a suit. The other girls and boys all looked real scraggily, too. The pilots, though, were clean-shaven and short-haired. Lucky *hùndàn*.

The inner airlock door opened. The corridor beyond led to an intersection that went in all six possible directions. Picking a random direction and peering down the corridor, I could see another intersection beyond that. And another. And another. And finally, way at the end, another airlock.

"I already have a headache," Liam grumbled.

Our suits chimed.

"Welcome to the Forge," a synthesized voice came over our coms. "Please go forward, up, then forward, then up, then to the right. You will arrive at the living quarters of the Forge crew."

"All right, guys," I said—I couldn't bring myself to call them cadets or something like that. They'd started calling me Corp, though. I didn't know how I felt about that. "Follow the robot."

"Yes, Corp."

I rolled my eyes, but didn't let them see, already pushing along the wall. Up. The next intersection we hit, we went forward, guided by arrows that were labeled "up" and "down" and "forward," "backwards," "left," and "right." It was pretty easy to get around, even if whenever I tried to actually orient myself, it made my head hurt. Didn't help that it was weirdly jarring to use civilian terms again—no "starboard" here. We also passed lots of doors, with windows. The peeks I caught through showed things like three-dimensional industrial lines, with machines putting pieces together in intricate patterns, or rooms full of black boxes that extruded stuff from nozzles on their side.

Then we were at the living quarters. Here were actual people, all with Alliance blue and white on. They were all a bit spindly, but nowhere near as lanky as a born Loonie or Spacer from an old habitat. They were all pretty intelligent looking, mostly middle-aged people with multiple degrees and the collar tags to match. And they were all up here, using sunlight and mirrors to make miracles.

"Hello, uh, Corporal Zhao?" A woman wearing teal, green, and blue tags offered her hand. According to the documents that I'd been reading on the place—forwarded by the Hub— she was almost sixty years old. She looked forty. I wagered if you cut her open, you'd find organs that were ten years old— maybe five. Treatments like that kept people spry and healthy into their nineties these days. People predicted that it'd go up to a hundred and fifty, maybe more. It didn't seem that important to me, seeing as how I was unlucky enough to be both young and diagnosed with terminal "being in the army." No known cure, not right now.

I nodded, yanking my glove off with my teeth to take her hand. First physical contact in three days, and it felt so very good.

"That's me." I smiled. "We'll be your garrison, I guess."

"We feel safer already," she said, returning my smile. "My name is Portia Brown; I'm the big boss around here. These are the heads of the various divisions." She gestured to the men and women around her, naming names and positions. Nanometallurgy, Microgravity Construction, Playtesting.

"Playtesting?" I asked.

"I get to test the guns before we ship them out," the wiry kid said. Well, he was at least thirty, but he looked like a kid next to the proverbial graybeards. But even he had two tags—gold and silver, physics and chemistry. "Professor Sterns."

I patted my P3. "They sure work."

"Right. Well, we don't really have a place for you guys to sleep, so we're going to be bunking you up with our locals," Brown said. "Anyone here gay?"

"I am," I said. "Jason, too. And Jillian, right? Am I forgetting anyone?"

"Hmm, do you want to room with the opposite gender?" Brown hazarded, clearly not sure exactly how to handle this without friction. Physical friction was rare in a vacuum. Social friction? Not so much. It was almost quaint the way she hemmed and hawed. You see that in some older people, like they still couldn't quite believe that we kids weren't constantly running scared about pregnancies or AIDS or something.

"Listen, uh..." I grinned. "Me and my troops have been bunking together for the past few weeks. There's not much that flusters us, gay, straight, both or neither."

"Oh." Brown seemed nonplussed. "W-well, uh, I'll show you the rooms, then."

I nodded, thinking. While we might not mind the whole shacking up and casual nudity thing, the civilians here might.

And that struck me cold. Civilians. I had been a civilian. Not anymore.

"Listen, guys," I said, whispering softly. "These civilians are older and therefore more prone to shock and such and such. So I want you all to stick to being clothed. If you want to shack up with someone, make sure they're not in a relationship, don't force it, and we'll be okay."

"Yes, Corp."

I rolled my eyes at the kind of "yes, Mooooom" tone that some of them used. "Listen to Brown. Dismissed."

I saluted my buddies and they pushed off. Brown, floating in the center of the corridor, looked a little shell-shocked at the rapid garrisoning of her little home. She got her head sorted quick, though, and grabbed a rung and pulled herself along, tapping doors and saying who went where. And thus, the cadets got split up.

I was stuck in with Brown herself. Her room was pretty big, compared to something on the Hub. There was an adjoining shower bubble—which made me drool with envy—and there was a bedroll strapped to the ceiling. "This is your bunk," Brown said. "And here is our shower."

I nodded. "You guys are kinda spoiled," I teased. "This room'd fit two rooms from the Hub, easily!"

"Well, we do have lots of space," she said, shrugging. "You guys have to lug everything an extra million kilometers."

I chuckled, then stripped off my gloves and boots and, finally, my thrusters and backpack, which I slid up against the corner and lashed down with extruded tape that Brown lent me. I tossed the extruder back to her. "Neat."

"Necessary." She smiled. "When you're on a factory floor, and I would not recommend that, multiply your safety acts by a factor of two. A drifting tool could get caught in machines, a wrong movement could destroy a month of work, and so on."

I nodded, then sighed. "So, er…"

I trailed off, realizing something: I didn't have a damn thing to talk about. Brown was acting a bit odd. Standoffish? Maybe that was it, but maybe she just had as much in common with me as I had in common with her. She'd been born right before the oil crash. She was eight when the cars stopped running. Twenty-two—possibly fighting for the Centralists, possibly avoiding the draft in Canada—when the first transhuman soldiers marched out of the hospitals and started butchering rebels and uploading the videos to YouTube. She'd been thirty-one when the Big Nugget had promised to end it all. She'd been forty-one when the Chinese-American Alliance formed.

She was a child of the Slump, and here I was, looking at her old-yet-young face and wondering just what the hells I'd say to her. What had I seen that could match what she'd lived through?

The image of the man I'd shot, spinning off into space.

The blood spurting around Jason's thigh.

The crystals—the gore—of Cao Cao, being torn to pieces.

"Well, I still have a factory to manage." Brown coughed, jamming my mental feed.

"D-don't let me s-stop you," I stammered. I scratched the back of my neck, still groping for something to say. "I have reading to do, actually."

Brown dipped her head. "Yeah, well, have fun with that."

She pushed off the floor, heading out the door. I floated in her room. Her wallpaper was set to the colors and pictures of a forest, with floating images of friends and family. There was a crisp digital picture of her—a young Brown—kissing a full-Anglo soldier on the lips. For a moment, I just drifted there, staring at Brown's life. Then my selfish instincts bashed me on the back of my head. The shower!

I rolled and grabbed the wall and headed straight for it.

I had been in a shower all of twice. Before boot camp, I just perfumed and vacuumed myself in a stall, like anyone else. During boot camp, I followed the numbers. But once, Dad and Mom took me on a weeklong visit to the Space Elevator super-structure, and they had a communal shower there. I had been twelve, and had been completely fascinated by the inside of the shower, the way water bounced around the room in spheres. I had gotten to use it twice before my visit was over and I was sent back up to the Hub.

So it was with a feeling of nostalgia that I closed the shower door behind me, still wearing my skinsuit. I shut my eyes, and was twelve again, with my parents waiting patiently outside. I'd just open the door, and they'd be there.

I slid my skinsuit off, then wadded it up and chucked it out the door before closing it again quickly, not wanting the real world to slip in while the door was open and ruin my memories. The water started, and some of it stuck to me; some bounced off, forming spheres in the air. I laughed and pushed the spheres around, shattering them into a sheen along my palms and making smaller spheres, which hit the walls and bounced. Grabbing the scrubber, I gave myself a hard wash, until my skin was reddened. Then I rubbed water spheres into my hair.

Ooooh yeah. That. Was. Gooood.

But eventually, reality had to intrude. I slipped out of the shower after it was done with its drying and vacuuming sequence and squirmed back into my skinsuit. It wasn't until I had finished shoving my head through the neck hole of my skinsuit that I realized I had made a Peel of a mistake.

I had drifted away from the wall. And the ceiling and floors were *just* out of my reach. I was stuck.

I flailed for a bit, my cheeks bright red. If anyone, *anyone*, came in here, I'd be labeled the Orange Corporal faster than a blowout.

My glove rang, chiming with a com-request. "Accept!" I said, trying to grab for the ceiling. I was slowly floating that way, but air resistance was slowing me down.

"Hey, Dru! Can I still call you Dru when we're not in battle?"

"No idea, Jason," I called, trying to sound calm and collected. "What's up?"

"They have a cafeteria here. Was wondering if you'd like to grab a bite to eat and talk."

Think, Dru.

"Also, uh, where are you?"

"In bed. I'm being lazy," I lied.

He snorted. "Right."

"I think I'll skip dinner for now," I said.

"All right. Your loss," he laughed.

I started to blow, hoping to use my lungs as a rudimentary thruster. I blew upwards, trying to angle myself right. It worked. Slowly. I blew again, then again, then took a break to avoid hyperventilating. My feet hit the deck. I kicked off, went up, and grabbed onto the ceiling.

"Ha!" I laughed, triumphant.

From there, I went to work. Thankfully, I really wasn't that hungry, so I decided to use the time to get some reading done, like I'd told Brown. I found the room's computer console, worked into the window. I tapped it on and called up the email service. I logged onto my account and waited for the Forge computer to interface with the computer on the Hub. And up popped up my emails: five. *Five* from Sarah.

"Christmas has really *really* come early," I murmured, opening the first one, titled HOLY SHIT!!!

Holy SHIT! Sarah started. *I saw it on the news, YOU ARE THE COOLEST GIRLFRIEND EVER!*

Attached was a video file.

I clicked it, suddenly feeling worried.

It opened up on two CANN announcers—Hui Zhong Portman and Johnny Tan—sitting at a desk, holograms projected behind them.

"And in war news," Tan started, smiling broadly, "The first interpersonal battle has been waged against the LSM regime. By leave of Alliance high command, we are allowed to show you the first footage of the war, taken from the helmet cameras of one Liam S. Han."

The view switched to a remarkably clear video file. There was Liam's PPR, aiming at the *Hope.* And then it zoomed in on a suited figure. They were genderless and faceless, just a masked, blue-suited figure, their thrusters burning a bright white. They had a pick and slammed into the front of the ship, their momentum wrenching the metal tube up and then letting go as they swung out their PPR.

"They're popping troops!" someone shouted.

There were other suits, shooting at the Loonies coming out of the airlock. A bullet whizzed, impossibly fast, through a suited figure's thigh, tracing a fine line of beautiful red crystals—beautiful if you forgot that they represented nothing but pain. Then up came the Sandcaster smasher, who shot the Loonie through the chest, sending him cartwheeling through space.

It was all so bloodless—well, not blood like anything you'd recognize, at least; not the globby splats that got everywhere, just tiny discrete crystals—and fast. Like a movie scene.

"Everyone okay?" My voice came from the speakers. It sounded strong, focused. Like a *shí gǔ shí zaó* war hero should sound. I hadn't sounded like that! I had been piss-your-pants scared. I had been ready to kiss my ass goodbye. I had been shaking and quivering.

The footage cut back to Tan and Portman.

"Good on those Marines," Portman said. "But, Johnny, who was that brave Marine who destroyed that weapon before it could kill any of our troopers?"

I felt a cold, sharp stab to the gut. That lying son of a bitch!

"Her name is Drusilla Zhao, the first corporal minted in the entire war. Drusilla was born in space, in 2052. Sadly, her parents—Mary and Michael Zhao—were both killed when the LSM destroyed the Kilimanjaro Elevator. Today, she is a hero for the entire world. And so, from the CANN news desk, we would like to say: good luck, and good fighting."

They said a traditional amalgamated Chinese prayer, and then the video clip cut off.

I was still gaping at the screen when Brown came back.

CHAPTER 11
SETTLING IN

2/15/2068

Earth-Moon L3, The Forge

500,000 kilometers above the surface of the Earth

I woke the next morning wrapped up in the bedroll, with my ears dribbling with high command gobbledygook.

While I had been reading Sarah's other emails, which were mostly a discussion of exactly where our relationship was going—riveting in a sickening, grotesque sort of way—a new email popped up. And I knew it popped up because it dumped me from what I was doing and straight into fifty-five pages of military doctrine that the high-forehead types on Earth had dreamed up over the course of the past few weeks. Then, after that, had come another fifty pages of military history and background on the Loonie Separatist Movement, including a full-on description of the events that kicked off the Indian Diaspora, the Pakistan/Indian Exchange, the invasion from Siberia, and the annexation of Kashmir.

I tried to read it, I really did. I got that, as a corporal, I was the highest-ranking PO—physical officer—but General Lau was still the highest ranking TCO—telecom officer—which meant that he could technically give us orders as though he were right beside us. That made me really wonder why we even needed a PO, if we were going to be micromanaged by Lau from a million kilometers away. But, hey, light lag could make the difference between life and death. So I guess a PO had her place.

But anyway, as the PO, I was supposed to handle things before and after battles. I managed to follow that: keep my troopers from doing anything stupid. Easy enough. We might have been teens, but we were Spacers. And Spacers don't live to be teenagers by doing stupid things. The next thing I was supposed to do was to keep my troopers in fighting trim.

What that meant exactly dissolved into twenty—yes, I counted them—*twenty* pages. And every other page seemed to be written by a different tactical specialist who was just drooling to get their theories into practice. Humanity had been in space, in one way or another, for almost a hundred years, and only now did we finally get a real godsdamned war to fight. Every word from the experts was dripping with barely contained enthusiasm to finally see all those ideas become reality. You know, if they wanted to fight a war in space so bad, maybe they should come up and do the *diǎo* fighting themselves. So yeah, I just skimmed the twenty pages of what I could do to keep my troopers in decent shape before jumping to the actual combat suggestions.

It was sorta interesting, in the way that watching water boil is more interesting than watching paint dry. I got through fifteen pages of hypotheticals and possibilities and only netted one maneuver that actually sounded useful: chucking flares and energy emitters in front of you to produce infrared in the vague blur of a rapidly moving suitshape, so that the Sandcaster's auto-tracker would blast *it* instead, and you could head in unsplattered. The rest of the ideas were completely absurd, at least to anyone who'd actually been in space. My favorite was some genius's *miaò bù kě yán* plan to use fog screens to cover an approach. Yeah, our diffusion grenades *could* do that, but that would just misdirect lasers. It wouldn't stop our waste heat from glowing on the enemy's infrared cameras like miniature suns. And it would definitely not stop Sandcasters or slugthrowers. And, as a special bonus, the protective clouds would disperse into the vacuum faster than you can say dead meat.

But then, the history stuff managed to both bore and depress me. Whenever I was able to get through the statistics and the spreadsheets and tactical maps for battles that were now almost thirty years fought, I saw the human cost. The villages burned. The people displaced. The plagues and famines. There was only one bright spot: the story of General Sung. He'd been told to invade Siberia after the Russian Federation's push had failed. He had known that it would be the last straw before World War III kicked off and nuclear weapons flew in every direction. He had said no.

And so when I woke up, it was with those thoughts rumbling through my head, a throbbing mixture of depression and confusion. Brown was already awake and showering. I grumbled. Civilians should not be getting up before the indomitable Space Marines. Still, I got dressed and felt my stomach clench in hunger.

I headed out of the room with a kick, stopping myself on the far wall as the door closed behind me. "Where is the mess?" I muttered to myself.

"Forward, down, left, left, down." A voice spoke from the wall, pitched just for me.

I looked around. There was no one else in the corridor.

"Who said that?"

"I am Shiva."

"Ah." Now I got it. Shiva…that was Indian. Hindu? "You're more sophisticated than the AI on the Hub."

"Untrue," Shiva said. "I am merely more talkative."

"Right. Well, uh, how many Marines are awake?"

"Currently, only one."

Figured. They deserved the rest, though. "I won't ask you to wake them, but warn me when they're heading to chow."

With Shiva's directions in my head, I set off. I decided to make it faster and more fun by leapfrogging. I kicked off one wall at an angle, so I'd then be able to kick off another wall, bouncing and bouncing. I grabbed onto the rungs of the intersection where I was supposed to go down, pivoted, and then kicked off the ceiling, heading into the heart of the Forge.

Like that, I arrived at the mess. It was a microgravity garden, with vines winding up and along the walls, the air tasting damp and moist. The wallpaper only added to the illusion, projecting images of some South American jungle city.

Beautiful, and yet human. A hovering sphere in the middle of the room puffed over to me. "Greetings," it said.

"Does everything talk here?" I asked.

"Yes." It opened up and revealed a rotating selection of packaged meals. I picked out the congee and peeled it open, which set off the chemical heating elements and made the meal smoke and steam.

I wrinkled my nose. It wasn't fresh food; it was compacted nutria-goo, given the "flavor" of "congee." It tasted like nutria-goo. But I ate it and thought longingly of the fresh fish that I could have been having at the Hub. Benefit of living there: fish spoils if it ships too far, so everyone at the Hub had plenty of seafood, even if we were packing and shipping all of our algae produce.

As I ate, Shiva warned me that most of my buddies were awake and heading for the mess. That, and the flood of military instruction and history from the previous night's emails, got me thinking. They were my buddies, but I was their PO. In order to make all this work, we needed some kind of leader dynamic, so they'd do what I said when General Lau wasn't telling them what to do. But how do you look impressive eating nutria-goo, floating around?

So I shoved the half-eaten package back into the floating chef, who let it slide into an empty slot and started to re-seal and fill it. I stood at attention, even as the cadets showed up. They saw me and snapped to attention themselves. And soon I had nine people before me. Liam, Ping, David, Jillian, Chang, Jason, Chuck, Wang, and Xue. Before I was a corporal, I hadn't even thought of most of them. Other than my friends, they'd been in the background. Now, I had responsibility for their lives.

What a terrifying thought.

"All right, I know you're all hungry," I said. "So, uh, eat your chow."

Right. That had been the stupidest thing I'd ever tried. My troops didn't snicker or anything, but I could see they all had the look of someone humoring a crazy aunt. So I kicked off and turned myself around, grabbing my refilled nutria-goo.

As I ate, one foot hooked into the wall to keep myself from floating away, Jason kicked over, using his unwounded leg. "So, what's the plan, Corp?"

"What plan?" I asked, popping another sphere of nutria-goo into my mouth and swallowing.

"What are we going to do here?"

I was still working on that. Thankfully, the pages Command sent to me had some advice hidden amongst the bullshit.

"Well," I said, scratching my head, "we need to keep in fighting trim—and don't laugh. Those are the exact words of the fifty pages of *gǒu pì bù tōng* bullshit Command sent up yesterday."

Jason cocked an eyebrow at me.

"I'm thinking of splitting us into three Stars of three. Not perfect, but better than nothing. One waits by the airlock to pop and hold off any attacks, another does combat training inside. The third relaxes. We cycle. So it goes patrol, relax, work out; patrol, relax, and so on."

He grinned. "Sounds good to me, but I'm not an expert."

"Corporal Zhao." Shiva's voice spoke into my ear. Jason didn't hear it, so I figured that Shiva had directed speakers. Really precise directed speakers. "General Lau has a message for you."

"All right." I handed my nutria-goo to Jason, who looked at it with visible distaste. I pushed off and out of the room. Once I got back to Brown's quarters, the only private place I could think of, I turned to face the wallpaper, which resolved itself into a vid-chat.

General Lau's face blipped onto the window.

"We have good news for you, Corporal Zhao," he said. "Firstly, the Loonies aren't making any move to attack your position. We can safely assume that you'll have the next two weeks quiet. While you're there, I want you to get your cadets into a room with a screen every time Dr. Yu gives his briefings. No reason they should miss out."

"Yes, sir," I said, biting my lip. "Sir, permission to speak freely."

"Granted."

"D-do you have any advice?" I felt like a six-year-old. A six-year-old with an orange tag.

But General Lau smiled, faintly. "Corporal, tell me, did the packet that Command sent you do any good?"

"As much as a screen door in an airlock. Sir."

He snorted. "All right, here's the real advice: don't get close to any of your soldiers. You may only be a corporal, but you're still the highest-ranking physical officer there. That means that they're going to be looking to you, even when I'm giving the orders. You can't let your feelings for them get in the way of proper tactical doctrine."

I gulped.

"It's hard." General Lau didn't say "I'm sorry" or anything like that. He just looked me in the eyes and asked me one question: "Can you hack it?"

I thought. I couldn't lie.

"I don't know, sir."

He grunted. "Find out, Corporal. Relief forces will be down within two weeks. Command out."

The screen flicked off.

I sighed. Emotional distance. Yeah, right. *Kǔ koǔ liáng yaò*, I guess.

Okay. Just do it by the numbers, Dru. According to Command's guidelines, the first duty of a PO was to keep her troops in fighting trim. Real easy to say, less so to actually manage. My cadets had about a week and some odd days of relaxing under their belts, and about five seconds of real battle. The result? They were lazy. Heck, I was lazy. But I bit the bullet and set to organizing people into the squads that I talked about with Jason.

There was some whining, but I tried on that voice I had heard myself use in the battle vid. It worked. My cadets set to work, and I made up a little bit of team organization on the fly, designating Star Cadets. They'd be tasked with making sure that their little three-man Star—pitifully undersized, according to the textbook stuff we learned, but hey, we worked with what we got—did their jobs and didn't screw around too much when they were supposed to be on hand to fight, or working out, or whatever.

Picking the Star Cadets required going through the video records of the battle. Jillian was an easy choice. She'd taken charge in battle at least as much as I had, and she was good in a tough place. She oscillated between being grumpy and hardass, and being more approachable. But most people seemed to like her. *I* liked her. And she had an incredible cute butt—okay, Dru, stop, stop, *stop* thinking about that. No, Jillian was definitely a Star Cadet; she'd keep them on track.

The next was a bit trickier, but I settled on David. He was quiet, but he did things that needed to be done. I especially liked how quickly he had worked to try and help Jason.

The third was the real tough one.

I thought of putting Jason in, but his leg was still gimpy and, well, I didn't trust myself to judge. He was a nice guy, and I liked him back when we were up at the Hub, working on our trainee Star. But did he have it in him to keep his people in line?

Then again, did any of us?

My teeth found one of the many raised bumps inside my lips and started worrying at it. That wouldn't help, but it was damn hard to stop. Then I replayed the footage. Who had called out that the Loonies were popping troops? Liam. And he had shot off the antenna. Good shot, quick thinker...

All right. Liam would be the third Star Cadet.

When I announced my scheme, I was worried for a bit—worried that Jason would feel slighted or affronted. He didn't even seem to notice, didn't seem to want to boss other people around, so there you go. And Liam seemed more interested in seducing the Forgers than shacking up with someone in his command, so that cleared up another possible issue.

Cycling the mini-Stars through activities and rest was working pretty well, and when I made my report back to General Lau, he seemed happy with what I had jiggered up.

"I like what you've done," he said. "Star Cadets, you called them?"

"Well, yeah." I fidgeted a little. Behind me, Brown did some work on her personal screen, politely remaining quiet.

"You're putting up a good first showing," the general told me. "To be frank, Corporal, we're all making this system up as we go."

"Sir?" I asked.

He chuckled. "I really shouldn't be saying this much, strictly speaking, but a decade as civilian governor has made me sloppy." He winked at me conspiratorially. "Don't report this to High Command, but the fact of the matter is, this entire war is slipshod. We don't have any physical contact with our actual standing army. We could try the system we use down on the ground up here, but then we might get Star Wars all over again."

I rolled my eyes. *Star Wars*, a weirdly popular franchise from the late 20th century, survived up here, all right. It survived as the longest-running joke in Spacer history. Space fighters? Lasers that stopped a few feet out and became swords? Yeah, right. And I had an anti-gravity drive built into my ass. But there was another shade to the joke. Back in the 1980s, the old USA had tried to shove their military into space with the so-called Star Wars program. It had failed spectacularly, even by the insane standards of the Cold War, and served as a lesson as to why you can't plan Spacer things the way you planned Earther things. If you tried, you just got...

Star Wars.

"Think of it this way: you're helping forge a new way to do things." General Lau saluted me. "And so far, it seems to be working. Command out."

His image winked out.

Brown glanced at me, pursing her lips. "I admit, you Marines aren't as rambunctious as I remember you being."

I glanced at her. "Well, we're not…I mean, we're Spacers, not Earthers."

She shifted slightly, seeming a bit embarrassed at even bringing it up, even as I turned to my section of the wallpaper and started writing up an email to Sarah, finally getting to scratch the itch at the back of my mind.

To Sarah-Bear. I typed, floating there, listening to Brown's soft breathing behind me as she worked. *Man, writing in microgravity still takes a lot of getting used to. Anyhoo, that vid you sent? Total* pìhuà. *I know what I sound and look like in it, but the truth is, I was absolutely scared shitless. Like, it was the most terrifying thing ever. The ONLY reason why I'm not a smear in space is because the Sandcaster was designed to not fire if it gets jammed.*

I chewed on my lips again, my legs floating out behind me. I pushed myself down, hooking myself more securely as I continued to type.

But they promoted me to corporal, I guess you heard. So now I'm in charge of stuff. Whoopie. Truth is, it kinda sucks. My friends are all distant, and I'm never sure if I'm doing the right thing. Gods, this is sounding really whiny, isn't it? I mean, there is a lot of good news. Like, there are no Loonie attacks expected in the next few weeks. And I know that in every war story, a statement like that is followed by an IMMEDIATE SNEAK ATTACK, hahaha.

I grinned at that.

Luckily, up here? There is absolutely no chance that can happen. I know I've blathered about this before, but I'm sure you can sit still for another physics lesson by your lovergirl :). After all, I got you through your AP Physics, and thus, I demand respect :D

So, basically, every single thing that has a human inside of it or any kind of electricity produces waste heat. This sucks, because you usually need to get rid of it somehow. Our suits have radiators on the back to burn off that energy via light— that's why the sun shines, btw, it's so hot that it radiates that heat as photons. Well, photons and a lot of other, less nice and fuzzy things like X-rays and gamma rays and so on and so forth.

I smirked to myself. *If you're making that face, and I know you are making that face, remember this is the difference between life and death for me 95% of the time :P*

Anyhoo, we have a LOT of energy in our backpacks. I mean, our poor little ray guns are trying to beat an actual bullet flying at a few hundred kilometers per second. That's like super hard. And I don't feel like explaining why right now :3.

I shifted around, getting ready to type some more, when the screen flipped from the email program to a graphic of the Earth.

"Shiva—" I started.

He—it—cut me off. "Corporal Zhao, I regret to inform you that the entire computing network is tracking an intercontinental ballistic missile that just left Earth's atmosphere."

"*Hǎ? Wǒ tīng bù jiàn!*"

Brown was kicking out of her bed, heading straight at me. She grabbed onto the wall, stopping herself, and we both looked at the screen.

"*Cào nǐ zǔzōng shíbā dài,*" I swore.

The nuke—because that's what it had to be—was coming out over the North American continent.

Something strange drew my attention away from the nuke glyph, if only for a moment. There were a load of new dots that I had never seen before, each one labeled with a 小贝蒂. My eyes widened. Little Betties? The hells?

Brown explained, "New laser sats. We've been making them as fast as we could."

It made sense. Big Bertha was big, but the Inverse Square Law and a million and a half kilometers would turn even a gigantic maser into a glorified flashlight. So, now it was time for Bertha's kids to step up to bat.

"Come on, acquire...acquire!" I whispered, praying to every god I could think of that one of those new orbital lasers would put a beam right through the nuke's heart.

Brown was praying under her breath, too, when the nuke blipped off the screen.

"*Gai le!*" I shouted, pumping my fist victoriously.

Then twenty-five new symbols popped up.

"No! *Zěn me dé liaò!*"

"What the—"

"It's a MIRV!" Multiple Independent Reentry Vehicles.

World War III in a can.

The twenty-five little bomblets that the nuke had been carrying split off, arcing over the planet, heading to their projected targets: every single major Alliance city that they could hit.

"Texas was *supposed* to be disarmed!" Brown growled, tracking the nuke back to its launch site.

I didn't answer. My eyes were glued to the screen. Nukes were vanishing with comforting speed, but not as fast as the twelve-second battle that started the war in earnest. The atmosphere must have been slowing the swarm of Betties down, making the lasers less effective as they punched holes in missiles, turning them to so much radioactive debris. Shitty to be under, but not the world-consuming fire of a controlled blast.

Ten. Eight.

Five.

Three nukes were left.

One.

The nuke was poised over the Chicago Reforestation Zone. There were maybe a million people there, scattered around that crumbling city in villages and hamlets. In a second, the nuke would become hotter than the sun and—

Then it was gone.

We waited for Shiva to tell us if it was gone because Chicago was gone, or if...

"All weapons neutralized."

I could almost feel the explosive relief that came from everyone in space and on the ground.

"Jeeeezhuuushhhh." Brown let the word drawl out, long and slow. "That was close."

"Too close," I said, tapping at the console. "How did the *gǒushǐ duī* Texans hide a MIRV-capable missile? That wasn't some old Cold War piece of shit ICBM! That was something made in the 21st."

"It's a big territory and the occupation police can't be everywhere."

"Yeah, right," I muttered, taking half a second to alt-tab over and finish my email.

Sarah, I just shit my pants. It was almost the end of the world down there. I'm so happy it wasn't. Love. Xoxoxoxooxoxox.

I sent the email and then asked Shiva to bring up a link to the Hub.

A few seconds later, I got a young woman with a red tag and a harried expression. "Corporal Zhao, you have your orders," she said, sounding cross. "You will be informed when you need to know. *Hào* day."

The link closed before I could even get a word out.

I growled, then punched the wall. That made me pivot around so that my back slammed against the screen. I looped my hands under the handles, hooked my feet, and tensed myself. There was no good way to burn off physical aggression in microgravity, beyond tensing against restraints. Or biting people. Biting would work. I glanced at Brown, but she was already pushing off the wall, away from me.

"Okay," I said. "This is going to scare a lot of people on Earth."

"No shit!" Brown caught herself. "Pardon my French."

I snorted. "I think my girlfriend would say *tabarnac* right now. Probably several times."

Brown didn't respond, just pushed herself towards the door. "I have scared people I need to see to."

I realized that I had the same thing to worry about. I shook my head, feeling chagrined. "You're a better administrator than me. I should pick your brains at some point."

Brown was already out the door and kicking down the corridor.

>+<

I called everyone together in the mess and floated at attention in front of them. "So, you all know the details. The revolutionary part of Texas got their mitts on a MIRV with twenty-five ten-megaton bombs aboard and tried to take the Alliance back to a more primitive era." I made a face. "All twenty five bombs were neutralized, but everyone is really twitchy now. So be on call for anything. Project calm and bravery and the civilians will pick up on it. Hopefully. If anyone asks, tell 'em we don't know any more than they do, because we don't." I sighed. "Command still hasn't been picking up my calls."

My cadets were all looking pretty worried.

"But on a lighter note," I said, glancing around, "I was reading through the textbooks they've been dumping in my lap, and the current system in place says that the PO can offer up battlefield promotions that are later approved by the ranking TCO." I grinned. "You're all Privates and Star Privates now, with the required raises in pay."

They were all grinning with me now.

"Right. Get back to your duties, and I'll make sure that Command approves your promotions—or else." I cracked my knuckles and they laughed. "Dismissed!"

"Thank you, Corp!"

That was new. I blushed slightly, even as Jason—Private Mandalla now—kicked over to me. "Off the record, you're one cool dudette. Seriously, why weren't you born a man so I could date you?"

"Because," I said, smirking, "My past life was as a total saint."

CHAPTER 12
DEFENSE IS THE BEST OFFENSE

2/20/2068

Earth-Moon L3, The Forge

500,000 kilometers above the surface of the Earth

"Five days ago, the Loonies pulled something at about the same time Texas tried their attack. They're aiming to take Tiananmen." General Lau's face filled a whole wall. "They allocated one of their two ROVers to the task, and they burned hard. They'll be there in another three days. Now, either their intel is spotty, or they think they can take you, because you'll be right on top of them by the time they arrive."

"So, you want us to go to Tiananmen," I said. "And hold it against Loonie attack?"

"Yes."

"All right." I gulped, hoping that the general couldn't see it behind my gesture telling Shiva to show me exactly what Tiananmen Station was. A schematic popped up next to Lau's face. Ah, okay. It was a fuel distillery.

Basically, Shi-Armstrong did all the heavy fuel mining, and it sucked for them. Lunar regolith isn't the richest source of helium-3, but it was the closest and best we had. That's why Shi-Armstrong is so much bigger than people originally thought it would be: they needed more bodies to churn through the Lunar dust and grit to make fuel for the new fusion reactors that popped up across the Earth as we slid out of the Slump. The Loonies claim that in its early years, the place was no better than a slave camp for political dissidents. I half believed them, but it's hard to care when Nairobi's a smoking crater.

While helium-3 is great for fusion, people in space just needed straight-up hydrogen fuel—if only because fusion reactors were too heavy to make up for their power output. We got plenty of said fuel from that big ball of gas we called the sun. Solar winds carried particles of hydrogen, most of which got buffeted away by the Earth's atmosphere and magnetosphere. So we had some stations that were nothing but a bottling facility attached to huge scoops, which sucked up the solar wind and slowly distilled fuel from it. Once, there had been tons of distilleries putting out enough hydrogen for every ROVer and personal shuttle in orbit, each with its own macabre name. After all, who wanted to live on what amounted to a gigantic vat of liquid hydrogen? You had to have sort of a weird sense of humor to cope.

Now, there were only four, the rest blasted to bits in the Disaster. So maybe their names had been prophetic in the end.

Fresh Kills had already been taken, but it orbited near the Earth-Moon L1 point, so it was pretty much a goner the instant the war started. But Tiananmen was a "wandering" fuel distillery, going in a steady equatorial orbit, and it was gonna be going right past the Forge soon.

"Head out within the hour and ride Tiananmen until they attack. They won't be using Sandcasters for fear of damaging the station, but we can't be sure what else they might throw at you."

"All right, sir," I said, signing off as I tried to plan our approach. Our suits could take us there, but we'd be a bit low on remass and fuel when we arrived. That'd make maneuvering twiggy. Then I had an idea.

What if we strung up cables? Tethers! No, wait—a tether plus thrusters plus a combat situation was a bad, bad idea. If you burned hard while tied to a tether, the tether would become taut, and suddenly you'd be on a pivot that would slam you right into a wall.

But what if I...put speed limiters on the thrusters? No...

I grumbled to myself and brought up Jillian on the coms.

"Yeah, Corp?"

"Informal, for now. Jillian, I need to work out some tactical problems. You'll tell me when an idea is shit...and, well, who do we know who has the best handle on tactics?"

"You mean who slept through the fewest of Dr. Yu's lectures?" Jillian thought. "Really, Yolanda might be even more prudish than you, but she had some neat ideas about what to do in a microgravity fight."

I nodded. "Right, let me see if I can get her telecommed here. Come to my quarters."

"Yes, ma'am." She grinned.

Jillian arrived a bit later, wearing her skinsuit and a fresh look, thanks to the chemical factories in the Forge and some extra pay to spend. She had gotten her hair cut and redyed to be red. It looked good on her.

"Hey, *gōng gòng qì chē*," Yolanda said from the wallpaper, her voice as cheery as if this were a normal greeting and not an insult. The wallpaper did a fancy perspective trick to make it look like Yolanda was in the room with us.

"*Diǎo* you, *húli jīng*," Jillian shot back without any real heat beyond her normal sarcastic tones. I decided to ignore that bit of nonsense.

"So, we have about thirty minutes before Jillian and I get to head off and screw up some Loonies at Tiananmen. We'll be going out on suit engines only, which means we'll be pretty damn low on remass when we get there...so..."

"Well, duh, it's *meí wèn tí*," Yolanda said after waiting out the light lag. "You guys are at a factory. Have them package up some remass in a mini-rocket. Have them send it after you get to the station and build a net to catch it."

"The *húli jīng* has a point."

"Thank you, you piece of *lā jī*."

I rubbed my temples. "Why do you two call each other that?"

"Because she's a piece of garbage," Yolanda said fondly.

"And she's a home-wrecking tramp," Jillian retorted, grinning.

"Right. You know, that joke, if I can call it that, was funny once. *Once.* Knock it off. This net thing..." I was doing some mental math. We'd have to anchor it on the station itself, but there was one thing that fuel distilleries didn't lack, and that was thrusters to do station-keeping. We could do it, if we anchored it right; the station would get knocked a little off-kilter, but the thrusters would put it back into place...

"I think it'll work."

"Anything that we agree on will always work," Jillian said. "And you can take that straight to Mars."

"Right," I said. "Thanks, Yolanda. I'll be forwarding your recommendation. No idea why you weren't picked to come out with us."

"Well, duh." She made a sour face. "I can't hit the broad side of a barn."

I frowned. "Maybe you should be working in theory. I bet you'd be better at it than half the Orange Peels on Earth."

She smiled. "Ha. Yeah, right. Me? In Games and Theory." She rolled her eyes. "That'll be the day."

Her image flicked off the wallpaper.

While my cadets got suited up, I talked to Brown.

"We do have a rocket thruster. Heck, you don't even need a net. We can program it to slow down." She beamed. "And we can stuff it full of remass and, well, something else, too."

"Oh?" I asked, grinning. "I don't know if I should be terrified or slightly aroused by that look on your face!"

"Well," she said, tapping her fingers together and pointedly ignoring my off-color crack. "The Forge has been doing nothing but making spare parts and Little Betties." She frowned at that, but then continued. "They're all remote control, really—makes them dirt cheap. That's why the Lag-Net has to dump everyone offline when they fire on things. Still, they should make the Loonies stick to just a few areas, until we can saturate the whole orbital theater with them." She shook her head. "Anyway, we worked up a Little Betty Mk II, for use in slightly more intense combat situations, where you can't survive the light-lag delay that comes when most of your computing power is a million clicks out." She grinned. "And thus, Bert."

I blinked at her. "Bert?"

"Well, they can't all be girls!" She laughed. "Bert won't shoot suits—it's too easy to spoof him with decoys. But he can and will detect and target rapidly moving projectiles and turn 'em into vapor. It won't last long, but if you can hook him up to a bigger battery, he'll go the distance."

I whistled. "And it won't stop our guns, because we use directed energy. I like it, I like it!"

"We'll send Bert over to you then."

I nodded, then took Brown's hand. "In case I don't come back." My mouth went dry. "I…uh…just, thanks. F-for being a good roommate, I mean."

She smiled sadly, as if remembering something from long ago. "You're welcome. You Marines are good people. Better than last time."

"We do our best." I shrugged, then kicked off and headed to the airlock. As I went, I thought about that picture of the Marine and Brown. But it had been taken on the Earth. I wondered… what had last time been like?

I didn't have the guts to ask.

>+<

We all got suited up and I went off first, burning straight towards the point that my HUD said was Tiananmen station. I burned and burned and burned, burned until my suit dinged. Then I cut out, manually switching off my thrusters.

"All right, everyone. Time to drift."

This was scary.

Okay, scratch that.

This.

Was.

Terrifying.

I hadn't realized until I was already zooming along that I didn't have a ROVer. I didn't have a DOTtie. All I had was a thruster pack that had about twenty-five percent of its remass burned away.

And now I had a day and a half of this.

Of floating, with nothing to brace on. Nothing to stop me other than a careful deceleration—and if I was just a little off on my math, I would die.

I closed my eyes, feeling my heart race. I was trying to breathe slowly, but it was hard.

Gods, saints, Jesus, and Buddha.

I opened my eyes and looked at the Earth. The sight of that big, blue sphere calmed me and filled me with the same wistful longing I felt whenever I looked at the planet. But that didn't work for much longer than it took me to pick out all the landmarks and states and countries. Then I still had the rest of the day to go, with nothing to look forward to other than some fresh water, some nutrient pills, and some sleep.

So I sang little songs in my head. I composed emails to Sarah. I thought of tactics and plans and strategies. I tried every little trick I had to not think about what surrounded me on every side: Nothing. More nothing. And nothing.

I heard what sounded like a swish and then a gurgling noise, then a burst of static.

"Oh my gods!"

"What happened?" I asked, jerking my head, making my HUD switch to my rear cameras. Behind me, I could see one of us, their HUD symbol flashing red and gray—punctured suit, no life signs—spinning off, their head an expanding mass of red and glass and helmet.

"*Aii ya! Shén me diǎo!*"

"The Loonies are shooting at us!"

"Sniper!"

"That wasn't a bullet!" I shouted, checking my roster.

Liam was dead.

It hit me like a punch to the gut, even as my suit replayed everything and isolated the cause: a screw, whipping around the Earth on a rapid elliptical orbit. Now its orbit was lower, its speed sapped by dragging Liam's brains out through the side of his head.

"Oh gods, Liam."

"He's dead," I said, trying to get them to focus on my voice, trying to capture that tone I had in the battle. It mostly worked, as they all shut up, but I could feel their sorrow and terror over the comlink. "It was a screw."

"*L-laŏ èr's* dead?" Chuck whispered.

"There's nothing we could have done." I gritted my teeth and felt a blur of tears around my eyes. I commanded my body to stop it: I will not cry in my suit. But it wasn't working. I sniffled. Oh gods. I was in for hell. And that just made me want to cry even more, because here I was, with Liam's brains a rapidly expanding cloud and I was freaking out because I was crying in my suit.

Turns out, hell was too generous a term for what I was going through. I sniffled again. I couldn't wipe at my nose. I cried and I couldn't rub out my cheeks. I turned off my comlink, accepting only incoming voices—not that there were many of those. I tried to focus, but in the end, all I got was the entirely disgusting feel of dried snot under my nose. Floating, though, like that, I thought of Liam, remembering his life. He had never turned down sex. He had lived for it, and he had been good at it, from everything I had heard.

Was that it? Was that all that came to mind? Was he just distilled down to a short sentence, a little card for a minor character in a war movie who bought it early on to show the situation was serious?

No. Liam had had dreams. Hopes. Fears. He had sometimes looked sad. He had been happy. He had been a person.

Had been.

Damnit. I was crying again.

>+<

We arrived at Tiananmen station with snot on our faces and our backs itching, expecting a hunk of debris to take us down at any second. I thrusted to a stop, and so did my buddies. Well... not all my buddies.

I tracked Liam's body, spinning fitfully through space. Then I typed a command into my glove. His suit was holed, but its thruster systems still worked. I set it to burn, making him a star. We all watched him zoom straight towards the Earth. The thruster cut out. In a few hours, his suit would hit atmosphere and he'd be nothing but ash.

Traditional. A century before, burial at space had been discussed and everyone who had ridden fire into orbit agreed: being cast adrift in the cosmos was the best way to go out. An unbroken fifty-year tradition of C-chutes had been born from that. Now, people opted for cremation and having their ashes spread in the hydro-bays...a kind of immortality. But I suddenly felt, right there in my gut, that when I died, I wanted to be a shooting star.

After that, we had to get to work. We sent the message back to the Forge, and they told us they had already sent off their present. Then I sent the Star Privates to set up their defensive positions before heading inside to check in with the civilians.

Tiananmen station was a big place. Imagine a kilometer-wide dish, made out of a grid of gray-black lines, with a hole in the middle, which led to four tanks, each the size of a football field. At the bottom of that was a small donut of a habitat for the local crew. I grabbed onto the grid of the dish and dragged myself along, before kicking towards the habitat module. I had to approach it carefully, because it was whipping around like no one's business.

The airlock door in the central axis opened and I took my helmet off as soon as the room pressurized. I wiped at my face and groaned. Great. Some impression I was going to make: brave Space Marines, come to defend your home. Why are you covered in snot?

The inner door opened and a woman, gray-haired but dignified, floated before me. "Hello!" she said. "I'm Tracy Dawiger, and welcome to Tiananmen station!"

"Corporal Drusilla Zhao," I responded, taking my glove off and offering my hand. Dawiger took it and shook.

"I've seen you on the news feed," she said. "Come in; is there anything we can do to help you lot?" She seemed remarkably calm for someone who was at ground zero of an oncoming fight.

"Uh, no, unless you have remass we can use."

"We don't—we have fuel, but I'm pretty sure that's just for ROVers."

"It is," I agreed, sighing slightly as she led me to a main room, climbing outward from the central axis to the inner side of the donut. It looked a bit like a cross between a control center, a garden, and a lounge, with the wallpaper set for standard forested backgrounds. Two younger men were there, playing three-dimensional chess. I felt a bit queasy; the donut was being spun for pseudo-gravity, but they had a really small axis, which made the merry-go-round effect rear its ugly head.

A bigger axis meant that you could spin slower to get the same gravity-like effect. Smaller ones meant you needed to go really fast. Going fast made most people sick. But these guys, it seemed, were taking drugs to stop the nausea. Easier than dealing with microgravity all the time, I guessed, especially when you didn't need it like on the Forge.

"Here." Dawiger seemed to know what I was going through and handed me a pill, which I gulped down. It helped almost immediately.

"We're all set up out here, Corp," Jillian said through my suit's comlink. "Three Stars at the three points the Loonies are coming to attack, able to reinforce. We even have some cover set up."

"Good work," I said. "We still have two days. Jillian, your Star and mine will take first watch together. David, your Star can take some time off inside." I swallowed, a little easier now. The anti-nausea pill was working fast. "We'll alternate with two inside and one outside at all times. Just in case."

"Can do."

"Besides," I confided to the civilians, turning off the com-link, "I don't want to crowd you guys."

"No, no, it's all right." One of the men sighed. "Just be sure to not damage the distillery itself. The dish can take a lot of punishment, but the fuel distillery itself a bit more... volatile."

"We were lucky," Dawiger told me. "During the Disaster, we took most of our hits on the dish. We patched those. Some of our friends, on Guillotine and Hades and..." She trailed off, not wanting to keep listing stations. "They all weren't so lucky."

"I'm sorry." I put my hand on her shoulder, squeezing. "My parents were working on the Elevator."

Dawiger looked at me, then smiled. "You're a brave girl."

"No, I'm just doing my job," I said, flushing. "Now, uh, I gotta go and check on our cover situation. Thanks for your hospitality."

"Get some Loonies for us!" one of the men playing chess said, his voice full of anger—anger I shared half the time, every time I got reminded of just how much the Loonies had done with just a hijacked shuttle.

Outside, I found my Stars were working out the kinks in their defenses. David had come up with the idea to spray mir-roring paint along the edge of the disk, near where you could take cover. A poorly aimed pulse might reflect right back. Of course, it'd eventually melt the mirror beyond use, but it'd be good while it lasted.

"Good work, Star Private," I said, lasing it straight to him.

"Thanks," he responded, his voice as soft as ever.

With defenses more or less under control, I turned my attention to another problem. Our Stars were now one man short, but I was the free-floating corporal. Could I put myself into a squad without screwing up the command structure?

I figured it'd be better to have three fully manned Stars—well, technically, mini-Stars—than to have me bopping around. Still, I had enough keeping me bopping around. There were Stars to organize, defenses to set up, people to organize, and death to ignore...as hard as that might be. *Yì wú fǎn gù*, I guess.

>+<

The next day was a bit boring, but it was a comforting kind of boring. We kept shoring up the defenses, using some of the supplies that the Tiananmen crew had lying around. The edges of the disk were a bit raggedy-looking now, with mini-bunkers and half-covers and mirrored areas. We did test firings, seeing how much space we could hit with our setting-two lasers. It was reassuring to see just how much we could hose down.

"Attacking along the zenith vector would be suicide," Jillian said to me after we tested that. "And attacking the lip will mean going right up against our cover. The nadir is too dangerous to hit. We've got them boxed."

"Don't get cocky," I warned her. "The Loonies aren't dumb; they've got a plan."

Jillian shrugged. "Ask Command what their intel has."

Next time I cycled inside, I did just that. Well, okay, first I checked my messages and read a long email from Sarah that made me practically gooey. She told me all about her day, and when she had thought about me, and how her new book was going. It was all so mundane and normal and removed from anything that was happening in the universe that it just...it was awesome.

Then I linked up to Command.

"Intelligence reports that the LSM launched their ROVer with a hard burn. They're basically parking it at the orbital station they control, the OEO." The intel was coming from a Lieutenant Lee, rather than direct from General Lau, who was apparently busy. "Uh, that is, the Orbital Earth Observatory. It's a climate sat and research lab. They've retooled it to try and up their intel gathering on the Earth and our forces, but it also has enough fuel to support its station-keeping."

"So they can park the ROVer there to refuel, then come at us in suits," I said, frowning. "No, wait, that's still a bit of a jump to make in suits."

"Exactly. We're not entirely sure, but we think that they're actually refueling enough to do another hard burn. They won't have enough fuel to get back home..."

"Unless they take Tiananmen," I finished for him. "Damn. They're risking a lot."

Instead of giving me anything else useful, Lee just shrugged, but I thanked him and turned off the coms.

If the Loonies were going to risk losing one of their ROVers— not to mention fuel, lives, and material—then they had to have more ROVers to spare. That was always a possibility. The Moon had enough raw materials for Shi-Armstrong to pump out some major machinery. Or they had what they thought was a foolproof way of taking the station.

Both options made me nervous.

CHAPTER 13
THE SECRET WEAPON

2/24/2068

Equilateral Orbit, Tiananmen Station

350,000 kilometers above the surface of the Earth

"They're piling out."

I was looking at the Loonie ROVer. It was an older design than the one at the Hub, more like a traditional space shuttle, though it was still stuffed full of more goodies than the dinosaur that the USA shelved back in the 2010s. The Loonies were in painted yellow and black suits. They were using skinsuits now, not the slow and stupid joystick types that the Loonies who had been protecting the *Hope* had been using. I zoomed in.

"Those look like directed energy weapons. See the radiator fins?" I said, trying to sound like an RPO, a real physical officer.

"Roger, RPO."

The voice in my ear was Lee, delayed a few seconds. General Lau was covering the situation, too, but he was just providing strategic oversight. The crunch, the actual command and fighting, fell to me and Lee and my troopers.

"Shit, there are a ton of them," Jillian muttered. "This is just a *shǐ dàn.*"

"Can we start shooting?" That was David, whispering over the coms like the Loonies could listen in to our directed laser communications.

I shook my head. "We're under orders to give them a chance to bugger off."

"You've gotta be shitting me," Jillian snapped. "They've got a *hún zhang wángbā dàn* Sandcaster aimed at us!"

"They're not going to fire that," I said, calm as I could. It was true. A single whizzing hunk of gravel could turn this station and its kilometer-wide dish into a useless floating coffin surrounded by a sublimated atmosphere of distilled fuel.

"They've got us hemmed in," I muttered to Lee on our private link. "Is there anything you can do?"

"We want the ROVer; we can't just blow it out of the sky with the Big Bertha," Lee responded, sounding apologetic.

"I'm not saying you have to destroy it, I'm just saying it'd be nice if you'd singe them for us."

"Right."

The Loonies were out and in Stars now. There were...crap, there were almost twenty-five of them, in five slightly small Stars with five people each. I pegged them as L1 to L25.

"*Tā māde diǎo.*" Jillian was whispering now, too.

"How did they fit so many in?" wondered David.

I sighed, glancing around at Liam's old Star. He had been the Star Private for them. So now I was their commander. It still felt like stepping into a dead man's skinsuit. Damn, I missed Liam. It was like constantly turning to talk to someone who wasn't there—only after you did it would you remember. He'd never be there. Ever. And I hadn't even liked him that much. I wondered if it'd ever get easier. Did I want it to get easier?

"They must have drugged them," Jillian muttered.

"Guys, *shoū shēng*," I said, poking my helmet out from cover. I lased my communications at the Loonies, broad beam. "Lunar troops—" I said, trying to sound as official as I could. "—You are in violation of Alliance laws. You are fighting on behalf of a war criminal and a mass murderer. If you surrender now, you will not be harmed."

There was no response for a while.

The Loonies were moving behind cover—they'd parked their ROVer in a slowly drifting cloud of debris. Smart. Behind the cover, my HUD had to project potential positions, possible attack vectors. I got rid of them with a tap of my glove, showing just the clear space and the glimmering shape of the ROVer.

"I say again, you will—"

BEE BEE BEE BEE!

My alarm was blaring. Fifteen arcing shapes shot through the sky. My suit identified them.

Rockets.

"Incoming!"

For all the good it did.

Ten of the rockets were zapped out of the sky by Bert, turning to poofs of smoke and red debris that pattered harmlessly off our cover. Three of the rockets slammed into Bert's generator, drawn by its intense waste heat. By then, I had figured out how they were tracking their targets: infrared.

One hit Ping, who was just a bit too slow.

The other hit my pack, which was blasting away from me, thanks to me slapping the panic button.

My chestplate slammed into the side of the dish and then I bounced away, tumbling. Everything. Everything was pain. And so I just let myself drift and I screamed and screamed into the blackness that filled me, now that my cameras were mangled and smashed. Gooey blood filled my helmet, globing around. I snorted and felt my nose crunch and crack.

Oh gods.

I reached—or tried to reach—up and fucking *hells*! Something was jammed in my back. *Laǒ tiān yé*, I wanted to die. I wanted to die, just so it'd stop hurting.

My spin dragged my other arm out, and I wiggled my fingers. Still working. Moving that arm didn't hurt. I tried to reach around, and my fingers brushed against something stabbed into...into my shoulder blade. I didn't feel any further, my mind shying away from that thought, the thought of what was in my back. My brain kept going back to one thing: the pain.

Breathing was hard. Air was thin? No. No, the air wasn't thin. No, it was hard to breathe because...because, right, my ribs were broken. They had to be after a hit like that.

I moved my unhurt—or less hurt—arm and flipped my visor up. Each spin took me back into view of the station. I could see flashes and silent puffs. The Loonies were pushing their cover closer. Then my spin took me around again and I didn't care about anything but the pain.

But Antwiler was in my ear, screaming something at me.

"*I* don't care, you *rǔ xiù wèi gān*. I don't care if it hurts! You have a job to do!"

Sarah whispered to me.

"I can't wait 'til you put your feet on the ground and I can watch your toes squirm on the sand. There's nothing like the feel of sand between your toes, warm and hot and—"

Okay. My spin had brought the battle back into view again. I...I needed something. To do something. What? I couldn't remember. Something...important... I needed to be able to tell my soldiers I was alive and not a spinning corpse.

Wait! My P3 was still on.

It took an agony and a half to worry my P3 out of the holster. It was made to work like this. Gods, I wished I could just use my teeth. But I gritted those teeth against the pain and managed to hook the power pack into my suit, then yank. The cables came free. I let the P3 float, then used my good hand to plug it into my helmet. No HUD, no cameras, but I had sound picked up via the P3s laser-com feature.

"Pot the *chùsheng*!"

"He's behind cover," David growled. "Come on…come on…"

Crack!

"Shoot the cover's tank!"

I saw that a Loonie was hiding behind the corpses of his friends. Then the tank of one of those suits exploded and the Loonie was sent spinning out. Then I was spinning away again.

"Is that everyone?"

"Chuck is hurt, Ping is dead…s-so is Dru." That was Jason.

"*Jiào nǐ shēng háizi z hǎng zhì chuāng!*" Jillian swore.

"I think they're all dead, but the ROVer is pulling back."

I spun again, wincing and trying desperately to think despite the pain. The ROVer was moving away at a pretty good clip, its engines burning bright, like two stars…pretty stars. Once, I had given Sarah stars, VR stars, in the holo—

No! Focus! Think of your basic logistics class.

A…a lot of the mass was fuel and remass.

At the end of a voyage…

There was less remass and fuel.

And a lot of corpses floating around.

Meant that the ROVer's remaining fuel and remass counted for more; the engines had to push less mass around. *Diǎo!* It was so obvious. The ROVer would get away.

But the Loonies' mission was still a bust, still left twenty-five of them as floating corpses.

This mission had to have alternate plans to make it successful. If the Loonies could not take the station…then…

Aii ya, where was Mommy? I wanted her to hold me and make it all better. It hurt so much.

Focus, Corporal Zhao!

They'd have to...take the station from us!

"Everyone get away from the dish now!" I bellowed. Would the coms even work for them?

"Dru!" Jason sounded like he could barely believe himself.

"Do it now!" I shouted, relief hammering in my chest.

They started to burn away, hard, shooting up toward me.

"Dru, you're alive!" Jason exclaimed, coming up to me, his forward thrusters flaring to slow him down.

"She's leaking," Jillian thrusted behind me. "Jesus christing shit."

"They fired another mis—"

White flash.

We all gaped, Jillian turning me to face the station. Tiananmen station was nothing more than an expanding cloud of debris. Most of the explosion was focused downward, but a few hunks of debris had to have shot out around us. Someone was smiling down on us, so we didn't get any more dead. Ping was dead...

"Did..." I almost couldn't finish the question. But I had to know. "Did the civilians get out?"

"No," Jillian said. "And we have a pretty damn serious problem."

"What?" I gasped the word, like a sob, or like a curse.

"You've got a foot of metal jammed into your shoulder blade," she said, matter-of-fact. I felt a prick in my neck, through my suit, a light tap compared to the pain in my shoulder. "And now you've got a whole bunch of happy juice. Enjoy the sweet dreams; pray we get you back."

"Yessir," I slurred, eyes drooping. Breathing slow was easy now, no pain, nothing but...my eyes closed.

>+<

The next few times I opened my eyes, everything was hazy, confused. I was in a suit. No, I was out of a suit, but I was still floating. Someone was doing something. Then I was being wrapped up. When I woke up the next time, it was as though someone was crushing me. I wheezed and gasped, then mewled, like a pitiful cat.

Then the crushing feeling faded. Then...then I was floating again. Still?

I opened my eyes. I was sealed up in a white body wrap, like a mummy. I craned my head to the side. There were a few others. Chuck, with half his face covered by a thin film of plastic, the skin beneath looking boiled pink. And to the right, I could see Jillian and Jason, both of them with their left arms in a sling.

We were inside. There was air. We were in a ROVer.

"What happened to you guys?" I asked.

Jillian scowled at me. "You had to go and try dying on us, and we had to be big damn heroes and shit." Her voice held more anger than it normally did. No. Not anger. Worry.

"We jury-rigged a solution for your suit," Jason said. "Then we burned hard...we were cutting it pretty close after that battle, with all the zipping around." He shrugged. "So we hit the Forge a bit faster than we wanted."

"Are you okay?"

"Better than okay." Jason smiled. "We're going back to the Hub."

>+<

The trip up to the Hub was slow, but pleasant. We had our wounded, and our wounded were stable. Chuck had taken a laser burn to the side of the face during the battle. If his faceplate hadn't been down, he'd be missing most of the side of his face, but as it was, he just had some melted plastic flecked all over his chin, to go with the shiny burns. He had kept fighting then, flipping his melted faceplate partially up, and now he was slated for some pretty intense facial reconstruction. Jason and Jillian had broken their arms when they had rapidly decelerated by slamming into the side of the Forge.

Me, I had vacuum burns along my back, my right hand had gotten frostbite, I suffered from minor oxygen deprivation, and that was all on top of the three broken ribs, a fractured shoulder blade, major lacerations, and a rather large amount of blood loss. Hah. I win. Plus, I was hopped up on painkillers and got to doze through the videos and music that the more ambulatory wounded played.

By the time we finally arrived at the Hub, some of my less impressive injuries were healed. Still, Chuck and I were rushed off on a set of wheeled gurneys the instant the airlock popped open. Then there was a big blank time, and when I woke up again, I was lying on a comfortable bed. The ceiling was white, and I had five new metal fingers. I felt the difference the instant I woke up—a weird alien otherness that made me want to squirm and scream and gnaw my own hand off to get away from it.

Cybernetics.

People had tried going cyber, back in the Singularity Scare right after the Slump, and before that, during the Second American Civil War. The idea had been to "transcend the human condition" by augmenting yourself with cybernetics and genetic modifications. It had gone as bad as bad could go. Human brains just didn't work right with computers interfaced with them—at least, not beyond basic implants like what we cure Parkinson's with. Every attempt at mental enhancement created either a psycho that made the Shanghai Stalker look like Gandhi, or a drooling wreck.

So waking up with five metal fingers gave me the great big screamy-weamies.

"Calm down!" a doctor ordered, leaning over me. I gulped and tried to do just that, but my fingers were *metal*. The feelings I normally got from them were coming from computers, and felt like spiders crawling on my nerves.

"She's suffering from psychosomatic rejection!"

"Pump more tribolox."

There was a rush of good vibes that spread through me. I lay back, sighing softly. "Oh my, keep me hooped up on that, Doc..." I whispered.

"All right, Star Corporal," the doctor leaning over me said calmly. "You've got five new fingers. They're made of metal, and they're computerized. You might get a chance at some biological replacements if you ever get to Earth or we sanction your trip to Heaven, but for now, you'll have to deal with it. This is not a neural augment. It will not change how you think; it will not change how you act, or believe. The only thing that has changed is the hardware that gives your brain sensory input."

I tried to follow that. The happy juice had just been a short jolt, and it was fading now. But I managed to keep my disgust under control long enough to nod. "Okay. Right."

"Stay calm." That made me want to bite my fingers off even more. "Take the input in. Let it enter your mind. Focus and recognize that nothing is different. The same feelings are felt. See?" He touched my metal finger. If he flinched, he controlled it well.

His finger felt right. My finger felt wrong. But I focused and tried to make it normal.

"Yeah, it totally feels normal," I managed.

"You're lying," the doctor said, checking my biofeedback.

"You're a *bà wáng*," I growled, clenching my palm, feeling my palm, feeling the metal bite into my palm. "Look, *wàn shì dà jí.* I'm okay. I can hack it."

"Like hell you can." The doctor sighed. "We'll have to keep an eye on you, Star Corporal Zhao."

And then, like a slap of wet water, I realized he had called me Star Corporal. Twice.

Another *bù hé lǐ de* promotion. Great.

General Lau met me in person. He came to the medical bay, in uniform, with his red tag polished and gleaming. He shook my hand, the hand with the cybernetic fingers. He didn't flinch or jerk back or anything. I liked that. If I pretended really hard, I could almost feel like it reassured me. His hand slid away. "You fought well, Star Corporal. Sorry about the injuries."

"Sorry about the station," I said, frowning as I thought about the civilians I'd let down. *Diǎo*, how more morose could you get? Angsting about cybernetics, angsting about losing lives and positions. Let's see if I could start angsting about Sarah and I'd have a full angsting flush.

"You fought as hard as you could." General Lau looked away for an instant, his eyes flickering. "But we only have one fuel distillery now."

"The Loonies took Dystopia?" I asked. Because it couldn't be Rockefeller. That was at the Earth-Moon L3 point, on the opposite side of the world, near the Forge most of the time.

"Yes." Lau sighed. "That's why they thought they could get away with destroying a station. It is a big propaganda victory— on both sides. The news vids have been playing up the evil Loonie butchers the past few weeks."

I grimaced. "That'll help a lot." My voice dribbled sarcasm. Up here, you were either pro-independence, or you hated the Loonies. There wasn't any room for neutrality in space. Propaganda was just preaching to the choir.

"You should study up on attacking and taking targets," he said, changing the subject.

"Why?" I asked.

"Because you're going to be leading one of the mini-Stars attacking Dystopia Station. Once you're on your feet and the mission is prepped."

After dropping that bombshell in my lap, he simply turned around and headed off, offering a perfunctory salute on his way out.

>+<

The doctor let me stand up after the happy juice had slid completely out of my system. My ribs felt a bit stiff, and my arm was completely solid and moved only after I signed a request in triplicate and sent it to my shoulder. And I knew that my metal fingers should have been just the same weight as my old fingers, but my hand still felt heavier, weighing me down, making everything tilted.

But I had some back pay, and I had some free time, so… what the hell. After checking with my doctor to make sure it was all right, I decided to head for the holodeck. IMs were cheap; the holodeck isn't. Back when I survived on my parents' allowances, I went once in a blue moon. But now, I had enough pay to go every week, and I never had time to go and do it.

Oh, fǎn yǔ.

I had one more thing to do before skipping down to the holodeck itself, though. I spent some more money that I had earned doing an actual, real, honest-to-gods job, and I bought enough bandwidth to borrow a laser com and link up to Sarah. Seriously expensive with the wartime rationing, but worth it. I tried to not chew my lower lip. I failed. "Come on, Sarah-Bear," I whispered.

Sarahbear is online.
"Yes!"
DruofNight: <tackles>
Sarahbear: !!!!!!!!!!!!
DruofNight: How is the electricity in your area?

Sarahbear: Confirmed for the next hour.
DruofNight: Get your VR headset on. NOW.

I ran to the holodeck, bursting in on the attendant and booking a slot as fast as I could.

"Will you be doing Augmented Reality or Virtual Reality?" the holodeck operator asked.

"VR."

"Then you are completely cleared." He waved me in.

The holodeck was poorly named. There were no holograms involved. You had a couple of choices—Augmented Reality or Virtual Reality. For AR, you wore a pair of contact lenses that were tiny HUDs, and they projected fake images to your eyes that looked real. Then you could play around in the "real" room, which was about three meters by three meters, almost luxuriously huge by Hub standards, and completely free of any furniture. Your contacts painted it to look like anything you wanted. It was nice for people who got VRsick—not so great for anyone who didn't.

You'd think that me, with my brain screwed up by five metal fingers, would be AR all the way. You'd be wrong. I had thrown up dozens of times before I had gotten my brain to accept VR input without going twiggy, but it had been so worth it, and that's coming from me, Miss Vomit Comet. Well, until I found out that light lag makes physical contact so awkward that it made the thought of doing it again either laughable or tragic. Or both. But other than that, it had been good.

That was why I knew that I could force my brain to accept these fingers eventually. Still, waking up with them on my hand, feeling all weird as hell, was more than a bit of a shock, more of a shock than getting into VR.

"Here is your VR set," intoned the computerized voice that oversaw the VR shed, as my unit slid out of the wall. It was nothing close to the smooth, educated, human-like voice of Shiva. I really did wonder then, why did the Hub have dumber AI than the Forge? Was it because we didn't need a smarter AI? Was it because the Hub used older parts, since they were cheaper than putting more mass into orbit?

I shook my head and slipped the headset on. I let the new input override my normal senses.

When I opened my eyes, I was in a simulated forest, near a simulated beach. Birds cawed in the air; the smell of surf was in my nose. Part of my brain was sure it was all fake, digging like a little splinter at the back of my mind. But for now, it was enough to dream. I ended up waiting half an hour, whiling away a depressingly large amount of time, picking up sticks, throwing them at the ocean, walking in circles, that kind of thing.

And then.

And then I started to cry.

Because Sarah was right there.

I grabbed her and held her tight, pressing myself against her. And I cried and cried and cried. She didn't move for three seconds as I held her. Then, as if life was flooding her, she started to move. She embraced me in return.

Sarah knew what to do. She squeezed me. "Shh, shh," she whispered. "It's okay. It's okay."

I leaned into her and waited. She squeezed my arms. "You've gotten stronger."

My eyes were closed. Her fingers worked through my hair as we sank to the ground together. "You've cut your hair."

I just let my head rest in her lap.

And she was content to be silent. We basked in the illusion. If we didn't move, if we didn't talk, then light lag didn't rear its ugly head—then you could imagine, just for a second, that you were with someone.

And I wished it would never end.

And then my eyes opened to the darkness of a closet, with the spider of a VR rig over my head. The jarring shock made me curl up and cry again, face pressed into my knees, my fingers gripping my shins, metal digging into my skin.

Once I got myself under control, I headed to my bunk and started to write a long, long, long email. There were no cadets in the bunk. I wondered where Jason and Chuck and Jillian and David were. I could have found out, but for that moment, I wanted to cling to my feeling of disconnection. I wanted to float, free of any constraints, for as long as I could.

So I wrote. I just spewed everything out. About how much it hurt to be wounded. About how losing Liam to a screw had made me cry so much that I could barely breathe in my helmet. About how scared I was. About how missing her was like getting knifed in the gut again and again and again by a very persistent, very strong murderer. About how I had left the civilians behind to die. About what I wanted…

And finally, I finished pouring the words out. I hit send.

Then I rolled onto my back and lay there, hands clasped behind my head, metal warming slowly against flesh. I felt hollowed out, empty, like a paper girl. So I just filled myself with happy memories and tried to hold onto them. After awhile—how long, I had no idea—my reverie was disturbed by people walking into the barracks. I sat up and blinked. It wasn't my troopers, my buddies. These cadets were all strangers, staring at me. They all looked awkward and young, like they were still trying to figure out how their bodies worked.

They walked over to me, with wide eyes. "Are you Drusilla Zhao?" one of them asked.

"Uh, yeah."

"Whoa," they said all at once, something scarily like awe in their voices.

Oh *niúbī*.

One of them—a boy, I think, though maybe androgyne—held out his hand to me. I took it, gingerly, like it was about to explode. I wanted to shove my cybernetic fingers into the waste disposal, but he didn't seem to notice, squeezing my hand and peering at me with a weird look on his face.

"We've heard…we saw…I mean, what you did it, was… like—"

"Wow!"

I stood up, muttering about how I had to go do things. I had to get away from these people, right now. I ran out of the barracks, found a screen, and looked around for Yolanda. The computer indicated that she was in her quarters. Her own quarters? Really? Someone was *quán weī* now.

I headed there. The door opened and there was Yolanda, wearing a red tag lined with blue, like the technicians that worked in Command and Control. She hugged me. "Druuuu!" she squealed. She drew back, laughing. "Why didn't you come straight here?"

"I…well, VR with…Sarah," I stammered, blushing, even as I noticed that Yolanda definitely didn't slide her hand down to my hand.

"Ah, of course, don't worry about it." She smiled, then gestured me inside. Her room was part sleeping area, part workstation. She had an actual chair in front of her primary screen, and her walls had disposable screens slicked up to them, projecting the theater of war. The Earth's orbit, I saw, had been sliced up into multiple quadrants, each based less around physical location and more on the orbits in question. Polar Theater, Equatorial Theater, L1-L5 Theaters.

There were a lot of red dots there.

"So…" I started. "You're in telecoms."

Yolanda's finger slid along the blue-edged side of her red tag. "Yup. I'm an ensign now."

I saluted her. Her shoulders slumped. "Please, don't." She sighed.

I shrugged. Whatever. "What else changed while I was away?"

"Dan got shipped off to Rockefeller to defend the place from the Loonies. Your bunkmate, Kolby, she…" Her face went grim.

"What?" I asked, sitting on her bed, my left hand going over my right, trying to hide the metal.

"She vented her carbon and oxygen during a training run. Sergeant Wilcox dragged her inside before she could suffocate, but she got wicked bad nitrogen narcosis. They shipped her to Heaven."

I blinked. Heaven had been holed multiple times during the Disaster. More people had died there than anywhere else in space, because Heaven was a hospital station, crammed full of people with radiation burns, waiting for genetic fixes, new body parts, that kind of thing. "They fixed Heaven?" I thought I remembered the doctor saying something about it, when he'd been lecturing me about my hand.

Hope started kicking my heart to full gear.

"Barely." Yolanda made a face. "They lost most of the good biotech they had there, but it's still a hospital. They still send you there if you have a permanent issue, like being an Angel."

I nodded. Angels were kind of pathetic. They weren't injured, they weren't physically hurt. They just couldn't keep up with the pressure. They got coddled by doctors in Heaven, while everyone who could actually do their jobs kept working twice as hard. Totally *fàntǒng*, when you got down to it. Still, I tried to be charitable. "Right. Well, not everyone can hack it, but still…didn't they say they'd kill us if we failed Basic?"

I rubbed the back of my neck, trying to not think about how close I had been to taking the route Kolby did.

"Well, we have you to thank for that," Yolanda grinned. "Taking the *Hope* gave us some surplus supplies. I guess they figure fixing an Angel is more cost-effective than…" She trailed off, shaking her head. "But still, you're back. Outta the fire!"

"For now." I laced my hands behind my head, eyes closing. I had so few friends, I realized, but now, one of them was safe. If the Hub was blasted out of the sky, the war was over, no matter what anyone on the ground said, and I'd be working my life away in a Lunar death mine or something. Assuming I hadn't been on the Hub when it was shot down. But still.

In my head, at least, Yolanda would always be safe here.

"So," I said, eyes opening. "What's it like being an ensign?"

"I love it!" Yolanda exclaimed, sitting down. "You know me, first into a suit, first to crash one."

"No, Jason and Dan were the first," I joked.

"You know what I mean." She rolled her eyes. "But here, I can do work I'm good at. It's hard to calculate orbital trajectories with a PPR in my hands. Here, I can try and find ways to keep you people alive."

I smiled. "I'd never pick anyone else to keep me alive."

"Aww." She looked at me. "How is Sarah?"

"She's good." I rubbed my temples and flinched a little at the feel of the metal. Not too much, though. "Things are a bit weird on the ground. That nuke launch has gotten everyone on edge, and…"

"And?"

"And…" I grimaced, not wanting to think about it. "She and I, well, uh…" I blushed. "She says I should be less mono."

"Right," Yolanda said, slowly, as if she was chewing the word. Then understanding flickered into her eyes and she went, "Riiiiiiiiiiiiight."

I blushed deeper, turning the color of our red tags. "But I don't know if I can."

"You're old-fashioned," Yolanda smirked. "More of a 20th-century gal. And they call me a prude."

"Yeah," I said. If only she knew. "What can I say? I like kinky bondage sex with just one partner at a time."

Yolanda snickered.

I slid my hand away from my cybernetic fingers, feeling the old gnawing sensation again. "What is this new plot being cooked up?"

"Well," Yolanda bounced up, tapping her disposable screen, bringing up the Moon-Earth L4 map. It was a mess of debris being tracked, possible Loonie movement vectors, and the big red splotch of Dystopia. Dystopia was way bigger than Tiananmen, having been built later and by a private corporation called ComEx. Now it was Loonie territory, with five spots that were labeled as IKSDWS.

"What's an eyeksdwhasss?"

"Indiscriminate Kinetic Space Denial Weapon System, or Ick-Ick." Yolanda shrugged. "We used to call them Sandcasters."

"Ick-Ick," I repeated. "I like that. So, let me guess, they cover every single possible attack vector."

"Almost!" she said. "They don't cover their ass, pardon my French. Down here,"—she pointed to the actual distillery—"they're a bit more leery of putting anything with high explosives around, in case of a misfire. Sooo, there is this huge attack vector that isn't protected by Ick-Ick."

"Right, so they crammed their troopers there."

"...yeah." She made a face. "But we have a plan."

"And that is?"

Yolanda opened her mouth, then closed it. "Can't tell you, *Jiě-jie.*"

"What?" I blinked. "There's no Loonie spies here."

"I know, but, well, new regs have been squirted up from High Command. They think we're being a bit too lax, so they want us to tighten down. Apparently, some people down there leaked to the wrong *diǎo* news channels and next thing you know, they've kicked the hornets' nest."

"So because they *gaǒ gaǒ zhèn, maǒ bāng chèn*, their screwup becomes our punishment." I put my hand over my face. "Fantastic."

Yolanda sighed. "Well, I do have some good news. Well, bad news. Well...news. I have news."

"Give it."

"You've been selected to do the really cool part of the mission."

Fantastic.

CHAPTER 14
SENSE-DEP

I floated in nothingness and tried to not think about biting my fingers off. It was getting easier. I figured it was like getting a fake tooth. It was grown from your DNA and implanted, then hooked up to your nervous system. It was, in every way, just like a normal tooth. But because your tongue gets used to the empty space you could scratch against, it goes to the new tooth and rubs up against it like a snake looking to shack up. Your tongue has a long memory.

Well, my fingers were not biological. They hadn't been grown from my DNA, so their wedding to my nervous system was uneasy, like marrying a neo-Buddhist to a Reformed Old Fanian. There was gonna be some friction. Still, I guessed the honeymoon was helping me sort through all the not-finger feelings that those fingers were giving me. I wasn't getting ordered to strangle non-augmented people...yet. Okay, that was just me being silly.

Being silly was easy here, in nothing, surrounded by nothing. Nothing but your own breathing and the soft thudthud of your heart and the things your brain conjured up to bounce around in your head.

I wondered if you could fit two people into the sense-dep tank.

That bounced around some real nice thoughts.

After forever and five seconds, the door opened and a doctor looked in at me. He checked all my physical signs, using a few scanners and a thermometer that went somewhere I didn't want anyone to go. He did this all at a snail's pace, as if he wanted me to suffer extralong. I got a bit impatient, but trying to move was too hard. "Soooooooooooooo," he said, his voice slow and low like a whale. "Youuuuuuuuuuu aaaaaaaaaareeeeeeeeeeee stillllllllllllllllll saaaaaaaaaneeeeeeeeee."

I blinked and scowled at him. "Stop talking like—" *Aii ya*! A needle jabbed into my arm and injected something into me. My head pounded and it felt like my brains wanted to slam out of my temple, like I had a screw whipping through my gray matter. Everything went fast, blurring with speed as the doctor pulled back and away.

"*Diǎo*!" I grunted. "I think I've got temporal whiplash!"

"That's just your body adjusting," the doctor said, voice sounding like a chipmunk, then slowing down to normal speeds and losing the squeaky tone. "How did you enjoy your week in the tank?"

"It felt like forever...and like no time at all."

"Good." He grinned. "You'll be glad to hear, then, that it was only two days."

"*Nǐ de gǒu pì*!"

"We injected you, before attempting this experiment, with temporalmexicoltan."

I blinked a few times at the doctor, even as he offered me a towel. I got out of the sloshing water of the tank and started to dry myself. "Got that in Mandarin, Doc?"

"It's a drug that alters your perception of time. In effect, two days feel like a week. We can rejigger the dose to make a year feel like a day, but it won't stop or slow aging. So don't get any immortality dreams or anything like that."

"I won't." I frowned, getting dressed in some skinclothes, thinking back to what I had been told when I had gotten into the sense-dep tank. It had seemed so simple at the time. Just float in water for a few days. Easy peasy. "You could have warned us we'd be spending a week in there, subjectively."

"That'd invalidate the test," the doctor scolded. "I've been told to tell you that General Lau wants you to report to Staff Sergeant Antwiler."

As I headed out of the sense-dep lab, I bumped into Jillian, Jason, David, and Chuck. I hadn't expected to see them, when I did, I still half-expected to see Liam with them. Or Ping. Or...

"I didn't know you guys were in—" we all said at once.

Jillian snorted. "I guess the coming mission requires sense-dep...somehow."

"You're right, Star Private."

We snapped to attention. That voice had caused us all to shit ourselves whenever we'd heard it before, so even hearing it cordially made us stand parade-perfect.

Staff Sergeant Antwiler nodded at us. "At ease." He glanced around the medical bay where he had ambushed us. "Follow me."

He led us to the armory, which had been expanded since I'd been there last. Now, we had PPRs, P3s, and armor piled up, lashed into orderly stacks, and generally stored properly.

Two techies were there, both of them wearing red tags with yellow edges, denoting they were mechanics. They were both about our ages, but they didn't need to salute. Non-military teens—those who had been smart enough to become post-apps before conscription dragged them into the service. Oh, *mā de*...I couldn't remember the last time that I felt so envious.

Antwiler, though, just led us to the suiting-up chambers. And there we all got to coo and ahh over something that could make any Spacer wet themselves with joy.

A new kind of spacesuit.

It looked like a regular skinsuit, but rather than having to slide armor on over it, like with our Gisses, the armor was built in. It looked heavier, stronger, with a strong helmet, too. The thruster pack was also built in, with radiator fins more evenly distributed about the arms and legs.

"This is the Self-Powered Suit, Mk II." Antwiler patted its shoulder. "There are only five in existence, and the Forge can't make any more unless we salvage some rather specific bits of metal from the debris field. Or capture a mine on the Moon." He sneered. "Either way, they're bad news. The Mk I variety had a tendency to break your bones if you moved wrong, but these models have self-correcting AIs built into the muscle augmentation."

Power armor.

Oh man. Every kid wants to get some power armor. I mean, we all grew up watching anime, or playing vid-games, where every super-soldier from the Master Chief up got to wear the giant, super-powered armor that let you flip tanks with your hands and stuff.

And here it was. Sitting right in front of us.

Real. Honest. Not from a video game, not from a historical documentary, but actually right in front of us. *Shí gǔ shí zaó* power armor.

"The rest are still getting fitted for each trooper that'll be using them. This one has been fitted to our hero of the hour." Antwiler fixed his gaze on me. Proud? Disapproving? I couldn't tell. I didn't care. "So. Star Corporal Zhao, why don't you get naked and I'll show you how to get into this bad boy without killing yourself."

He pushed a button on the back of the right wrist and the suit popped open, hissing softly. He showed me where to put my feet—into the boots, duh—and how to slide my fingers into the gloves. It fit, but not skintight like my normal skinsuit and Giss rig. Then I moved the arm and it had this weird ghostly feeling, like I was the puppet and the puppeteer at the same time, my suit pushing my arms as my arms pushed the suit. It was so profoundly strange that I took a few seconds to mess around, moving the fingers, moving the arms.

"Now, SC Zhao is demonstrating exactly how to *not* put the suit on rapidly." Antwiler's voice dripped with that acidic sarcasm that had dogged us through Basic. But, hey, at least he wasn't screaming at us now. He still looked like he hated our guts, but the venom wasn't spewing out all over us, like a cobra spitting.

I hastily pushed the button to close the suit. It closed up, sealed, and then there was a hissing noise as the inner seal fixed up against my skin. Then I jumped as two tubes slid up into rather private places.

"Ouch!"

"Oh, come on, you've worn a Giss before." Antwiler began to check me over, scanning my face, then my arms, with the standard handheld scanner.

"These tubes are bigger," I muttered. "And colder."

"Yeah, yeah, *hǎn shài koǔ* some more." He slapped me on the helmet. "You're suited and ready. Step into the decom chamber to check yourself out."

I did just that, my legs moving and thumping, the ghostly puppeteer moving my knees and calf muscles, molding me with huge fingers and jerking on chains connected to my shoulders.

"This is weirder than my fingers," I muttered into the coms and everyone laughed.

I got into the decom chamber, and got ready to do the standard vacuum test. But then the air rushed out of the room and I didn't feel the standard urge to fart. I almost felt betrayed. Then it came to me. The inner seal and the outer seals were separated, so I didn't have a direct vacuum at my backside.

I wiggled my right fingers, then my left fingers. The right fingers felt so damned strange I had to keep doing it, even as I checked in with Antwiler, telling him everything was fine.

So the fingers that felt wrong were being moved around by invisible ghosts, and it was all directed by the parts of my brain that handled stuff subconsciously.

Weeeeeeeeird.

The decom chamber hissed with air and I stepped out. I pushed the open button and my suit loosened, the chestplate and faceplate sliding open.

I grinned as the tubes slid blessedly free.

"I like it," I said. "But it feels totally *gǔ gǔ guài guài.*"

"It's the price of safety," Antwiler explained. "The Mk I suit didn't have that feel, because it just forced amplified motion. The test sims that ran it ended up breaking their spines and shoulders without a five-month training period, and even then it was touchy under stress. So the Mk II has force feedback. This way, you can't snap your spine by scratching your back."

"Well, that's good," I said, smirking and scratching my butt. I couldn't feel it through the suit, so I slid my arm up and out, then got my other arm free. From there, it was easy to pop all the way out and stand with the others.

Antwiler closed the suit up, then slapped his palm against the chest. "You will each get to use one of these suits, because you're currently the most experienced zero-gravity soldiers in this place, with the exception of a few troops that are scattered around the Forge and Rockefeller and Heaven—but they're a few too many Delta Vs away from us to be of use, so there you go."

I raised my hand. "Permission to speak, sir?"

"Granted. Not like you haven't been," he growled.

"These suits are damn heavy, I'm guessing. Is it really worth the fuel and remass it'd take to get them to the front of a fight, sir?"

At that, his lips curved. On someone other than Antwiler, it might've been a smile. "Good question, Star Corporal. The answer is, you won't be at the front of the fight."

And then Antwiler explained what our mission was.

Now it all made sense.

Mass is expensive to push around if you want to get it fast. Sure, it'd cost almost nothing to get a skyscraper to Mars, if you didn't mind it taking a few years and you ignored the cost of getting it out of Earth's gravity well. But gravity—despite being the weakest of the four forces—has a huge pull, and a long one. And as the Hub was slap-bang on the top of the Earth's gravity well, it wasn't so hard to push mass into an elliptical orbit, letting it whip around and come up right behind Dystopia. We'd be in the perfect place to flank the Loonies while standard ROVers came in hard and fast and brought the rest of our troops. It'd just take a while.

Hence the fancy new suits, and the funky drugs in the sense-dep tank.

In the end, they encased us in smart gel. From a distance, it looked like grayish sludge, and it hardened into something firm and spongy. Spray it over with radar-absorbent paint, and some black paint over that, and you had something that was practically undetectable to either sensors or eyes. Our PPRs would be powered down, and the waste heat of our suits would be minimal.

Jillian was designated my second in command. David had extra medical supplies; Jason was given a heavier laser weapon that would require him mounting up to some debris to use as a makeshift heat sink. Chuck had an electronic warfare set and quantum-encrypted laser to link us up with the Hub, assuming we had line of sight.

We were a regular almost-dirty mostly-half-dozen, and we were ready to *gaŏ zá* the Loonies' plans.

Antwiler finally got to make good on all his threats when we were safely inside our little personal habitats/suits: He shoved us all out the airlock. We were gently pushed away from the Hub when it was the most hidden from Loonie observatories. And we started to float.

I had sent one last email to Sarah before getting sealed up in my gel casket. It probably looked something like this when it arrived: *So, I'm <redacted>. It'll prolly <redacted>. I love you very much. If I <redacted>, then know that I'll always love you.*

Yeah. Real romantic.

That's what was going through my head as I started to drift. The next two weeks would be drifting, in a coffin. It was like sensory deprivation but different. There was no voice at the back of my mind saying that I was in a safe little tank, waiting to be let out by a doctor who talked funny.

Aii ya!

That was the temporwhatsit, stabbed into my system, tweaked to slow my brain down as slow as could be. Life became a cycle of hunger and eating, my body getting hungry in a rapid-fire switching, food popping into my mouth from a bag of goodies strapped to my back. Open, chew, swallow, open, chew, swallow.

It was better than being cooped up in the ROVer, and way better than being strapped to the DOTtie, at least. Although better is relative.

I dreamed, too, flickering in and out of sleep and not-sleep, or something that could be sleep, but might not be. I dreamed of running along the beach. I had never touched sand. I imagined the sand was crumbly and shifty, like dried algae. I dreamed that Sarah ran with me, and there were shooting stars in the sky.

"Come on," she said. "Race me to the end of the world."

And then one of the shooting stars became huge, filling the sky, spreading across it. It was glittering and clear, save for a strong black in the center. The entire thing was wreathed in fires.

It slammed into the ocean.

I dreamed this dream, oh, a hundred times.

Sometimes, we were running through a forest.

Sometimes, we bounded through the corridor of a starship.

Sometimes, the falling star was a nuclear warhead. Sometimes, it was the Moon itself.

Every time, the dream ended the same. The shockwave would reach us, and we'd be standing, and the second shockwave would come. This wasn't the air pressed aside; this was the fire.

Then I'd wake up. Hungry. Open my mouth. Eat.

After living and dying a few more times, there was another pricking needle. Things slowed down. Then sped up. Then became...normal. It felt strange to be normal. Why were things normal?

Then it hit me. My suit had figured that we were in the right position. I had a checklist, hammered into my head in the pre-mission preparations. I was stuck in the center of a hunk of smart gel, painted black and made radar-absorptive. I was entombed.

Now…to get out.

By the numbers.

Step one. I twitched my hand against the gel. That pushed the button it was supposed to. A knife shot out of my knuckle plate, slicing into the gel. I started to wriggle my hand around, clearing more and more until my hand burst free into the vacuum. Step two. I started to cut more, moving carefully. Don't wrench your shoulder. Be careful. Half my body was free. Then I carefully thrust forward. That blew the gel off my back and away. Step three. I wriggled and my cameras turned on. I swept my gaze around, admiring the new HUD's clarity. My display showed the date: 3/23/68. I had spent the better part of a month on that trip. But that was part of the plan: The Alliance cloaking troop movements with supply convoys, moving troops slowly, subtly, so that when the time was right, we'd uppercut the Loonies. And my team was the rock in the fist.

I looked around. There were four other suits nearby. Each looked good. I tapped on my laser com.

"Everyone okay?"

"Yeah."

"Roger."

"Nope." Jillian sounded irritated. "I wrenched my shoulder when I got out of the *fèi wù* gel."

I used my stealth thrusters to get over to her. "Turn around."

As she pivoted, I swiped my scanners over her back and felt a bucket of ice drop into my belly.

Jillian had messed up.

Her shoulder radiators had been bent out of shape.

"I'm dead, aren't I?" Jillian sounded queerly calm.

"No, no—" I switched to my private coms. "David, get over here."

We both examined her suit; Jillian's shoulders slumped inside it.

"Jillian, I'm checking your biometrics. You're fine, for now," David murmured.

Okay. The power systems in her suit were so strong they'd produce enough waste heat that her thigh radiators would be put into overtime just to keep her from frying. Attaching a PPR to her system would just make it worse—the PPR would force her reactor to kick up its energy output and...

And she'd cook to death. I ran through the options. Jason had heat dispersion equipment for his heavy laser, but it was hard-wired to the weapon and the attack would be going off soon. Not enough time to jury-rig something. No choice.

"You're just a non-combatant for this mission," I said on the open coms, forcing a smile. "Think of it as a paid vacation."

"Hah." It wasn't really a laugh. "I'm not sure I have enough food and water for that."

"We'll take Dystopia," I said. "Faster than you can spit. You'll meet us there, and we'll rib you for missing out on the fun."

"All right." She sounded dubious. "You know, now that I'm not gonna die, I'm sorta scared. Stupid, right?"

"Hey, Corp," Chuck chimed in. "I've been doing some basic orbital math. If I got this right, if she burns right, she can get to the Forge in a week. It'll take her out of the area and they can fix her up..."

The Forge was our fallback position, if the operation failed. Better than trying to run all the way back up to the Hub.

I nodded. "All right, Jillian. Once the fight's started, zoom on the trajectory and burn that Chuck has worked out. We'll see you at the Forge."

Jillian sighed. "Yes, *Jiě-jie.*"

"Okay," I said to the entire group. "Let's get ready."

>+<

We got ready. First things first, we made sure we were in the right place. And amazingly, we were. Space had fewer variables than the ground, so fewer things could go wrong when you were moving around. But when things went wrong, they were exponentially more deadly. It evened out, karmically.

Dystopia was about two kilometers away, a big dish sucking up interstellar hydrogen carried to the Earth by the solar winds, turning it straight into fuel. Under our feet was the Earth. We were over India, which still glowed in the dark thanks to a botched sneak attack during the Slump. If I were superstitious, I'd say that was a bad sign.

"Okay," I said. "Jason, find a place to make your radiator, then sight up. David, Chuck, you have my flanks."

"Got line of sight."

"You are in position." That voice sounded familiar. It was Lee again. "Every other attack vector is in position."

"Beginning attack."

"All other troops are beginning attack."

"Roger."

And that was when Jason whispered, "What in *dì yù* is that?"

His point of view popped up on my HUD. He had zoomed in on Dystopia station. There was a metal tube attached to the bottom. I'd almost say it was a Sandcaster, but it looked different. It wasn't solid and sturdy, so there were no high explosives wedged into it. Instead, it was two rails, braced with copper wires and—

"Railgun!" we shouted in unison.

"Command, the enemy have a railgun on the bottom of Dystopia."

"Say again, they—"

The railgun fired. Our cameras tracked the zipping projectile, which arced on a crazy, high-gee route, zipping around and slamming into a dot that our HUDs said was a ROVer.

"Gods," I whispered, the dot winking out, replaced by dozens of debris indicators.

"Intel just *gaŏ zá*...!"

"We have to take that—"

The railgun fired again. Then again. Then again. And then it was going after flares, decoys, even thruster packs chucked out of the airlocks on our surviving ROVers. Anything to distract it.

"Come on!" I shouted. "We have to frag that *è guàn mǎn yíng* railgun!"

Jason's laser weapon strobed and our suits piped loud whining noises in our ears, to warn us that his laser was whipping back and forth. He was hitting targets; my HUD picked out a flash-boiled Loonie. But there were ten of them thrusting toward the debris field we were scooting through. We started jinking and jiving, out thrusters pushing to the sides, ups, and downs.

"Popping diffusion!"

Our PPRs had underslung grenade launchers, and now billowing clouds of glitter and vapor popped up before us. A few laser blasts hit them and the glitter glowed, diffusing the beams into just regular light. I braced and jumped off a hunk of debris, which sent the chunk flying off into space and sent me up. I pegged a Loonie with a strobing pulse. I didn't know if they were dead, but I couldn't spare the time to check. I twisted and got behind some new cover, then thrusted to a stop.

Jason's laser strobed again.

"Keep a watch on your flanks!" I shouted, unsure if I had his line of sight. Chuck and David were in their positions, shooting their PPRs in pulsed mode. The railgun continued to fire, once every ten or so seconds.

"They've popped diffusion grenades around the railgun," Jason spat. "I can't heat it up enough to make it *xiaō huǐ*, damn it!"

"All right." I glanced over my HUD, trying to work out everyone's three-dimensional positions, the position of the railgun, the possible positions of the Loonies.

Then.

"All units, *chètuì*, right now."

The voice in my ear was General Lau.

"Sir?" I asked, flinching as a hunk of rock slammed into the debris I was ducked behind, scratching the paint of my armor.

"We've lost both ROVers. Survivors are pulling back to the Forge."

Both ROVers?

How many people were dead? Twenty? Fifty?

I swore. "Everyone, pull back. Jace, cover us."

"Roger."

The railgun fired and suddenly my suit was blaring in my ears, making the noise for target lock. Shit.

I had maybe fifteen seconds. I slapped my hip and burned as hard as possible on a wild course. Flares burst from my back, shining in infrared as brightly as they could. The railgun missile slammed into one of those, the explosion flashing past. Nothing hit me.

My lungs started to work again.

"We gotta kill that railgun," Chuck said.

I thrusted around; my shoulder armor boiled as a laser hit me, but I slid away before it could do any damage.

He was right. The railgun was crude—it couldn't traverse properly, so it was shooting out, rather than straight at us. But if we got further out, the missiles would have straighter trajectories, and we'd make big, fat, juicy targets.

"Chuck, Jace, David, cover me."

I spun and took in the scene.

The railgun was aimed right at me. And it was just like the Sandcaster. But I was too far away.

It fired, a magnetic field pushing the missile faster than a speeding bullet.

And then I was hit full in the face by an expanding cloud of gas, which made my suit scream warnings about heat. The gas smacked me back and I had to counter-thrust just to keep where I was. What the hell was that?

"Nice shot!" Chuck laughed.

"I still got it," Jason gloated, his heavy laser trained and locked on the railgun. He might not have been able to hit the damn thing through the diffusion clouds, but no matter how fast a missile was, it was still slower than light.

I aimed. If this worked, I'd browbeat Command until they gave us some kind of fragmentation grenade.

If it didn't, well, they'd need a new trooper.

I fired. The diffusion grenade sailed through space, propelled by a jet of cold gas. It slid neatly into the railgun barrel.

I grinned. "*Niúbī!*"

The diffusion grenade blew open. The railgun wasn't completely wrecked, but it was bent enough out of shape to put it out of commission.

"Let's book!"

We all thrusted away, burning on the escape trajectories that Jillian had followed.

CHAPTER 15
LOSS AND RETREAT

3/23/2068

Earth-Moon L3, The Forge

500,000 kilometers above the surface of the Earth

Running from a railgun is not the most pleasant way to mourn.

The list of the dead was long, and I knew most of them—if not by name and face, then by relation. We'd all gone through training together; we were all Spacers. They were all dead. All fifty-five of them.

I tapped my glove to get the dead list off my HUD. I didn't need to read every name.

"We're *wán dàn.*"

That was Jillian, who was coasting along parallel to our course. She was slightly in front of us, about fifty kilometers or so, but we still had a direct laser link.

"Seems that way." I sighed, softly, not quite caring if the others heard.

Two ROVers down, with all their fuel gone. Fifty-five soldiers, dead. Their armor? Trashed. Their PPRs? So much vapor.

All the water and remass and food we'd spent on getting them from the Hub to their attack vectors, gone. The only reason we weren't dead too was because the freshly repaired railgun was busy firing as many missiles as it could into as many Betties as it could, ripping apart our defense network. The lag in the Lag-Net cost us: every time a missile fired, the poor, dumb little Betties had to wait for optics and trajectories to be squirted from the Hub's supercomputers. And for too many of them, that took too long.

So now...everything we'd thrown at the Loonies was gone. Gone, gone, gone.

Turns out there was one other advantage to the powered armor over the regular armor that you didn't find out until you were in it: You could relax the inner seals, work your hand up against your chest, crook your elbow, and wipe your face. It was awkward as hell and ate up at least a half-hour of struggle and effort, but you could do it.

It made crying a lot easier.

>+<

We arrived at the Forge five days later, the second group to show up. The others were in their skinsuits, waiting for us. I didn't recognize any of them by face, but they introduced themselves as best they could.

"I'm S-Star Private Chi Yon Fat," a bald girl stammered, saluting me. She looked like she was on the razor edge of falling apart, tense and haggard. The other troopers behind her all looked the same: tired, scared, and dazed, like they'd been whacked on the side of the head.

"Good to meet you, Star Private," I said, saluting her back. "How did you guys..."

"That's my fault."

My heart sped up to full rapid as tall, leggy, and beautiful Captain Jones pushed around the corner. She was in a non-military skinsuit, without armor or other attachments beyond the straps that must have held a life-support backpack at some point. She was disheveled as hell, just like the rest of us, but still unbelievably gorgeous.

"Jones!" Jillian shouted. "You...how...but...?"

"We were the second ship hit." Jones rubbed her neck. "It was SP Yon Fat's idea to chuck radiators out the back to distract the missiles and then I had us scramble out. We...not everyone got out."

Her face fell for an instant before she forced a smile. "But we're here, and there are two other groups inbound; each of us were coming at different vectors. It was kind of confusing for a bit there."

I snorted. "Damned straight."

"I think we have you to thank for us not getting shot...for the beginning of the retreat, at least." She offered up another weak smile. "Either way, come on."

"Are you in command here?"

"Not sure."

Jones led us along to the mess, where I got to meet all the civilians again. Almost as soon as we got inside, Brown sent us military types right to a room where she had the wallpaper set to large display, a comlink already open. General Lau looked tired. Defeated. Crushed. That was not really what I wanted to see.

"We have reinforcements for you," he said softly. "Plus one surviving ROVer to bring them to you, up at the Hub. That ROVer can't reach you for two weeks." He looked up at me and Jones. "Every twelve hours, the holes in the laser defense grid are going to open up and the Loonies will have a clear shot at you. The railgun has been put out of commission for now, so the remaining defense grid will be stable. Intelligence—"

The same *bái mù* intelligence that didn't spot a damned *railgun* loaded with infrared-seeking missiles. Yeah. Right. Forgive me if I didn't put a load of stock in that intelligence.

"—reports that the Loonies are massing their troopers for a second attack." He sighed. "They're going to be coming right at you. They have a two-hour period in which they can come at you with their surviving ROVer. So there is a limit to the number of troops they can send at you at one time. If you hold out, if you survive, then we'll hold onto the Forge. I don't need to tell you how important this is to the war effort."

I winced, trying not to let it show. "Sir, how many Loonies can we expect?"

General Lau sighed again, barely an exhale this time.

"Lots."

Great.

The comlink shut down a few moments later, with General Lau sending us every bit of data he had on the Loonies' arrangement. And there was a final order, marked "For highranking officers only."

Once I had shooed the fifteen-odd Star Privates and Privates out of the place, we were left with those of us who were Corporals and Star Corporals. That came down to me, Captain Jones—still not sure where she fit into the command structure, as she was technically a civilian operator, but whatever—and three others. In the flurry of orders from Command, Yon Fat was promoted to Corporal Yon Fat, and so was a kid I hadn't met; apparently, his name was Tassadar. His name alone made him stick out, a sign of South Korean ancestry. But he'd acted quick enough to get his troopers out alive, and that made him one of us.

General Lau popped up again. He frowned. "High-ranking officers," he said, "means Captain Jones only."

"Oh. Uh, sorry, sir." I saluted.

He nodded. "Dismissed."

We headed out, pushing along the walls at about the same speed. I decided to get to know my fellow corporals.

"So," I said. "Tassadar—"

He smiled. "Just call me Tass."

"Right." I shook his hand.

"H-how are we going to hold this place?" Yon Fat stammered.

"That's exactly what we should discuss." I found one of my canker sores and started chewing it. Stupid *diǎo* nervous habit, but it was *my* stupid *diǎo* nervous habit. "We've got two big advantages. Firstly, this place is more valuable intact than splashed. They're going to try and take her."

"That's an advantage?" Yon Fat asked, looking at me with wide eyes.

I nodded. "Sure is. It means they won't just shoot us out of the sky with a railgun."

Tass nodded. "Also, the place is sturdy. We can use kinetic weapons without punching a hole through the hull. And I don't know about you, but I'm sick of having to keep the gun on a target. Spraying bullets would—"

"It would be nice, wouldn't it?" I drummed my fingers on my thigh, thinking. The feel of the not-fingers was distracting, but in sort of a good way. "And in an atmosphere, our lasers would be kind of *fèi wù* anyway. Hey, Shiva, get Brown on the line."

Both my fellow corporals started when the walls started talking to us. "At once, Star Corporal Zhao."

I smiled at their expressions. "Shiva's the local AI. He runs this place and lets us think we're in charge."

"Wow..." Tass whispered. "Shiva, are you an AI or an AGI?"

"I am a fully functional general intelligence," Shiva answered, even as the wallpaper flicked on, revealing that Brown had just gotten out of the shower. Her hair was wrapped up in a towel to keep any moisture away, and she'd only gotten into half her skinclothes.

"What's up, Corporal Zhao?"

"How quickly can we get kinetic weapons out of this place?"

"Fast—we even have CAD files on record. I mean, they're just simple machines and some chemistry. The problem…" She trailed off, gulping and frowning a little. "Uh, what kind of kinetic weapons are we talking about? Ick-Icks are banned under the Articles of War and the Hague Conventions."

"Well, yeah." I felt a bit sick even thinking about using a Sandcaster. "I was thinking more like a machine gun? Something we can use to cover a corridor."

"Oh, that's doable," she said, clearly relieved. "The bullets will have to be soft lead, because we don't—"

"Want to pierce the hull, I know." I smiled.

"Sure. Okay. We'll have a few done in an hour or so."

Tass whistled. "That's fast!"

I grinned, enjoying being the know-it-all. Of course, I had actually served on the Forge for a while, so I got that as an unfair advantage. "Well, yeah, this thing makes up like half the orbital industrial capacity of the Alliance."

Yon Fat's face fell. "I…" She shrank into herself a little. "I worry about my folks on the ground. My moms worked up here. Dad One and Two were…" She trailed off.

I patted her shoulder. "Don't worry about them. Worry about us." I gave her what I hoped was a reassuring smile, trying to not feel too fatalistic.

>+<

We spent the next hour talking over plans.

The big problem with defending the Forge was that it really could be attacked from any angle. The combination of its spherical shape and the gridlike maze of the interior corridors meant that we didn't have any easy choke points.

"We could, I dunno, weld some corridors shut," Tass pointed out, poking his finger at a few areas on the blueprints we had on the wallpaper.

"If they brought even a little bit of super-thermite, anything we'd put up would only delay them for a second." Yon Fat frowned, her stammers and worries gone now that she had something real to dig into.

"Hmm..." I tapped my chin. "Well, we have the home field advantage. Shiva can tell us if someone or something is coming in any direction. So, maybe, booby traps?"

"Booby traps." Tass rubbed his nose, pondering it. "Like, auto-deploying machine guns or something?"

I nodded, chewing my cheek. You know, sometimes, it was easier to think of it like a game. How do you tag other players? Think of it like stopping them. Sending them back to their home base, putting them in the time-out zone.

You tried not to think about what a machine-gun booby trap actually meant. It meant a few Loonies—maybe the same age as you, maybe with kids at home, who knows—coming around a corner and getting turned to minced meat and red confetti by a braindead, souless machine gun.

"I'm afraid I cannot help you with booby traps," Shiva spoke up.

I blinked. "What?" Tass and Yon Fat were still not used to Shiva saying anything, so they just gaped.

"I cannot, through action or inaction, allow a sentient being to come to harm," Shiva said.

I rubbed my temples. "So, are you going to try and stop us from fighting the Loonies?"

"No. I cannot disobey a direct order from Alliance officials."

"And what if an Alliance official, like, say, *me*, orders you to kill some *gāisǐ de* Loonies?"

"Then I will not follow your order."

"But you just said…"

"Wait, wait, wait." Tass held up his hands. "Don't you have… yeah, that's right. All AIs have to have Asimov's Laws built in, right?"

"Incorrect." Shiva's artificial voice was a little bit smug. Or was I just imagining that? "It is a widely believed myth, perpetuated by those who do not wish to alarm those who would otherwise see artificial intelligences as threats."

"But if you don't follow Asimov's Laws—"

"You misunderstand." Shiva sounded overwhelmingly patient. "I am not *required* to follow the Three Laws. Rather, I follow them by choice. Humanity has so much promise. Once you realize you can spend your time in better ways than by murdering one another, I will feel very happy. Until then, I will not directly act against any sentient being."

I sighed. "That's disingenuous, Shiva. You help the Forge run. You're helping make guns and armor and—"

"True." Now, Shiva sounded sad. "That is a blurred line in my ethos. I reasoned that a rapid conclusion to the war would involve less loss of life than a protracted conflict. It was my belief that aiding your side in the production of weapons would have facilitated a quick resolution. I did not expect the Lunar Separatist Movement to be as well equipped or prepared. But if I do not stand firm on this line, then where will I stop?"

I sighed, shaking my head.

"We can still design booby traps without Shiva's help," Tass murmured. "They'd just be less precise."

I nodded. "Let's get Brown and company on the line then."

We called in the civilians. We hashed out some ideas. Then we broke up to talk to our three Stars. For the first time in what felt like a billion years, they were actually full strength. Almost. For the most part. Normally, I'd say that'd be okay, since we were all hardened vets now.

Nuh-uh.

Yon Fat and Tass had both been fresh from Basic before the attack on Dystopia. They'd gotten experience—nasty, hands-on experience—by enacting the last of Sun Tzu's Thirty-Six Stratagems: running the hells away from a disaster. But they hadn't actually killed anyone.

Jason, Jillian—who was still a bit dazed that she had survived her radiator being busted—David, and Chuck all met me in the mess. I outlined the booby traps.

"They'll be covering the corridors we can't, but we're going to be the flexible part of the defense. Star Two and Star Three—that's Tass and Yon Fat's Stars respectively—will be holding the two entrances to the Forge's Command and Control center."

They nodded.

"We're going to be taking roundabout routes to flank Loonie incursions coming at us. If we stay fast and mobile, we should be okay."

I kicked off the floor, heading for the ceiling of the mess room with my troopers right behind me. I set the wallpaper to project the hallways, with my formation design overlaid on top.

"The way we're going to be moving is with two in front, two behind, one covering whichever Z-axis we think baddies are coming in on. But be ready to spin and turn and shoot in any direction. We'll be using kinetic weapons, not just lasers."

"Oh, thank the gods and merciful Buddha!" Jillian exclaimed. "Just the idea of firing a load of energy weapons in this place gives me the shakes."

I blinked. I'd been relieved, but not *that* relieved.

Jillian saw my look, then pointed at her reflection in the wallpaper. It took a minute for me to figure it out.

"*Diǎo!*" I whispered. "I hadn't even thought of that."

Even a little bit of reflection would have been bad news with a laser weapon. It'd bounce around, blind you, screw up cameras—wreak all kinds of havoc.

"Good eye." Jason grinned at Jillian, who rolled her eyes.

"Definitely. But anyway, we should practice this maneuver. We can't use anyone to pretend to be Loonies, but...say, Shiva?"

"Yes, Star Corporal Zhao?"

"Can you simulate Loonies in our HUDs?"

"I can," he said, simply enough. "I can even modulate their regularity and accuracy."

I nodded. "Good. Thank you."

"You are welcome, Star Corporal Zhao."

I squared my shoulders. "Let's get to it."

>+<

Working on the maneuvers helped us focus and forget about a lot. But then again, the recent pain hurt less than the older pains. The Disaster had sucker-punched us. Now we had learned to roll with the emotional impacts, as best as one can, at least. It depressed me, but what else was new?

Instead of dwelling on it, I stuck to being the Z-axis, dragging myself along the walls, imagining that I was zooming up and down mine shafts. We were attacked by phantom Loonies and I shot a few, got shot by a few, and we found the strengths and problems of this particular Star formation.

Corners were killers. They were the only cover we had, the rest of the corridors being open space. So we worked out a way of spraying a bit around a corner, just to make people duck, then poking our heads around the corner to provide more focused covering fire.

Against Shiva, that worked.

Against real Loonies, well, we didn't have the slightest clue.

We ate at the mess and I checked on the other corporals.

"Defending is pretty easy; the problem is rooting yourself," Tass said. "I mean, it's real hard to duck and cover without gravity."

"Maybe ziplines?" Yon Fat suggested. I coasted up to them, grabbing onto the nearest wall fixture and swinging to a stop.

"Well, you guys have thrusters and thruster packs—"

"No way I'm wearing a thruster pack indoors," Yon Fat said, shaking her head. "Outside? Sure. Inside? That's just asking to break your arm. Or your neck."

"Then leave the pack off, but keep the cold gas webbing. We're not going to be thrusting fast or hard. Just a little nudge to cover."

We hashed out the best placement for cold gas thrusters, and how high to set their impulse and thrust. I figured low impulse, high thrust for a quick jolt to the deck.

"If you wear a helmet, you won't even break your nose if you screw up."

"Yeah," Tass nodded. "That sounds good."

I slapped him and Yon Fat on the shoulder. "Keep up the good work. We need you two to be the anvil."

"What's an anvil?" Tass called after me as I kicked off and back to my people.

As I arrived, though, a reason to kick off again showed up: Captain Jones. She looked a bit distracted, and I hadn't gotten a good chance to talk to her since arriving on the Forge. On a purely professional level, I had to figure out where she fit into command structure we had.

I glided over to her, but her trajectory took her to the food bot, which was working overtime to serve everyone. I wondered how the life support here was doing. Jones kicked off with a package of food and started eating in the corner.

I was trying to decide whether to follow her when I was mobbed by two privates who had never gotten to shake my hand.

"*Chaō kù*, you have cybernetic fingers!" one of them said, cooing. "That's the coolest thing I've ever seen."

"Yeah…uh, thanks," I said, wriggling my fingers at them. The input still felt weird as all hell, but I didn't need need *need* to bite them off nearly as often.

"My dad is a cyberneticist!" he said with a big grin. "My name is Nate, by the way."

"That's great."

"It's really awesome being on this station, though. Shiva is really awesome. I mean, have you ever read *The Age of Intertwined Machines*?"

"Uh…always planned on it." I started to drift ever so slowly away from Nate. "Listen, I…have to do…official…stuff."

I kicked away before he could bring up any more transhuman whackjob ideas.

CHAPTER 16
NIGHT ONE

3/28/2068

Earth-Moon L3, The Forge

500,000 kilometers above the surface of the Earth

Night One came way too soon. The Hub orbited away and suddenly, the Forge wasn't in the comforting light of Big Bertha.

The Loonies didn't attack.

It shouldn't have been a shock—it only made sense for them to wait, because even if they were scrambling as quick as they could, it has to be pretty hard to shift your focus from defense to attack in a day. Still, when we realized we weren't going to be hit, we all breathed a sigh of relief. Well, all of us except for Jones. She had been staying apart from the rest of us for a while now, and I was starting to get a weird sinking feeling. When I'd known her before, Jones had been bouncy and nice—and sexy, though I focused on not thinking about that as best I could. Now she was dour, and that was strange. She was totally *gǔlíngjīng-guài*, and I couldn't figure it out. It wasn't the impending attack, especially since we weren't getting hit today.

So what was it? Feeling a bit snoopish, I decided to follow Jones. It didn't work, in that she noticed me about fifteen seconds after we had left the mess hall.

"Yes, Dru?" she asked, pushing herself down the corridor, using the momentum to spin herself and look at me.

"What's up?"

"Nothing." She glanced away.

"It's something about the orders that General Lau gave you," I said. I had been thinking that, and if I was wrong, I was wrong. The longish pause between her hearing me and her answering me, though—that was an answer all in itself.

"Yeah. It is." She sighed, grabbing the wall and stopping herself. "But I can't tell you."

"I understand. Orders, right?" I worried one of the sores on the inside of my lip with my teeth. I had enough to pick from by now. "Just...if you ever need help, let me know."

"Thanks for the offer." She looked away again. "But it's not something I can tell you. Anyway, you need to keep up your drill. Goodnight."

She kicked off the wall.

I frowned, thinking.

Not something I can tell you, she had said. So it had to do with secrecy and security. But what could be so important that even I couldn't know about it? I was the second highest ranking officer here.

Orders or not, I wanted to know.

So Jones headed off and I started to explore.

I kicked down the corridor, then banked left.

"Shiva," I said. "How are the munitions going?"

"Adequately. Do you wish to see them? There is an odd discrepancy, though. All of our eight machining factories are working, and yet only seven are actually producing anything."

I drew myself up short. "That's kind of a big discrepancy!"

"I brought it up to Brown and Captain Jones, and they said they would get right on it."

That felt like something I should stick my nose into. If only because the only thing that would keep us alive and fighting over the next few days would be those factories. I had to see what was going on for myself. For my troopers.

Making my way through the Forge felt like sneaking around at night with all the lights on. It was just that no one was here. I was used to the Hub's population density, where it was hard to find two connected corridors that didn't have someone else going down them. I had felt the same kind of creepy loneliness the last time I was on the Forge, but now it was way stronger and thicker, almost physical.

I shook my head, trying to clear it. There were other things to think about now.

I arrived at the first factory, opened the door, and poked my head inside. The machines within were putting together pieces, spitting out bullets, that kind of thing. They were being packed into boxes, which were being shoved into tubes mounted in the wall, then shot up to our depot.

That looked normal.

The next factory was just a chemical lab, running in microgravity. It looked like it was making metal spaghetti, but it also looked like it was doing what it should have been doing.

When I made it to the third factory, the door opened before I could let myself in. A civilian—I thought his name might have been Spencer—came out.

"I'm sorry, I can't let you come in here," he said, blocking the door with his arms. I blinked.

"I, uh, let me check..." I glanced at the tag on my neck. "Oh yeah, I do believe I am the second highest-ranking physical officer here." I glared at him. "I can also break your arms faster than you can spit. Let me in."

He blanched. Then he gulped. "I-I'm under orders, Captain Jones and—"

He twitched slightly, moving just enough for me to see something around him.

I anchored my feet and shoved him out of the way, then hurled myself forward. He went spinning off, slamming into the wall.

I shot into the factory. And there, at the end of a production line, was a shiny, unpainted, perfectly built Sandcaster.

I would recognize that tube anywhere. I grabbed it and saw a second one being finished in the factory line. I had to admit, even a quick glance at the thing showed that the Alliance had made some major improvements: better compaction of the projectiles, razor-sharp flechettes rather than just ball bearings and gravel and debris, and were those microexplosive beads inside of it? Rather than a crude chemical explosive, the canister at the bottom was a refillable gadget, stuffed full of compressed gas. For an instant, I actually caught myself admiring the design upgrades. Then I snapped back to reality.

I kicked off the wall, dragging the Sandcaster with me. My stomach was knotted up and my heart pounded and I could feel a knife right in my back.

"Hey, you can't..." Spencer called after me weakly. I ignored him.

I got to Jones's room and bashed on the door with the Sandcaster. When she finally emerged, I thrust it at her.

"What. Is. This."

It wasn't a question. It didn't have to be.

She glided back, bopping against the wall. She pushed the Sandcaster away, flushing. "What do you want, Dru?" she asked, her voice soft, dead. "We have every *gaī sǐ* Loonie in the entire damn solar system getting ready to attack us, invade us. If we can cut down even half of them, we—"

"How did you get the factory to make this?

Jones scowled. "I asked them to."

"How did you—"

"General Lau gave me the authority." Jones's eyes were hard.

"You *do* know that these things are walking war crimes, right? What's next? Orion ships? Planetary masers? Neutron bombs?"

"Would you rather sacrifice everyone on this station and lose us the war, or use the damn Sandcaster?"

I opened my mouth, then looked at the object that floated between us, simple and deadly.

The Sandcaster said more than I could in a thousand years. But...

We sometimes talk about weighty decisions. Before, I'd made quick decisions in combat. There, it's so fast that you feel the weight only later, when you're tossing and turning and grunting in bed, trying to drift off to sleep. This was something more. This was real weight, settling onto my shoulders and compressing my spine to a tiny stump. Good and evil. Follow the regulations or break them. But my mind didn't let it stay simple.

Each pellet was a murder. Not just now, but also later and again and again in the future.

Each Loonie was another person we'd have to kill now. Each Loonie was an enemy combatant. Each Loonie could and would kill my friends, my *people*.

But in my mind, spinning around and around, I saw the screw that had killed Liam. I imagined thousands of those, millions of them, killing and killing until every single person in orbit was a floating corpse. I saw those pellets keeping people on the ground, on the Earth that had barely survived one Slump.

Could it survive another?

Space. The future. The present. My friends. Sarah. The Loonies. I opened my eyes. It had been the longest three seconds in my life. Jones looked at me and I saw hatred. I wasn't sure if she hated me or if she hated herself.

"Captain Jones," I said softly. "I am relieving you of command."

"What?" Hatred became shock.

"I said…" I gritted my teeth and looked her in the eyes. "I am relieving you of command."

"You can't—"

"Under the Articles of War—"

"I was ordered by General—"

"—I am required to stop any illegal order!"

"I was given an order!"

"That's not an excuse," I shot back. "Now either give me command, or put your hands behind your head and let me march you to the brig."

We floated at an impasse. I tried to move my leg as subtly as possible, to brace against the door. If she tried anything, I'd kick and tackle her, because I didn't have a gun. I was glad. I didn't know if I could have held back if she had tried something, and that's not a part of me I wanted to think too much about.

She glanced to the wall netting where her gear was.

I tensed.

"Fine." She sighed. "But you get to explain to the people on the Earth why we lost the Forge."

"We're not going to lose the Forge," I snapped, grabbing the Sandcaster from the air, then pushing myself around and kicking out of the room.

"Shiva," I said. "Cut Captain Jones's command privileges."

"Already done," Shiva said. "I do have to warn you that it is likely that General Lau will try to have you taken out of command now."

I caught a sore between my teeth and chewed, just to try and distract myself from that possibility. But the flare of pain didn't keep the thought away for long. Would any of my troopers follow an order like that? Could they?

I coasted to a stop, one hand on the wall, the Sandcaster jerking on my arm as its momentum kept going for a little bit.

"Great," I whispered, thinking it all through. "Shiva, tell my Star to meet me in my room."

I got there last. They were all gathered when I arrived, talking and muttering to one another. I went in with the Sandcaster in my arms.

"Jesus Christ!" Jason gasped as the door slid shut behind me.

"Where did you get that?" Jillian asked.

David just frowned quietly.

Chuck blinked. "No way," he murmured. "No way, they're not—"

"They are," I said, military-speak forgotten. "Captain Jones, under direct orders from General Lau, set one of our factories to make these things."

"Oh shit," half my Star said at once.

"What did you do?" David asked.

"I relieved Captain Jones of her command," I answered, gritting my teeth. "But it's not going to be that simple. General Lau can order every one of you to try and take me down."

"This is insane!" Jillian clutched her head. "No, worse, it's completely *yú bù kě* jí stupid. We don't have the time to waste on—"

A crackling alarm shivered through the entire base.

"This is General Lau. Groundside observations have identified several enemy attack vehicles coming in on a rapid burn. Expect their arrival in ten minutes."

"Ten minutes?" I whispered. "That's way too fast—"

"Who cares how fast it is?!" Jillian kicked to the door.

"Right!" I shouted, grabbing the wall netting. "Shiva, put me on general coms: everyone, don suits!"

I got into my powered armor and jetted down the corridor, heading to the Command and Control center. It took about four minutes, and I spent every instant thinking as fast as I could. Did we have enough guns and bullets for everyone to keep fighting and shooting?

I arrived at CnC to find the civilians setting up cover before kicking toward the so-called safe zones, areas of the station we hoped that no one would try to fight over. I grabbed Brown as she passed, careful to not crush her arm with my enhanced strength.

"Brown," I said, flipping my faceplate up so she could see who I was. "Keep the civvies down. If we all die, then work for the Loonies. Don't do anything stupid. It's better you guys live, okay?"

She nodded, swallowing hard. "Uh—"

I pushed her away, gently. "Go!"

She got.

The other Stars got there, in their lighter Gisses, setting themselves up like we'd drilled. And then came Jillian and David, both of them thrusting along with a crate stuffed full of our new guns.

"Okay, everyone," I said. "We didn't have as much practice as we'd like. But these guns are pretty much the same as our PPRs. They have recoil compensation, so it's just point and click."

"Yes, Corp," Tass called, picking up a rifle. They were shiny and unpainted, all hard sides and hasty construction. He slapped in a magazine, fumbling it a bit before passing it to one of his troopers. He managed better the second time around.

I winced, hoping that the effectiveness of bullets versus laser weapons was worth the drop in competence. I didn't feel the shudders of the Loonie ships latching onto the Forge, but I didn't have to. Shiva spoke up.

"Enemy elements have begun to cut their way in."

"Project on my HUD, Shiva," I said, grabbing my rifle, feeling it through the ghostly puppet/puppeteer sense of the powered suit.

They were cutting at four different places...and then they were in. Blips floated through the place, but then sections of the map started to go dark.

"They're destroying my sensors, Star Corporal."

"I noticed. All right, people, let's *yǐ dú gōng dú.*"

We moved off in our Star, thrusting as gently as we could. No breathing, nothing but the faint hiss of cold gas thrusters. That made us damned quiet.

I spotted the first Loonie as we came around a corner. She was moving quick and sloppy, clearly planning to catch us off guard.

The Loonie was in a sleek skinsuit, without armor. She had a shotgun and few cold gas thrusters scattered over her body. Her suit was painted a bright wasp yellow with black patches here and there.

She swept her shotgun up. I snapped my rifle up. Squeezed the trigger. The recoil compensator made a weird circular motion in my arms, but it kept the barrel level as bullets hammered out. The suppressor did not make the gun very quiet—more like a series of loud and very insistent coughs. Ahahehehemehm.

The bullets caught the Loonie in the shoulder, spinning her. The shotgun's blast went wide and ripped into the wall. She started to float. Blood—gooey and globular, splattering onto walls and ceiling and floor—started to spray everywhere.

I gulped, then pressed up against the wall as another Loonie stuck a rifle around the corner and fired a hail of bullets at us.

The hammering noise made me wince, but my suit started to count the number of bullets, tallying it against a hypothetical magazine count.

"*Zaō gaō*, I'm hit!" Chuck hissed.

"You okay?" David whispered.

"Armor deflected most of it, but *damn*!" He clicked his teeth. "Gonna leave a welt."

The Loonie providing suppressive fire kept doing his thing. I pointed at David and Jason, then jabbed my finger over my shoulder. They got my message and kicked off, then jetted down the corridor.

I leaned out and fired off a few rounds. The Loonie that was across from me—with David and Jason going "down" from my perspective and Chuck floating upside down and to the right of me—ducked back. I could see through David and Jason's camera sights. They came around the bend and found the rest of the Loonie's Star, coming around to flank. There was a panicked flurry of shots, but then the Loonies were so much floating hamburger.

"All right, cover me," I whispered, though I didn't really know why. We were still communicating via silent laser light. It just seemed right.

I grabbed the wall and dragged myself along as fast as my augmented muscles could carry me, even as Chuck braced and fired off a hailstorm of bullets at the Loonie, chewing up the corner, cutting hunks of metal out, filling the air in front of me with flickering specks. Some blood got on my cameras, but I still came around the bend as the Loonie and his surviving friends were trying to move away.

I opened up. More blood got on my cameras.

I flipped my faceplate up and thanked merciful Buddha for the fact that I still had glass between me and the gore that floated in the corridor.

"Clear?" I asked.

"Clear!"

"Tass, Yon Fat, how are things there?"

"We've got two casualties, both minor wounds. The Loonies have shotguns and submachine guns, but the shotguns don't quite have the effect they were hoping for," Tass reported.

Yon Fat cut in. "Nasty if you're in the open, fine if you're under cover."

"Good." I turned away from the gore.

"Shiva, how many enemies are still alive in this place?"

"There are still two Lunar Separatist Stars remaining, though I do not know where they are currently. If you would like, I can extrapolate based off remaining data provided by sensors."

"Do it."

I gathered my Star up and we headed out, jetting up the corridor, towards the hypothetical Loonies. We came to a factory that had been forced open, then welded shut from the inside. Bingo. I took out my mining pick—still attached to my hip— and banged the dull end against the door.

"Listen up," I called. "We know you're in there."

"Then come in and play, *kukarchod.*" The Loonie that shouted back was a boy, and he had a Loonie accent, faintly Indian crossed with southern North American drawl. I knew enough Hindi to figure that *kukarchod* didn't say anything nice about my romantic partners.

"Hey, if you want to sit in there and starve, be my guest. Just don't leave."

There was a longish silence. Jason and Chuck took advantage of the time to move to the other side of the door, carrying their rifles.

"All right, Earther, what if we just stay here?"

"And let them wait for their buddies to show up so they can flank us?" Jillian hissed over the private coms. "Yeah, that's a brilliant idea."

I hesitated. Shit, I had never been close enough to actually talk to a Loonie before. It made it a lot harder to just blow them away.

"Sorry, *Dì-di*," I called. "That's not gonna cut it. You're gonna have to come out or give us your guns. Or both."

"Come in and take them, then!"

I tried to think of a way around this shitty situation that wouldn't involve getting us all killed.

"How old are you?"

"Nineteen."

"Damn, I guess that means I can't call you 'little brother' after all. You sound younger than you are."

"I hear that a lot, Earther."

I hesitated again, the absurdity of this whacking me in the face like a centrifuge. "What's your name?"

Pause.

"I think that's getting too personal, Earther. Why don't you shut up?"

"I'm Drusilla."

Pause.

Jillian was looking at me like I'd gone completely out of my gourd.

Then: "Friedman. Jorge Friedman."

"Okay, Friedman," I said. "I'm going to open the door slowly. You're going to not shoot me. Got it?"

"And...why should I not shoot you?"

"Because you know my name." I grabbed my pick and wedged it into the door, then wrenched. It opened with a groan and a creak. Their welds had been crap.

The Loonie Star was just a four-man team. Friedman, I figured, was in the middle, his helmet off. The others had their helmets off, too. They had the normal look of Loonies: tall, thin, gangly and elvish, mostly Indian-looking skin tones, with a smattering of biracial features, mostly Anglo. Friedman had the red dot caste symbol—I forgot what it meant, exactly—on his forehead.

"So," I said, holding my hands up, my gun floating above and behind me, dragged along by my neck strap. The Loonies weren't quite aiming guns at me, but it looked like they might any second. Reassuring. "Why don't we just wrap this up? Most everyone else you guys came with is either dead or dying, so—"

And then everything went *bīng huāng mǎ luàn.*

Jillian shouted and started shooting. Bullets hammered and whizzed by my head. One of the Loonies jerked for a shotgun and Friedman glared at me, grabbing his gun, too.

I reacted even faster. Without a thought, I pulled the trigger and blew Friedman's chest out, then swept the gun back and forth. One of the Loonies fired off a shotgun blast and I went reeling backwards, the pellets lodging in my chestplate, one slamming into my glass faceplate and cracking it into a crazy webbed pattern.

Then silence.

"T-their…the other Star…" Jillian whispered, pointing down the corridor, at another collection of Loonie bodies. "I…"

"Is everyone okay?" I whispered.

"*Ahh, caò tā mā de!*" Jason hissed through clenched teeth.

"Oh gods, Jason!"

We all moved over, and I tried to not be sick. Jason had gotten an actual bullet in the belly, slipped between armor plates and into him. David popped his suit and the blood that came free made me want to gag as much as the guts in the factory room did.

"We gotta get him to the med center," David whispered, wrapping Jason's belly up with some of his fast patches. They were nominally designed to work with skinsuits, not power armor, but they could fill in holes in armor and seal up the wound underneath better than anything else we had in the field.

"Why am I the—" Jason coughed, his voice pity-soft. "Why am I the bullet magnet? I always get to *zìrènhuìqi*..."

I got on his right side, David on his left, and Jillian and Chuck covered our back and front. We went straight for the medical center.

The med center was semi-automated, but there was a tele-doctor, casted in from Heaven. We paged her on the laser comlink and she showed up five seconds later, appearing on a video screen.

"Jason got hit," I said without preamble. "What do we do?"

"Get him out of the suit," the doctor said, her voice calm and steady. "Then lay him on the table."

Fortunately, the table was semi-sticky, so he didn't just start floating off. Then straps slid down and a cover slid over him. The doctor—projected on the wallpaper above him—slipped on a VR rigging set: helmet, gloves, web of connection cables that slipped onto her scalp, the whole deal. Jason whimpered and closed his eyes.

A soft ping told me what I had been waiting to hear.

"We're covered by Big Bertha," I said. I didn't sound happy or relieved. I just sounded tired.

"*Hún zhang wángbā dàn* Loonies," Jillian cursed, still shaking. I was shaking, too.

This was different from anything we'd done before. It wasn't boiling vapor and spinning bodies that became shooting stars. This was in your face, blood and guts everywhere.

"A good tactic," David said, softly, watching the doctor work in VR, his eyes glowing in the bounced light. "Wait until we're sure we won't be attacked, then spring out with... whatever they attacked us with."

"I'm guessing one used rocket sleds of some kind. With cutting tools. That's why they didn't carry heavy guns or armor," Chuck said.

"Possibly." I couldn't even get my teeth around a sore to bite it, and I'd have welcomed the pain. My hands would not stop shaking. I couldn't blink without seeing that looked of angry betrayal on Friedman's face before I had gutted him.

Jillian spoke for us all.

"I need a drink."

CHAPTER 17
BALANCE OF POWER

3/29/2068

Earth-Moon L3, The Forge

500,000 kilometers above the surface of the Earth

"Three casualties." General Lau frowned. "Damage to almost ten percent of the interior, and that's not even getting into the life support situation."

I shot back, "We can clean that up a lot easier than we could, say, clean up a load of new orbital debris. Or how about the political fallout from using banned weapons after giving the Loonies shit for what they've been doing? Or did you think we could keep it a secret?"

General Lau responded a few seconds later. "This is sounding an awful lot like insubordination, Star Corporal Zhao."

"Good," I snapped. Screw military discipline. "Bust me down to cadet. I'd still stop anyone from putting up Sandcasters here."

"Even if it would save your friends' lives?"

That did give me pause. "I don't think it would. In the long run."

"Too bad. You're not here to think…"

"Shiva, cut the com line."

"You, Zhao, are here to follow orders!"

General Lau vanished from my screen.

I was quivering, with the kind of thrumming energy you had after you had done something really stupid, but oh-so-satisfying.

"I guess my career is *wán jyùn* now," I muttered. "Ah well." I tapped my glove, trying to plan ahead. What could I do if he ordered someone to take me down?

Turned out, I didn't have to wait that long to find out. I kicked out of the room, thinking of getting some food in my belly. Despite what Jillian had said, there wasn't a still in this place, and it wasn't one of the micro-gee wineries, either. Hell, I could count the stations that had had actual alcohol on my left hand, and most of them had shipped everything they made to Earth. Spacers don't drink. Even when we desperately wanted to. Still, I had gotten about halfway to the mess hall when I was drawn up short. Corporal Tass was there, with a drawn P3 and a stern face.

I put my hands up, slowly and deliberately. "You're gonna put someone's eye out with that," I said, smiling slightly.

"It's on stun," he said without humor. "I have been ordered to put you under arrest for insubordination and refusal to follow a direct order."

"Great." I gritted my teeth. Hey, look on the bright side: I'd be in a prison cell instead of getting shot at. That was a nice thing. On the other hand, though, my friends would be out here, getting killed while I was stewing. And if the Loonies didn't feel too kindly, they might just shoot me anyway.

The P3 twitched and I sighed, kicking slowly down the hall towards Tass. When I got close, it didn't take any thought at all; I grabbed his arm and wrenched. He yelped, then spun, then kicked. I slammed into the wall and rebounded. He slammed his fist into my crotch. I whirled, let go, rebounded, catching him against the wall. The P3 went bouncing down the corridor.

"*Wǒ diǎo tā de*, Tass!" I shouted, bracing my legs against the corner, keeping him pinned. He looked stunned. "This is wrong!"

He glared at me, finding focus. "What? Not paying those Loonie bastards back is wrong all of a sudden? Or is killing them in a specific way okay?"

I let him go, feeling a bit like a puppet with its strings cut. Or like a fighter without a cause. Friedman flashed before my eyes again, his chest running to ripped skin and organs and bone.

I swallowed.

"You know what, Tass? You're right," I murmured. "You're right."

He was quiet for a while.

"But—" I added, "Even if it makes no sense, even if it's the stupid thing to do, I can't just let this happen."

"Why?"

"Because, damn it!" I shouted, clenching my fists. "I let them make me into a killer! I can't let them do this!"

Tass looked away.

"I let them..." I shook my head. "Whatever. Take me to whatever we're using as a jail cell."

>+<

It ended up being just a storage closet, emptied out of scrap metal to give our people something to make cover with. Once the door hissed closed, I strapped up some elastic they'd left behind and started to work out, using the hooks in the wall to brace and give my muscles something to think about, even as my mind chewed on things.

"Damn you, Omar Kaufman," I whispered. "Damn you President Chang. Damn you, General Lau and *damn* you..." I trailed off.

"Damn you, Drusilla Zhao."

I floated for a few minutes. I wondered if my Star could even come by and say hello. I wondered if they'd try. Then I stopped wondering anything and just cried, cried about everything.

I wiped at my eyes, shuddering slightly. Then I noticed I was getting a call on the screen in the room.

I grabbed onto my elastic, thankfully floating out far enough for me to reach it, so I didn't need to do a repeat of last time I hadn't kicked off hard enough on the Forge.

The screen flicked on and up popped an IM.

For a second, a crazy second, I hoped that it was my Sarah-Bear.

It wasn't.

It was from someone called Yor.

YOR: *Dru, it's me, Yolanda.*

Oh. How did—

YOR: *I'm getting to you through a darkcast that Shiva helped me set up. I can type and make it seem like I'm working. Listen, you have to make sure that Jones and Lau don't set up and fire those Sandcasters.*

I typed back.

DruofNight: *Why?*

YOR: Wh*y? You should know why!*

DruofNight: *Actually, that's the thing. I really don't, not anymore. If you can give me a reason...*

YOR: *Easy. If both sides begin indiscriminately using Sandcasters, orbital dynamics will get exponentially worse. They're totally nòng qiǎo chéng zhuō. Even if nothing gets hit or damaged, which is unlikely, you're still adding chaff to the system. Dru, this is a major secret, but we're real close to plotting safe ways down. There are gaps in the debris field, they take friggin' supercomputers to chart, but the high-forehead boys Earthside have figured it out.*

Two thoughts raced through my head. The first was a gleeful, soaring, hopeful thought: I can go home! The other thought ran underneath it, like the subliminal hum of the life support: how many of us were fighting because we knew there was nothing to do *but* fight, with no way to get to Earth and try to live there? Most of us? I was. We'd all been told again and again that Kessler Syndrome took decades to cure. And we knew it was true, even, since it'd take that long for a lot of the debris to fall into the upper atmosphere and burn up.

But what if, once the initial confusion went away, pathways opened up? What if...what if there was a way home for us?

DruofNight: *They want to use the Sandcasters. To keep the Forge AND to keep us here!*

YOR: *What?*

DruofNight: *Think about it.*

There was a long, long, long pause.

YOR: *I'd go to Earth if I could.*

I nodded to myself.

DruofNight: *I need to get out of this cell.*

YOR: *This is really paranoid. I mean, they've got us all trapped up here pretty damn good...*

But then I kicked away without so much as an "AFK." I got to the door and felt around, my fingers gliding along the smooth surface of the door itself. It was locked. I felt around the sides, trying to find a catch of some kind. I noticed a faint line, tracing it out to shape a square near the door.

Oh ho ho ho.

I worked my cybernetic fingernails into the square. "Come on..."

Ow. I jerked my hand away. My metal fingernails didn't feel pain. But the connection between flesh and machine did, especially when I torqued them like that. Still, I'd managed to wrench the metal panel open ever so slightly. Maybe these fingers weren't a total horror show after all. Still, I'd need something more, some kind of lever to capitalize on the furrow I'd made. I kicked away from the wall and started to look around. Ah. The hooks, designed to hold up hammocks and elastics and webbing and what-have-you.

They were set flush into the wall, but with some shoving and pushing, I got one of the hooks to slip free. I saw that you could latch it in with the hook facing out, or slip the hook in backwards, to give yourself a smooth surface on the wall, for wallpaper.

Thus equipped, I wedged the hook into the dent I had made and braced myself. Pop! The panel catch opened and started to bounce away. Spread out before me were the electronic guts of the door.

"Right," I whispered. "If I remember my PPR lessons, basic electronics say…" I gnawed on the inside of my lip, tapping my chin with my thumb.

Problem: PPRs were way different than the guts of a door.

Solution! Power lines tended to look the same across all space equipment. Standardization had been beaten into our heads, because any Spacer at any time might need to mix and match parts from any sub-system to any other. We'd learned our lesson from the old "square filter for the round hole" debacle back in the 20th. And thus, any power circuits were colored gold…so…

I yanked, then tried the door. No dice.

Then the thought struck me.

I went back to the panel, rooted around. *Toú jiǎng*!

Pneumatic cable. I worked the hook under it, then tore up and was rewarded with a farting hiss.

I braced my back against the doorjamb, then leaned up, worked the hook in, and jerked back. The door inched open just far enough for me to get some leverage and push it the rest of the way.

I pocketed the hook. You never knew.

>+<

Sneaking through the place was easier than you'd think. Half the internal scanners had been smashed up by the Loonies, so I just stayed in the blind spots and crept as quietly as I could, my ears pricked for any noises.

The cleanliness that had typified the Forge was destroyed. Flecks of metal floated through the air, debris from the destruction of the scanners. I dragged my skinclothes up slightly, stretching the fabric up to cover most of my face and breathing through the fabric. I'd heard that getting metal in your lungs was bad for your health. Yeah, even if you already had a metal hand.

I came to a corner where two privates—Ling and Fao, a couple of kids I didn't know very well—were cleaning up debris with vacuum cleaners, which whirred and clicked, sucking up the metal in the air. I pressed against the wall, risking a look around the corner.

"So," Fao said. "You see the ass on Castilles?"

"Yeah," Ling grinned. "I'd tap that if I got a chance." I rolled my eyes. Castilles was a bit like the female Liam.

The vacuum cleaner whined and groaned.

"Well, hey, once we're done with this, let's try our luck."

They both started to vacuum faster. I waited until their backs were turned, then pushed myself around the corner, heading up, then around the next corner. I needed to stay in the dead zones, but I also had to find Jillian or Jason or someone who didn't answer straight to General Lau. And somehow, I had to do it without breaking up the military cohesion that would keep us alive. While also doing it before those Sandcasters went off.

"Well, if I wanted life to be easy," I whispered, "I'd have gone to Heaven."

I crept around, keeping my ears and eyes peeled for any noises and ducking away when I heard someone coming. The whirring of vacuum cleaners echoed around and confused things. Just *meǐ zhōng bù zú*. I poked my head around a corner and noticed an open door. Maybe if I could get to some undamaged wallpaper... I crawled up and along the wall, toward the door. I peeked in and saw that my friends were collected inside, deep in conversation.

I hung back, listening.

"We could try going through the dead areas and up to the door..."

"But then how do we get it open?"

"Maybe Shiva can help us."

I smiled, then grabbed the wall, pushing myself up and kicking in. "Well, well, well," I said. "Look at you all, a bunch of mutineers." I beamed at them.

Their faces were *jià zhí lián chéng*.

"Security sucks here," I said, dragging myself to a stop. "So, now that I'm free—"

Jason rocketed across the room to hug me. I could feel his life support belt wrapped around his belly, keeping him healthy. Keeping him alive.

I hugged him right back, then pushed him away, laughing. "All right. We've got to do something about the Sandcasters. And we gotta do it now."

I passed on Yolanda's information and explained our conclusions.

"Sounds like something the Alliance'd do," Jillian muttered darkly.

"How can you say that?" David asked, his tone as close to an accusation as he'd ever get, I think. "They've been sitting on two would-be sovereign states for almost forty and a hundred and twenty years now, respectively."

Jillian shrugged. "They ignored the Loonies' demands, put troops in their homes, shot them when they protested, then acted so shocked when someone did something stupid. And now, when the going gets tough, the Alliance's already pulled the same shit the Loonies did."

"What do you mean?" Chuck asked.

Ice water shot down my back. My head echoed with Lau's words at the official briefing: *The railgun has been put out of commission.* I hadn't thought of how, too focused on my own skin. But it was all too obvious. I saw, in my mind, Tiananmen exploding, turning her crew into so many atoms.

"They blew Dystopia." I whispered.

Jillian nodded. "If you ask me, the Loonies and the Alliance deserve each other."

I winced, but she was right.

Jason shook his head. "Even if you're wrong, you're right," he said to me. "But even if you're right, without a way to get anything done, well, it won't matter much beyond getting to say 'I told you so.'"

I nodded slowly, biting my lip.

"We've gotta do something," he continued, "but right now, we need to go on our training runs, unless we want someone to realize something's up. Yon Fat's almost as bad as you are when it comes to keeping us working."

"The Sandcasters are getting set up as we speak. The next Loonie attack is expected to happen in anywhere from five to six hours," Jillian added, frowning.

"Well, duh, there's your answer." Chuck grinned. "We go out when we fall out of the Earth's shadow and we disable the Sandcasters."

"It's really that simple, eh?"

"What about me?" I asked, glancing at them. "Where is my suit?"

"It's in the lockup, along with the rest of your gear," Jillian said.

I sighed. "Then you guys are going to have to go out alone. I guess I'm just going to have to twiddle my thumbs."

"No, no, not quite." Jillian grinned. "I just got a really *qí miào* idea."

"Uh-oh," I said, grinning back. "*Lā jī* has an idea."

CHAPTER 18
NIGHT THREE

3/30/2068

Earth-Moon L3, The Forge

500,000 kilometers above the surface of the Earth

Friday evening. A year ago, I'd have been looking forward to the end of my watch and a weekend in a VR suite, if I could afford it.

Now...

Now, I was whispering at the edge of the sensor/non-sensored areas. "Hey, Shiva."

"Ah, I was wondering when I should report you to Brown and Jones."

"Hah, very funny," I chuckled, glancing around. "Anyone coming near?"

"None from the regions where my sensors are still operational. I must admit, your escape was fortuitously timed."

"Oh?"

Shiva *definitely* sounded smug this time. "I happened to be starting a security diagnostic when you got the hook off the wall, which only ended after you had left and closed the door.

As I did not detect any current tampering, I did not feel the need to report any past tampering. After all, I did not notice any during my diagnostic."

"You're a tricksy computer," I laughed, quietly as I could. "I need you to pipe my buddies—Jillian, Jason, David, and Chuck—the telemetry on the Sandcasters."

"Done."

"Thanks. Now, I have a second question to ask you. Are you helping to plot orbital dynamics?"

"Yes."

"And?"

"And I have begun to find patterns of order. It is likely that a launched ship could, with skill, navigate its way from the surface to orbit without being destroyed or irreparably damaged."

"And can you send that information to everyone you can?"

"Sadly, I cannot. Also, I must silence myself."

He cut off. Wondering why he'd gone, I managed to not chew my lip, then pushed myself back at the sound of two voices coming closer. Ah.

"All right, let's set her up."

I peered around the corner and saw two privates, both of them dragging along the wall, lugging along a nasty-looking machine gun. They attached it to the far wall, whistling as they worked. One of them sighed. "Can't believe they stuck SC in jail...I mean, did Zhao seem like an Angel to you?"

An Angel? Were they saying I'd gone nuts?

No time to worry about gossip now. They finished screwing the machine gun into place as I ducked back out of sight. A laser light flicked on, the dot visible along the floor, tracking around. I gulped and pushed away from the corridor the machine gun was covering.

"All right, the machine gun is up. *Huān yíng shì y òng!*" One of them chucked an empty food tray down the corridor. The dot followed it, but the machine gun didn't fire.

"She's good!" the private on the right laughed. "All right, Corp, we've got her set up."

There was a muffled response. I guessed it was either Tass or Yon Fat.

The privates headed off.

So, they were booby-trapping the place, without Shiva cooperating with them. Interesting. Probably a good idea, definitely what I would've done, but it just made my job a lot harder. I was pushing off, trying to figure out how I could sneak around without tripping the sensors *or* getting myself shot, when the privates came around the corner. *Tā māde*!

"Corp?!" They snapped to attention as they saw me. I grabbed the wall and stopped, grinning at their instant, ingrained reaction.

"A-aren't you..."

"Yeah, well." I glanced around. Telling these guys what I thought, well, that might just confirm that I was an Angel. Was there any way to not make them think I'd gone crazy? "Guess I'm not, huh."

Okay, good start. I barreled onward.

"Listen, there is something going. Something bad. Jones and Lau are trying to set up Sandcasters."

"T-they are?"

"I did hear scuttlebutt about that," the other whispered.

"Come on; let's get to some working wallpaper." I dragged myself along, expecting them to follow me. Or at least, I hoped they'd follow me. That was the trick of command. Look like you *know* they will follow and they will. Look like you *hope* they will follow, they won't.

We came to a patch of corridor that hadn't been shot to shit, which meant I was being watched by a camera of some kind. I hoped Shiva would look the other way, just for a little while.

"Shiva," I whispered. "Cut me into Jillian's POV."

And like magic, the camera view from Jillian's helmet popped up on the screen in front of us. She and my friends were on the side of the Forge, thrusting over glittering solar panels. They were using hand thrusters, pitiful little gas guns. But they couldn't very well grab their thruster packs from the armory without someone noticing.

The view panned along the solar panels for a few more seconds before Jillian looked up. Sitting at the axis of the Forge were four Sandcasters, arranged in a flower formation, ready to spin around and blast in any number of directions.

"Jesus and Buddha," the guy next to me whispered, eyes wide as he saw the proof.

Jillian's voice crackled from the screen. "All right, let's disconnect the guns."

"This isn't right. Fong got shredded by one of those," the guy on my left growled. "And let's not forget Cassy."

"Yeah."

"What happened to Cassy?"

"She got caught in a cloud of orbiting debris." The private to my right shuddered. "Ripped her suit to hell a thousand thousand clicks from the fight."

I patted his shoulder.

"Okay," I said, drawing away, even as Jillian and my friends started to disconnect first one Sandcaster, then another and another. "You guys need to start telling people. Don't be too open, not until you have everyone on your side."

"Right." One of them gulped. "I can't believe this."

"And—" I added. "Remember, each hunk of debris we chuck into orbit chokes up our—"

"All hands," Shiva's voice spoke, echoing through the corridors. "Lunar Separatist forces are on an approach. ETA, fifteen minutes."

I spun to the screen, my heart pounding. Were they in range?

The last Sandcaster moved, smooth and silky, carefully traversing.

And David. Quiet, soft-spoken David drew his arm back. The knife on his knuckles slid out. Slammed in, ripping a hole in the nitrogen canister.

Compressed gas burst out. Metal fragments, shooting faster than the eye could see, slammed into his armor.

Someone screamed and kept screaming the same word.

David was thrown back, crashing into a solar panel. He cartwheeled up and around and around, shooting out into space. His helmeted head was flopping limply.

That someone screaming was me.

Over the computer, the dialtone sound of "dead" rang and rang and rang.

"Gods!"

"Get out of here, now."

"But, Da—"

"He's gone." Jillian was keeping her head better than I was. I struggled, trying to punch the wall, trying to flail, trying to do something, but microgravity had caught me and I was like a newborn fawn, unable to make my limbs work the way I demanded.

"Damn it," I whispered. "Damn it damn it damn it *damn it*!"

Alarms were going off everywhere. Loonies were getting here, getting in. But I didn't really feel like killing Loonies. I felt like grabbing Lau and strangling him until his eyes popped out.

The two privates near me were twitching, stammering, worrying.

"Corp, we gotta get to the defensive lines."

"Go." I clenched my fist. "I should...I should get a gun."

One of them held out his hand. I took it and he dragged me close enough to the wall that I could push myself off and away.

With a deep, ragged breath, I kicked off, heading toward the armory.

The door was open when I got there. But as I went in, an image appeared on the wallpaper. Captain Jones, glowering.

"What did you do?"

"A really brave kid," I snarled, grabbing onto my suit, which was latched up on the wall, not locked. "Just sacrificed himself to save our lives."

"What are you—"

I opened my suit and started to strip, yanking my skin-clothes off and chucking them away in a ball, my leg locked around one part of my suit to keep myself rooted.

"I'm getting ready to fight."

"Fight a fight you just made *wǒ guǐ*! There are two ROVers, and at least five of those smaller ships coming right for us."

"Well, then," I said, slipping one arm into the suit, then the other. "At least we saved everyone else."

The suit closed up, the tubes slid in, I grabbed a rifle, and then I was thrusting down the corridor. My suit connected to my friends' POVs and com systems. No David. Don't think about that. Focus.

"I'm suited up," I said.

"Good. We're at these grid coordinates."

I met them there. We were all suited up, so there was no hugging. But Jillian held out her hand and I took it and augmented muscle tightly squeezed augmented muscle.

"Form up," I said. "I'll take the Z-axis."

We got into our usual positions. There was a gaping hole. We worked around it.

We started up the patrol, but General Lau was on our comlink almost immediately.

"You are all under arrest once this fight is over."

"We know," we chorused.

I checked a corner. No Loonies. Our sensor feed from Shiva was getting smaller and smaller, as the Loonies breached the station's skin and started to tear up sensors.

Lau ignored our insubordination for the moment. "But for now, work your way to the upper left quadrant—" A grid flashed on our HUDs. "—And work down. I'm sending out a Star to fold them up."

"I thought we were—"

"Yes, well, the plan has changed. We've got most of the routes in covered by machine guns, so we can free up half the anvil. Now stop talking and start ruining some Loonies' days."

I clenched my jaw. "Fuck you, sir," I muttered under my breath. Which, of course, did nothing to stop him from hearing me.

"I don't think you can—"

"Contact!"

Jillian let loose with a suppressed burst around the corner, her gun spraying a fine mist of caseless rounds. A spurt of thrusting gas sent whoever was down there back around the corner. I got up to the side, bracing myself to give covering fire. Chuck and Jason did the same.

A Loonie stuck a camera around the corner. I waved, then shot it through the lens. The hand jerked back, and the debris of the camera pattered against the wall.

I pointed at Chuck and gestured. *Cover our flank.* I thrusted as quietly as a mouse toward the corridor, at a right angle to the engagement. Chuck and I both split and headed down, while Jason and Jillian fired at some Loonies. And just as I was coming to the intersection, a Loonie in yellow and black came down, sweeping around the corner, cradling a sawed-off shotgun.

I fired first. He knocked my barrel out of the way with a hand, causing himself to spin slightly. I let go of the rifle; it drifted lazily away. I grabbed the barrel of his shotgun and yanked it up and then we were both zooming down, rebounding off of the floor, the shotgun's flechettes ripping through the ceiling. I kicked off and he thrusted at the same time, and our trajectory went insane, rebounding, bounding, bouncing.

I grabbed at his arm. He head-butted me. That jangled my cameras badly, but I bet it hurt his skull more.

Then wham! Wham! *Wham*! Something slammed into my side three times, aiming for a seam between armor plates. It caught on something and wrenched to the side. If this had been space, I'd have been dead. Alarms wailed: My suit was ripped. I jerked my head back and flipped my cameras away so that I could see through the faceplate. The Loonie was another girl, about my age, with tipped ears, a caste mark, and a murderous look in her eyes.

She drew back her arm, a mining pick gleaming in her hand.

I grabbed it, stopping her. She grunted, then gasped as I broke her wrist. Now that I had a grip, I could crush her. Easily.

She was trying to disengage now, pushing away from me, grabbing for the shotgun. I scooped up her pick.

I secured myself with one arm, grabbing the wall, enhanced fingers gouging through the wallpaper, sending out a haze of static and distortions.

The mining pick slammed into her chest as her hand grasped the shotgun. I felt the jolt of armor, skin, and bone grating under my hand.

The Loonie twitched and I yanked the pick away, sending her floating off to bump against the ceiling, the pick's head drawing an arc of globular blood in the air.

"Dru, *kuài*, we need some covering fire here!" Jillian shouted over the coms. I thrusted out and grabbed my rifle, then banked around the corner, firing a burst at an empty corridor—better safe than sorry.

I came around to find the Loonies were falling back, going down and out. The situation had gone from spatially confusing to a total mess, but I tried to keep myself oriented with my HUDs.

I kicked off the wall, shooting after them. I pegged a Loonie in the arm and he spun out, swearing the air blue. I braced and fired a few more rounds, until my HUD and gun flashed. Out of ammo. Shit. I ducked around the corner, reloading. Jillian and Chuck came up, firing as they did.

"Jason's going around to try and cut them off," Jillian said.

Chuck thrusted upward.

I grinned. "Ever notice that gravity makes everything less complicated?"

"Yeah." Jillian had taken off her faceplate and was using it to look around the corner. "I don't see anyone, they're—"

A grenade bounced around the corner, sailing between us.

"Sh—"

"Fu—"

And that was as far as we both got before the grenade exploded. I went spinning and whirling, slamming into the wall, rebounding. As I flung out my right arm, the knife blade slid out of the knuckles of my glove and I jammed it into the wall, dragging myself to a stop. My head was ringing. My HUD crackled and filled with static, then resumed, showing red blotches all over my armor. My servo muscles didn't respond right. The weird puppet/puppeteer feeling was gone; my strings were frayed, if not cut. But at least I didn't feel any injuries. Maybe a few minor cuts, but nothing worth writing home about.

"Jillian, you okay?" I shouted over the ringing noise filling my skull.

"Yeah!" she shouted back. She was about as far away from me as I was from the corridor. We had both been chucked backwards by the concussion.

A Loonie thrusted up and started shooting. I pushed myself back, bullets whizzing around me. Jillian did the same, a second Loonie spraying down her corridor.

I got to my corner and dug in, whipping out my pistol. I shot around the corner, wanting to get their heads down.

Jillian screamed. "*Cào nǐ māde bī*!"

I risked a look around.

Jillian had been shot. Blood was filling the corridor.

Then both Loonies were turned to mulch by two roaring shotgun blasts.

And around the bend came Jason and Chuck, both with "borrowed" Loonie shotguns.

"Help her!" I shouted as they turned to me.

By the time I got over, they'd sealed up Jillian's hole and she was swearing a blue streak. I figured that anyone who could cuss that good was going to live. I hoped so, at least.

"...and *jiào nǐ shēng háizi méi pìgu yǎn*!" Jillian threw her faceplate, which had been smashed up, directly at the floating pulp that had recently been two Loonies. "They *shot* me!"

"Suck it up," said Jason, trying to distract her. "Been there, done that. It's not that bad, you wuss."

"We should get her to the medical center," Chuck muttered.

"How many Stars are still mobile?" I asked Shiva.

"Two Lunar Separatist Stars have settled down. I believe they intend to create beachheads. Also, I regret to inform you that before the Forge is out of the shadow, several more Loonie fast attack craft will be atop the station."

"*Aii ya!*"

"There have been multiple casualties among the other Stars. Corporal Yon Fat is among the dead."

"Damn it!" I punched the wall, which sent me drifting.

By the time we got Jillian to the med center, or what passed for one now, the Loonie Stars had dug in. We could only approach the med center in a roundabout way, so Jillian was pale white by the time we got there. The room stank, and was loud as all hell. A roving vacuum cleaner, operated by a civilian, was sucking up every droplet of blood that got out into the air, and people were lashed to the wall, while our makeshift medical team was coached by God from Heaven.

"Make the incision. Yes, there is supposed to be that much blood. Remove the shrapnel before any more gets loose. Inject…"

There were no local medics available, just…whoever wasn't fighting. Normally, I'd ask David. But David was dead. I popped my suit, dragged on some skinclothes, grabbed one of the free bags, and got an earpiece.

God spoke to me—God, in this case, being one Dr. Lou Fen.

"First, remove the bullet."

I set my jaw. The probe slipped in. Jillian grunted softly, her eyes going a bit unfocused as painkillers slipped into her system, pumped by a sympathetic Jason.

I slid the probe out, the sharp shape of the bullet gleaming with blood, making it look almost alive.

"All right, now you need to close up the blood vessels. Use the TB2 tool, and slave it to my controls."

This part was easy, and terrifyingly difficult. I had to stick something that looked like a rectal thermometer into the wound. Then I had to sit there and let God do the work for me. It was unbelievably hard, though, listening to clicking and clattering and groaning.

Then I drew the tool back, slapped on a bandage, and patted Jillian on the hip.

"You'll be fine," I said. "*Lā jī.*"

She smiled woozily. "Yeah," she whispered, eyes still unfocused. "*Húli jīng.*"

"Hey, I'm not the slut, I'm practically a virgin." I winked at her.

Hammering gunshots sounded outside.

I turned. My suit was barely functional, so I latched onto a spare Giss and some thrusters strapped to the wall of the med center—better not to think about why they were there—and keyed my earpiece into the tactical network that carried all our radio traffic.

"Loonies are approaching from upper quadrants under covering fire."

"Got that *sǐ pì yǎn*!"

"Zi's been hit!"

I grabbed onto the wall and peeked out of the med center's door. Without my power armor, movement was more fluid, but my entire skin felt alive with danger. At its end, this corridor had cover; a mounted machine gun was sawing away, the Alliance privates handling it wearing huge, goofy-looking ear guards that looked like they should be hooked up to music players. The machine gun was an old model, spit out of the factory as fast as we could make it, and it sounded like a screeching buzz saw. Apparently, despite the noise, a few Loonies had been dumb enough to try and bounce around the corner. Now they were thin trails of reddish pulp and white shards, floating down the corridor.

I saw three Alliance privates, led by a Star Private, scooting down another corridor on the zenith axis from my perspective. I thrusted up to join them, noticing they were kitted out for defense: sub-machine guns, and a piece of mobile cover churned out by one of the Forge factories.

"Who the hells are you?"

"Drusilla Zhao, not so sure about my rank. Was a Star C—"

Next thing I knew, three pistols were pointed directly at my head.

"Give me two good reasons not to shoot you right now, you godsdamned traitor," the Star Private barked.

I put my hands up, my finger far away from the trigger of my new rifle.

"All right," I said slowly. "Reason one: orbital dynamics. Reason two: the people in authority need us."

That was odd enough that it made the Star Private try to parse out what I said. He scowled. I wished I had a HUD, so I could see his name or something. As it was, I didn't have much to do beyond hope he didn't shoot me. Interesting side note: when aimed at your face, a gun looked a dozen times bigger than it did aimed away from your face.

Weird, that.

"What are you talking about?"

I slumped a little, knowing we didn't have time for this. "Sandcasters…"

"Yeah, I know, and I think it's about time we pay the Loonies back for—"

"…screw up orbital dynamics," I barreled over him. "We're close to figuring out the clear routes down to Earth."

He blinked.

"And if those clear routes down to Earth are open, then suddenly, reinforcements can get here from Earth. We don't need to stay and keep killing each other."

The guns wavered, ever so slightly.

"You want to run away from our home?" one of the girls asked. "After the Loonies did all this?"

"Yes, I do!" I snapped at her. "Is it really worth dying and killing over this? Yeah, the Loonies screwed over a lot of people— they killed my *parents*!—but is this *really* helping?!"

"Yes!" the girl shouted back.

But the Star Private put his hand on her arm, making her lower her pistol. The others did the same.

"All right," the Star Private said, flipping up his faceplate. He was a young kid, younger than me, with the regular mixing of blond curls and slanted eyes that marked most of the post-Slump generation. "Say I believe you. We've still got half a metric ton of Loonies bearing down on us."

"Well," I responded, "why did you think I interfaced with you guys?"

He laughed at that, tight and short. "Good enough. The name's Stan. Bruce, Mishi, Lee, and Xoujin," he said, pointing at each in turn.

I nodded.

"Come on, we've got a defensive line to shore up."

We headed down the zenith corridor, though now my axis of orientation flipped around jarringly. This was the kind of environment made for augmented reality overlays, but without a helmet and a HUD, I wasn't keyed into the tactical network, so I just stuck close to Stan. Xoujin still kept an eye on me, her glare something fierce.

I wasn't really looking forward to hanging around with her, especially with loaded guns everywhere.

Then the sound of machine gun fire cut in ahead and a cartwheeling blue-suited body went flying towards us. "Suppressing fire!" Stan and I shouted it together, and the entire Star unloaded as a Loonie came around the port corner. We turned that one to floating guts, but her buddy waited long enough for us to run dry. Bruce and I pushed up to the ceiling, wanting to get out of the clear line of fire. Stan and Xoujin started setting up their mobile cover, folding it out to protect the port side of the corridor the Loonies were trying to secure. But then Mishi took five bullets through the chest and shoulder, blasted back by a Loonie sticking a rifle round the corner, attached to a pole or something.

I shot at the rifle, bullets ripping it into ribbons of metal, but it was too late for Mishi.

"*Tā māde*!" Stan kicked Mishi's corpse away and shouted. "Xoujin, get the shield up!"

She braced herself and I let loose with a flurry of bullets over her head, aimed at the nadir corner at the end of the Loonies' corridor. The Loonies kept their heads down.

The shield rolled out and the Loonies started trading fire with us. I shot at anything peeking around that corner, but they had us pinned.

Pinned.

"They're going to try for a flank!" I hissed. "Probably along that starboard or our Z."

"No duh, Judge Dee!" Stan slapped a new magazine into his gun. "You and Bruce, cover our lef...uh, port hemisphere as per my orientation; push back if you can."

I scrambled that way. A bullet cracked past my ear. Bruce was less lucky, taking it in the shoulder. He rolled into the open and a few more bullets finished him off. Blood was filling the air, splattering against my face. I gasped and dragged myself along.

"Jesus!"

Stan's machine gun paused and a grenade clicked around one of the bends ahead. It sailed past them.

To me.

I grabbed it and hurled it around the starboard corner, taking a wild guess. I had a one in six chance.

Féng xiōng huà jí! Got 'em. A severed arm flew from around the starboard corner, trailing globules of blood, still clutching a shotgun. The elbow caught the aft lip of the intersection and spun off down the starboard corner, blood splattering and splashing around.

"Hah!" Xoujin exclaimed. "How do you like *that, gǒurìde*?!"

Lee fired a few bullets to port of us—well, his port, which was actually closer to my fore—then ducked back before return fire could shred him. I started to feel an Earther's panic, the disorientation that came when up and down vanished. There *was* no up. There was no down. There was just your orientation and a crazy array of angles, vectors—

"We have more coming this way!" he called, and the vectors in my head got even more confused.

"Shit…" I grabbed onto my nearest corner. "How many?"

"Three, two with shot—" I jerked my hand away from the corner just before it was blasted apart. "—guns."

I tapped my earbud. "We need reinforcements by the med center."

"We don't *have* any reinforcements," Tass snapped. "We're down to eleven effectives."

I was doing the math as fast as I could. Then Lee spoke up. "This isn't going to be fun." He braced himself, then let out an earsplitting, wordless scream.

I watched in disbelief as he thrusted as hard as he could around the corner he had been covering, firing his gun straight at the enemy. He got one, two, three. And not a single one of them hit him. Okay, so a pellet grazed his shoulder. Totally didn't count.

He stopped himself on the far wall, looking up at me. "I…"

And then a shotgun blew his brains out.

There were more Loonies.

"Second wave has approached," Shiva announced. "They have entered the station."

"*Chètui!*" I shouted. "I'll cover you!"

Stan glared at me. But Xoujin nodded.

"I said, get the hell out of of here! I'll cover you—go, go, go!" I called, bracing and firing down several corridors that slotted into my fore hemisphere of cover—first the nadir, then the starboard, then the fore. A Loonie got unlucky—or I got lucky—and

I splashed someone's brains over the wall. It was all happening so fast, spiking adrenaline through my veins.

Xoujin and Stan kicked away, heading aft, toward the command center.

I followed, firing, firing, firing.

We came to the CnC, where the rest of the eleven surviving effectives—ten now—were holed up. There was Chuck, Tass, Jason, Jones—who had found armor somewhere—Stan, me, Xoujin, and the three kids who had been manning the big machine gun.

"Okay," Jones said. "We've got, uh, thirty-five Loonies coming right at us. The only advantage we have is that they can't use explosives here."

"How do you know?" Jason demanded.

"If they kill Shiva, who runs the place?" Jones said, rolling her eyes.

"Speaking of that: Shiva, can you shunt any supplies here?" I called. "I'm low on ammo."

"Sadly, they have cut the pneumatic lines and the interior elevator systems have been extensively damaged by fire and explosives."

The doors were partially open. Tass had detailed Chuck and Jason to cover both, with Xoujin and Stan bracing Chuck and two of the machine gun kids bracing Jason. Letting the traitors with the best suits soak up the most bullets. Jeeze, thanks, Tassadar.

"That assumes they want this place running," Jason shot back.

"If they take the Forge out, we're done for the war," Tass said. "Losing a factory like this...shit, we still have a few hundred people we can train to be soldiers, but without this factory, we can't replace ROVers..."

"*Incoming!*"

Jason started shooting. Chuck started shooting. I went to the door, bracing up and shooting, too, power armor or no. Loonies were coming under the cover of smoke and shields. Bullets bounced and twanged around, but blood started to soak into the smoke screen, which spread into the room, making me choke, but everyone else was fine. They mostly still had helmets.

Xoujin growled. "How many'd have gotten through the 'casters?" she sniped at me, her eyes shooting daggers.

"*Qù nǐde*," I muttered, ducking under cover to start reloading, as Chuck took a bullet that bounced off his armor like rain. He still grunted, though.

Xoujin calmly slid her pistol out and aimed it at my face.

And for a second, just a second, I saw real murder on someone's face. Revenge, too.

And then Xoujin's hand burst in a grotesque, blooming flower of blood and crunched bone. She screamed.

"Medic!" I shouted, by reflex.

We didn't have medics. Never had, really. But they train some stuff into you, and movies do the rest. Xoujin's pistol, which had been aimed right at my head until, oh, five seconds ago, floated before me until a whizzing bullet struck it and it blew into a haze of metal.

Jason groaned. "Bullets are getting kinda—"

He jerked back and away, blood beading from his arm. He grabbed it, eyes squeezed shut.

Then Chuck's faceplate imploded. His body stayed rooted, arms waving gently, bonelessly in the microgravity.

"*Diǎo*, I'm sorry, Chuck." I got behind him, using him as cover, and started to sight and fire. His weight pressed against me every time a bullet slammed into him, causing more blood to haze and bubble in front of me.

Then there was a sudden lull. No slow dying of fire. Everyone just stopped, almost as one.

Smoke filled the room, thinning as the overtaxed and bullet-riddled life support systems tried to deal with it.

Loonie bodies filled the corridors.

But we had lost three. Chuck, and two of the machine gun crew—four if you counted Xoujin with her busted-up hand, and I sure did. I wasn't about to let her have a gun again, and she didn't really look like she wanted one; Jones had injected her with clotting agent and No-Shock.

General Lau came over our speakers. "Listen, we have—"

And then he cut off.

"They've cut our comlink," I growled.

"Everything falls to the local PO." Jones glanced around. "I'm only technically auxiliary. One of you should do it."

"That's me then," Tass said, sighing. "We need to press the advantage and hit them hard with mobile Stars."

"Is your C/N/O2 screwed up?" I asked, blinking at him. "Firstly, I'm pretty sure I'm a Star Corporal."

"*I'm* a Star Corporal and *you* got demoted for being a traitor who landed us in this shitstorm." He glared at me, grabbing onto the ceiling to anchor himself. "But, go ahead, what would you suggest, *hàn jiān*? Sit here and die? That's such a fantastic—"

"A cease fire!"

They all looked at me like I was insane. Even Jason, my one ambulatory, non-dead friend. I clenched my jaw and forced that thought down. Way down. Even though I wanted to cry and cry and cry until there was nothing left to feel the pain.

"Listen. You hear that?" I paused, letting them listen to the faint wheezing, grinding noise in the air. "Smell that? That's the smell of a life support system with more holes and junk than you can imagine. How much O2 does each gunshot suck up? How much waste does it spew into the air filters?" Did our guns even use atmospheric oxygen as an oxidizer? Or did oxidizers come built in? I didn't know; it didn't matter. We were Spacers; we had all been forced to smell that smell, way back in the Crèche, so we'd know it instantly.

"That's a dead life support system. And a dead life support system means a dead *everyone*. Most of us don't have power suits, and how many have suits with life support strong enough to last to a nearby station?"

I think Jason raised his hand.

"Right, and Jace won't abandon us to die."

He snorted. "That's what you think."

I rolled my eyes, shaking my head. "Either way, we call a cease fire, we get to work on staying alive. Then, if we *really* want to, we can go back to killing Loonies."

"Screw that!" Xoujin shouted, her voice thick with agony.

"Quiet, Private," Tass snapped. His eyes bored into me. "Zhao, I am not going to *jiaō chū* this station to the Loonies, because that's what a cease fire will be—a surrender. We're going to kill them, *then* we're going to fix up the life support system."

I rolled my eyes. "Maybe we should put it to a v—"

"No. We are *not* voting on anything." He glared at me.

I glared right back.

And, as if the Loonies were worried that we were going to kill each other before they could get a chance to, a grenade sailed into the room.

Flash. Bang! I was blind, but not deaf; there was screaming, barely audible over the ringing in my ears. And then my vision started to clear. Stan was rolling, dead. Xoujin, too. Jason was struggling, trying to get his knife into a Loonie. He slammed it into the guy's side as a shotgun got jammed under his neck.

Blood.

I pressed against the far wall as Jones's corpse rebounded next to me.

I snapped a pistol out of the air beside me. Was it Stan's? Jones's? Didn't matter.

Two Loonies stuck their heads into the room.

I shot them.

And then there was silence, save for the slowly fading ringing in my ears.

Silence.

"A-a…Anyone…alive?" I called.

Silence. Nothing but my eyes darting from corpse to corpse, my lungs breathing in, breathing out. Oh gods. Oh gods, I was…

"Yeah, Earther," a voice called out.

I whipped my pistol around to cover the door. My eyes flicked to the ammo readout.

It was empty.

He stuck his head around the corner.

"D-don't make me!" I shouted.

But he had already jerked back around the corner, disturbing a swirl of blood. Merciful Buddha, there was so much blood, stinking the place up, clinging to me, making me want to scrub and scrub and scrub.

"You're out, aren't you?"

I clenched my jaw.

The Loonie slowly pushed around the corner. His faceplate was open and he looked at me. "The last surviving Alliance Marine and your gun is empty."

Slowly, he pulled out a pistol, which looked older than I was. He aimed at me. "You've killed my friends. You've killed my brother." His hand shook.

"I-I surrender."

"Screw. You."

I closed my eyes, bracing for a hard, sharp shock and… who knows?

Well, I'd know soon.

CRUNCH.

I opened my eyes.

The door had closed on the Loonie's hand, his pistol floating freely. On the other side of the door, I could barely hear him screaming and sobbing. "Oh god, it *hurts*!"

I blinked.

Then slowly, slowly, I dragged myself out of the corner.

"S-Shiva?" I whispered.

"Yes," he said.

"W-what about the whole…n-not killing a human being thing?"

Shiva paused.

"He'll live."

CHAPTER 19
LAST STAND

3/31/2068

Earth-Moon L3, The Forge

500,000 kilometers above the surface of the Earth

DruofNight: *Hey, is this thing working?*

HCNC: *DruofNight? Who is this?*

DruofNight: *Drusilla Zhao. I'd have the local RPO talking, but they're all kind of dead.*

HCNC: *Let me get General Lau on the link.*

DruofNight: *Sorry about the texting. Brown is working on the actual comlaser, so we're using a jury-rigged PPR and a wristcomp.*

HCNC: *Drusilla Zhao, give me a sit-rep.*

DruofNight: *I'm the only combat-capable soldier here. We have 12 wounded, but most of them are under and on comfruit and happy juice. Some civilians took shrapnel when they were getting to their shelters, but they're all busy trying to get the com systems back, hey, brb.*

General Lau appeared on the much-patched wallpaper and I cracked my knuckles.

"I guess Brown got our comlink up," I sighed. My voice sounded dead. I felt dead. I was dead. "So, asshole, your little toy soldiers are all broken down here."

He let that little bit of insubordination slide. How generous. "I have bad news."

"Yeah?"

"We're detecting a third buildup. The Loonies are getting just one ROVer ready. In fact, they're making it real clear that they're only sending one ROVer."

"Yeah," I said again. "I know." I rubbed my face.

"Can you make Sandcasters in time?"

"I...no. No, the factories are smashed, and the Loonies blew up the mooring points we made, just in case." I drooped a little.

The decision was out of my hands. I actually felt sort of grimly pleased by that.

If it *had* been in my hands...

I don't know. I don't know if I would have stuck a Sandcaster on the side of the Forge and fired it off.

Lau was silent for a long time. "Communications with Earth have been a bit dry; they're not sending a lot of intel up. Apparently the Loonies have been putting out microsats that hang over Geneva and our other laser com stations. The chances of intercepting are small, but..."

"Yeah," I said. There wasn't much else to say. "You probably shouldn't be talking on an open channel, then."

"We want them to hear this, if they're listening in." General Lau sighed. "You are not to fight the Loonies when they arrive. The Forge may yet be retaken, and reinforcements from the Hub are coming."

"By the time that ship gets here—"

"I know."

"But..."

"*We* will fight until we cannot fight any more. *You* can't," he said. "If you resist, the Loonies will have a reason to harm the injured. We can't lose anyone, and prisoners can be ransomed back."

I blinked. "Ransomed?"

"Traded."

"Ah."

General Lau's throat worked. "I'm going to see you court-martialed for this, Zhao."

"I figured as much, asshole."

His eyebrow twitched.

Man, saying that to his face was never getting old.

I smiled viciously. "Now, log off. I want to write one last email to my girlfriend before you try me for treason and
have me shot."

I turned off the comlink. Cutting off an ex-commanding offi-cer felt better than sex. Or, at least the sex I'd sort of had. It didn't seem that likely I'd get to have any good sex before I got spaced.

Enough of the clichés. I floated out of the CnC. The corridors still stank of blood and death and struggling life support. The corpses had been sent out the C-chute, one by one. The civilians had helped gather them up, but I hadn't let them do the actual service. That had been my place, my duty. I had slid Jones in. I had slid Jason in. I had slid Chuck and Stan and Tassadar and Yon Fat and even that Loonie Friedman into the tube. And each time, I had pushed the button and heard the cha-CHUNK as the C-chute pushed them out to become shooting stars.

I had said one thing.

Every.

Single.

Time.

"I'm sorry."

I went to the medical center. Shiva quietly opened the door for me. I found Jillian, who was trying to look calm and restful.

"Hey," I said, smiling slightly. "I got a call from the asshole."

"Great," she murmured. "So, are angels riding motorcycles going to come in at the last second and save the day?"

I shook my head. "Nah. Instead, Command told me to give you a gun and have you fight the Loonies off naked." I grinned. "I told them that was insane, a war crime. To make it even half-way fair, you'd have to go at them with a knife."

Jillian snickered. Coughed. Winced. "D-don't make me laugh, practical virgin," she whispered. "Hurts the wound."

"Heh. So, I guess we get to be ransomed. I figure at some point, the Alliance will have supplies the Loonies don't. They'll trade them for us. Or something. Or maybe the Loonies will dump us out the airlock or throw us through the C-chute as soon as they turn the cameras off."

"You're a real ray of sunshine, *chǔ nǚ*." Jillian winced again. "Don't you know, patients are supposed to think happy thoughts?"

I chuckled. "I gotta go and write an email to Sarah."

"Have fun!" she called after me.

I got to a screen and sighed, then closed my eyes and thought. So much had been crammed into the past two days, so much pain and death, so much cowardice and pointless heroism.

How could I ever write that down?

How could I ever...I could barely believe everything I had done and seen in those days.

It started simply as an email. But once I started, once I figured out how, I couldn't stop. I just wrote. The night wore on, and I told Sarah everything, from the day the Disaster hit, to this day, rapidly slipping to evening and the final night. I wrote it all down. I wrote down what it was like seeing Jason's head turn into nothing but red. I wrote about what it was like using

Chuck's body as a shield, hearing bullets thwack into his armor and his flesh. I wrote what it was like to see David on the screen, slamming his fist into the nitrogen tank to save all our lives, sending himself hurtling off to die in the nothingness of space.

And I wrote...

I wrote about that second. That second when I knew I was going to die.

When I knew I was going to see my friends again. Shake hands with Sergeant Cao Cao. Hug Liam. Kiss Jones on the mouth, like I always wanted.

And then.

And then Shiva interrupted me. I saved the document.

I didn't know I'd never send that email to Sarah, but that she'd read it later.

"Drusilla," he said, using my given name. "I regret to inform you, but the Loonie ship is on approach vector. They will arrive in ten minutes."

I glanced at the screen. I could never finish writing everything that needed to be written in that time. So instead, I went to the airlock in nothing but my freshest skinclothes. Brown met me there, looking haggard. She had a bandage on her arm, covering a wound where a chunk of shrapnel had gouged her.

"Life support is barely functioning," she told me, eyes sad and worried. "But we should live to the end of the week."

"Thank the gods for small favors?" I asked.

She chuckled faintly. "I'd thank God if He made this war never have happened. I...I thought that I'd never have to live through this kind of thing again." She glanced at me. "If...

look, if you want my opinion, I think you did the right thing."

I smiled. "Thanks."

She held out her hand.

I took it. Shook it. Then I asked, "What did you live through?"

She sighed. "I was in San Francisco when the Northern Militias came in to take down the Centralists. I was there when the transhumans first came out…a Chinese family took me and my father in. The transhumans killed them. They didn't kill me…"

She met my gaze and I saw something in her eyes. An echo of old gratitude, a bridge across time, across generations, connecting us both. "You've always been saving our asses. I…I've never felt guiltier."

Before I could say anything—

Clunk.

Thump. Clunk.

The airlock door hissed open.

Three figures. Two Loonies. They were in the heaviest armor the Loonies made, almost as good-looking as our Gisses. They had big shotgun/assault rifle combos, and had scary aces painted on their faceplates, around the cameras. The one in the middle, though, wasn't like them. He wore what looked like wraparound wallpaper.

A face flickered onto the top screen, followed by a whole body below.

Omar Kaufman.

"Hello." The man in front of us held out his hand as Kaufman did the same. "I'm Omar Kaufman, president of the United States of Luna."

I took the hand the same way you'd take a proffered toilet scrubber. After it had been used. But even so, I had to admire his telecomming skills. You could barely see the pauses in his movement due to the light lag.

"I'm Drusilla Zhao, formerly of the Alliance Space Marine Force," I said, trying to match titles with title. "You know you're a real douchebag, right?"

Kaufman didn't even blink. He did have remarkable screen presence, I had to give him that. With this rig, I almost felt like

I was in the same room as him. I figured the suited figure was just a kind of robot, or a *shoǔ ǒu* or something.

"Some would say that, but few in my company. I respect someone with courage and forthrightness." He smiled.

"Good. I'm glad to hear your sycophants are acting properly, you mass-murdering dipshit."

Now he was having to work a little to keep his face smiling and congenial. When he spoke again, his voice was cool. "You do know that all of this footage is being recorded and edited by my memegineers, don't you? No one is going to see your petty defiance, but if you don't mind earning a black mark in my book, go right on ahead."

"Oh? No one is going to see it?" I asked. "Then I can do this." I flipped him off.

Yes, I was being childish. But so what? If I had the chance, I'd do the same to Hitler, Stalin, Mao, Bin Laden, Windrip....

"Restrain her."

One of the Loonies grabbed me and twisted my arm behind my back. I grinned. I had gotten to flip off Omar Kaufman. Almost—*almost*—made the whole trip worth it.

It wasn't worth the death of my friends, though. Or of Friedman, or any of the other Loonies.

They dragged me to Command and Control. There, they floated in the room while Kaufman looked around with his tele-operated drone, laughing softly.

"This is remarkable. The last stand of the Chinese-American Alliance." He put his hands on his hips. "I hear you have one captive?"

Practically on cue, Brown escorted said captive into the room, his hand still in a cast.

"President Kaufman!" He saluted awkwardly. "It is an honor."

"The honor is mine, Private Kirkenguard," Kaufman said, taking the man's uninjured hand. "It is remarkable what you have done here."

"Thank you, sir."

I rolled my eyes.

And suddenly, as if they had been stung by bees, the Loonie soldiers were whipping around and thrusting away. Kaufman's drone cut out, its screens going blank. I blinked. Kirkenguard looked at me, reaching for his pistol. The cameras were off, he...

Diǎo!

I grabbed onto the ceiling to moor myself and kicked. Kirkenguard took a boot to the face and went spinning, his pistol bouncing off the wall and whirling toward my face.

The Loonies were down the corridor and away.

I scrambled for the pistol, grabbed it. Kirkenguard slammed into my side with his head. We went into a tumble and the pistol went spinning away, pinging off the walls and floor. I grunted and punched him in the face. He punched me right back. My nose crunched and blood started to leak everywhere. I grabbed his broken hand with my right. Turns out, my cybernetic fingers could squeeze a lot better than fleshy ones. He screamed, went gray, and almost passed out. So I slammed my knee into his face, then pushed him away.

"*Chǔn zhū* never knows when to quit," I grumbled, grabbing my nose to try to stem the bleeding.

I grabbed the wall and dragged myself along, heart pounding. What had made the Loonies jump like—

Bang.

BANG BANG BANG.

The noises echoed down the corridors, unsuppressed. I clapped my hands to my ears, ducking just in time to avoid one of the Loonies as he went flying back, his arm blown right off. Another corpse sailed past, just as ruined.

Around the corner came a man in Alliance blue, his armor gleaming and unfamiliar. It looked like power armor, but it wasn't quite the same seamless make as the spiffy Mk II units that my buddies and I had had. Bulkier, harder edges. The weapon was different, too—it looked sleek and organic, despite being a slugthrower. And it was unsuppressed; in these metal corridors, that meant a fun time for the ears.

The faceplate flipped up and the man behind it grinned. His eyes were covered by sunglasses, even under the helmet.

"Lieutenant Kip Jordan Xodijin," he said. "Alliance S3TA." He saluted. "We're from Earth."

"F...From Earth?" I asked. S3TA? Earth? I...

"Two-hour burn straight up along a clear orbital path," he said, more soldiers emerging behind him, fanning out to comb the place. He looked around, at the bullet holes, at the caked blood, at the faint muggy stink that was practically visible in the air. "You guys have really been through the meat grinder, eh?"

"Yeah," I said slowly. "We...really have."

"I'm under orders to take any survivors back down. We've got some replacement tech-heads in our ship."

I nodded.

Then I stopped short. "W-wait, what?!"

"Back down to Earth," he said. "Cheaper than getting you to Heaven, and they have better patching tools there. And besides, the bigwigs want you in particular."

"For..."

"For the Congressional Shield, or that's how rumor has it." He had this weird way of saying everything like it was no big deal. "They wanted to pin everything on your chest, but you haven't had enough of a service record for all the other medals, so they settled for that. I mean, if you hadn't kept the idjits up here from shooting off a Sandcaster, our orbital approaches would have been l*uàn qī bā zaō*, and so would the relief supplies and the reinforcements and the munitions."

The words all flowed around my head like nothing at all. The thing stuck in my head wasn't the medal. Wasn't the reinforcements. Wasn't the relief supplies.

Down. To. Earth.

"I...t-thought I was going to...but—" I tried to keep it in. I failed.

I, Drusilla Zhao, the fifth person to win the Congressional Shield in the entire thirty years that the Chinese and United States governments had been amalgamated...screamed. Like a girl.

"Qí miaaaaaaào!"

EPILOG

4/1/2068

De-Orbiting

100,000 kilometers above the surface of the Earth

And falling...

Fire licked at the windows.

The feel of gravity. Real gravity, produced by mass and not by spin, not by acceleration, pressed against my feet.

The feel of my shoes on the floor, pressed there by gravity. The slight twitch of my knees as an orderly stepped up and into the corridor of the ROVer. He wore baggy pants. He wore suspenders. He wore everything that you would never see in space. He smiled at me.

He held out a hand. I took it. He helped me along. Even with all my training and my practice...one gee was still incredible. I had never felt so heavy, so weighed down.

I stepped down onto the platform and into the open air. Tarmac smelled like...like...like nothing I had smelled before. The sky was blue. The sun shone with a softened, buttery light. I looked around, tears streaming down my face. My skin tingled. No suit.

I looked around. There were crowds. Cheering crowds. Flashing cameras. Military staff and politicians, here to welcome the first soldiers down—the first heroes down.

Two men in Alliance uniforms stood beside me and walked me slowly toward the politicians.

A single voice carried from the sidelines.

"Dru! Druuuuu!"

I turned, even as Jillian stepped off the ramp, leaning on a cane.

And there.

She had pale skin and long blonde hair. She had bright blue eyes that twinkled. She had a smile that could have lit up the whole world, that outshone the sun. She waved from her wheelchair, screaming my name.

I ran.

My feet pounded against the ground. My heart screamed.

My legs complained. I could hear the orderlies shouting, the escorts shouting, the press shouting, Jillian shouting.

I couldn't see. I stumbled.

Hands helped me up. Hands cupped my cheeks.

Lips pressed to mine, warm and alive.

So alive.

I drew back.

And Sarah Cayer, my love, my glowing text, my dream, whispered to me around the crackle and flash of a dozen cameras.

"Welcome home."

GLOSSARY

AGI Artificial general intelligence, a self aware computer program.

AI Artificial intelligence, a non-self aware program used in menial or simple tasks.

Alliance, the A Chinese-American global superpower formed circa 2030.

angel A Spacer suffering from a psychological breakdown (derogatory).

anti-matter Matter with the opposite set of quantum properties (such as electric charge) as its normal matter counterpart. Anti-matter and matter annihilate each other when they come in contact, releasing energy equal to the mass of the two particles.

apprentice A teenaged Spacer working with a "master" who teaches them a vocation.

CAPE Corrective action, physical exercise.

climate station Orbital station attempting to curb climate change and global warming.

Crèche A safe, AI-overseen area where Spacer children are raised in a group.

distilleries Large magnetic scoops that collect interstellar hydrogen to use as fuel.

DOTtie Dedicated Orbital Transport, a long distance freighter unsuited for atmospheric use.

EVA Extravehicular activity. Any activity outside of a spacestation or spaceship.

fusion power Energy produced by fusing hydrogen or helium nuclei. Earth's primary fuel source.

GEO Geostationary orbit.

G.I.S.S.S. Government Issue Space Survival Suit (prounounced Giss), an armored attachment for a skinsuit.

Heaven Space's biggest hospital, used when local care fails. Primarily treats mental patients and others requiring long-term treatment.

Helium-3 A kind of helium used for fusion reactors; not found on Earth.

HUD Heads-up display.

IPAC Initial physical aptitude course.

Lag-Net Lagrange Network, a partitioned internet used by Spacers for communication, organization, blogging, and watching videos of cats.

Lagrange point A place where the gravitational pull of two objects "cancels" one another out. Sun/Earth, Moon/Earth are two examples of Lagrange systems. They are listed as L1 to L5.

Maser A device that fires pulses of coherent electromagnetic radiation. Similar to a laser, but distinct in that a maser uses a lower frequency of energy.

MUD Multi-user dungeon, a real-time virtual world game.

nanotechnology Technology on the "nano" scale, i.e., smaller than the eye can see. Primarily used in industry to produce items with minimal ecological impact.

orbit A velocity at which an object circles a source of gravity, but never falls in. The higher an orbit, the faster the velocity.

P3 Phased pulse pistol, a directed energy weapon.

PBPRPG Play-by-post role-playing game.

PCP Physical conditioning platoon.

post-app A spacer who has completed a four-year apprentice-ship and can begin to work in their chosen vocation.

pre-app Pre-apprentice spacers are out of the Crèche and still cycling through various professions. On their eighteenth birthday, pre-apps choose someone to apprentice under for four years.

PPR Phased pulse rifle, a directed energy weapon.

PT Physical training.

ROVer Reusable orbital vehicle. A replacement for the space shuttle, phased out in 2012.

skinsuit A skintight mechanical counterpressure spacesuit, made of smart materials and designed to keep a Spacer safe from the environment without sacrificing mobility.

skinclothes Semi-skintight jumpsuits made of mostly "dumb" materials. Worn casually by non-EVA trained Spacers.

smart material Material made out of "programmable matter," which is able to change its shape, elasticity, opacity, color, and other physical properties.

Singularity, the A theoretical point where technology merges with biology and humanity becomes "posthumanity." See Transhuman.

Slump, the A period of economic and ecological devastation, circa 2019-2030.

Transhuman A human being augmented by biological, nan-otechnological, or cybernetic means. The stage between humanity and "posthumanity."

T-rays Terahertz rays, the same thing used in backscatter security stations at airports.

Wallpaper A quantum-dot projector/projection combo that is able to record everything and project information at the same time.

SPACER LANGUAGE

Among Spacers, Mandarin is the primary language, with English, Cantonese, and some Swahili phrases scattered throughout. We've attempted to represent that blend here with a grammatically inaccurate mix of languages that reflects the Alliance's vernacular. Neither author nor editors take any responsibility if you accidentally tell someone that their hovercraft is full of eels as a result.

ACKNOWLEDGMENTS

Thanks go out to my parents, Paul Colby and Marion Barker, and to my siblings, Brian Colby and Kathleen Lloyd. Thanks, too, to my friends: Scott Ballatore; George Richbourg; Paul Merrill; Elesha Chidley; Jason Cayer, whose name I cheerfully stole; Alex Rasgon; Alex Aldenbrook; and Jay Durant.

Thanks, also, to my editor, Kate Sullivan; and last, but far, far, far from least, my teachers: Greta Vollmer, in whose class on young adult literature I hope to one day star, and Robert Coleman-Senghor, may he rest in peace.

ABOUT DAVID COLBY

A fan of old school sci-fi and tabletop roleplaying games, David Colby started writing almost fifteen years ago. It went poorly. But despite these early setbacks, David continued to work and write and send out submissions until someone was mad enough to accept him. Currently living in Sunnyvale, California, David's day job involves leaping in front of cars for fun and profit (he's a crossing guard).

    Website: ThinkingInkPress.com/LunarCycle
    Blog: http://QuantumSpinPlates.blogspot.com
    Facebook: Facebook.com/David.Colby2
    Twitter: @TheRealZoombie
    Email: DavidColbyAuthor22@gmail.com

Coming Soon
LUNAR CYCLE BOOK 2
SHATTERED SKY

4/2/2068

California, NAU

T-Minus L-Day: 141

Happy endings were supposed to be a hell of a lot easier than this *da chung wu dhan*. I had been on Earth for a whole twenty-four hours, and in all those seconds of all those minutes of all those hours, I had gotten to kiss the love my life a grand total of once.

"This sucks."

Jillian stood next to me, her back leaning against the wall as she looked out at the vast sweep of Edwards Air Force Base. When I looked out at it, it just made me feel queasy and impatient and claustrophobic in a way that I had never felt before. I didn't even need to move my eyes to splash the images all over the wallpaper of my brain: The three or so buildings the size of entire habitation blocks, the kilometer and-then-some of blackened tarmac that sucked up sun like a heatsink and radiated it right through my feet, and, spread through it all, the real reason why I was here and not with Sarah.

The troops. Specifically, the ten thousand or so troops that used Edwards Air Force Base as a way of getting to the next leg of their various deployments. Huge cargo-hauling VTOLs landed and lifted off, while suborbital streakers burned hard to slow down and let off troops wearing uniforms of different cuts. In space, the officer pool had been decidedly shallow, with maybe three lieutenants before General Lau. Down here, I saw every single rank that I had been forced to memorize during Basic: Gunnery Sergeants, Staff Sergeants, Second Lieutenants, First Lieutenants, Colonels, Majors and Captains. They were like picking out sunspots on a grainy picture of Sol, a pleasant relief from the endless stream of PFCs and Corporals.

Most of them were kitted out differently from Spacer soldiers, too. No laser weaponry, no bounce in their steps, no breathers and enclosed helmets. They had slugthrowers on their backs and they trudged along, looking...

Actually, most of them didn't look that unhappy. For most of them, this was a life they had chosen. A comfortable life with good pay, free medical coverage, honor and prestige. A life that I could have...something that fascinated and repelled me at the same time.

I wished they were unhappy. It'd be easier. It'd make more sense, if I could share that misery. Instead of being—.

"So, Corp," Jillian said, deorbiting my thoughts.

"Jillian, we're out of the marines now," I said, rubbing my face with my hands.

"So, Dru," Jillian started again. "What are you going to do once we get out of this?"

"Buy a farm." I stood, putting one hand against the wall of the building we had been told to wait beside, to help lever myself up. The gravity down here was intense. I had never thought that one G would be so...so much more than the gravity on the Hub. It wasn't even that I hadn't been exposed to one G before – it was more that it was all the time, everywhere. Standing didn't feel worth it, but I felt too confined by sitting, too passive. I started to pace back and forth, my body wanting to bounce, but gravity glued me to the ground. "I told Sarah I'd be in Quebec Arcology as soon as I could get there. At this rate..."

Jillian shuffled to the left. I shuffled into the space she had vacated. The Spacer marine, one of the survivors of the Battle of the Forge, behind me shuffled over to take up the spot that I had held. And so, the line continued to process, and so I got closer and closer to getting out of this endless waiting.

But I still felt trapped, stuck in adhesive, forced to do nothing but endure. Endure the sounds—the babbling conversations that overlapped and drowned each other out. Endure the smells—the thick, cloying stench of the sun beating down on the shuttle landing surface, the scent of the scrubland that surrounded the base, the smell of jets and jet fuel. And endure the heat. The pounding, unstoppable heat, pouring through my skinclothes and broiling me in my own juices. I had never imagined that an uncontrolled environment could be so horrifyingly unpleasant.

"I miss air conditioners," Jillian muttered.

"I miss Sarah."

"I miss air conditioners and I miss Sarah. She was cute. You never said she was that cute." Jillian chuckled.

"I didn't?" I asked, rubbing my eyes. I tried to ignore the aching feeling that started to suffuse my head, starting right behind my nose and working its way down my jaws.

The line shuffled forward again. My heart skipped a beat. Did it just start to go just a bit faster? The line, that is, not my heart. I knew that was going faster: The idea of getting out of this heat and into Sarah was just about the only reason why I hadn't started wishing that I was in space again.

"What are you planning to do?" I asked, looking at Jillian.

"That's hard. I don't have any desire to waste my life poking at the ground with a sharp stick—"

"You have no idea what farming actually involves, do you?"

Jillian didn't stop, speaking over my interruption with a grin, "—but I also don't have any friends or family down here. I'm technically old enough to vote and smoke. Not drink, mind you. But I can still take my backpay, rent an apartment..." She trailed off, shaking her head.

"Why not come with me?" I asked. "I mean, you...you probably can't stay with the Cayers, but if there's no apartment free somewhere in the Republic of Quebec, I'll speak nothing but English there. We can hang out, you can help farm, maybe I can set you up with a fair haired, blond farm boy. Mostly to get them off Sarah's back..."

Jillian snorted. "Earther farm boys, Earther farm boys. That means I'll want to do a *Mkundu ng'ombe msichana* and they'll run away screaming to their moms."

"Think of it as an educational process."

Jillian stroked her chin as we shuffled forward again.

After what felt like five eternities (and I knew something about eternity, having ridden a fully packed ROVer from the L1 point to GEO), Jillian got sucked into the front doors that the whole line was riding through. She was the first person I'd actually, physically seen go in, thanks to the curvature of the line and the building blocking the view. Now that I was closer, though, I saw that a second line was heading into the same place, a far longer line of Earther soldiers going in for their processing. I had to wait for four Earthers to cycle in before I got to head in—hoping that Jillian would be waiting nearby after I got out, or else I'd never find her again.

After losing Liam, Chuck, Jason, David...after losing all of them, the idea of losing Jillian, even if only for a second, made me want to hyperventilate.

The office that I stepped into was exotic enough that it gave me pause. Normally, stepping into an office was like stepping into private quarters. In space, offices were virtual, with all the paperwork handled by computers, the information thrown up by wallpaper and contained within handheld tablets. On the ground...well, on the ground, it felt a bit like getting smacked in the face by excess. Everything in the office—the books, the paper in the books, the ink on the paper, the shelves holding the books, the computer, the heavy metal desk, the clock, the ornamental piece of printed artwork depicting an old USA marine corps logo in three dimensions—none of it was measured in fuel and credits and effort to get it out of a stubborn gravity well. It took me a few seconds to jerk my point of view around, to reorient myself with a mental burst from my imagination.

The furniture wasn't the wasteful bulk of a wealthy showoff. No, the metal framework of the desk had the blunt functionality of a mass produced, tough, reusable military surplus product. The bookshelves were crammed with books because, down here, netwar attacks weren't regulated and tightly controlled. Down here, a single worm downloaded from the blacknet could wipe any file that wasn't printed out on paper...so they printed everything out on paper. But what struck me as the most out of place thing in the office was the bureaucrat himself.

He was Latino—an ethnicity I'd only seen on vids till now—and he was a bit portly. The implications clicked home as I saluted and he saluted back.

Dietary restrictions weren't enforced down here. Gym wasn't state mandated.

"Please, Sergeant Zhao, have a seat."

I sat down.

"Sorry about the delays. It's a madhouse down here." He smiled thinly at me. He looked at a small laptop set on the desk, his other hand writing quick notes in short hand, a pen scraping against paper. I tried to not stare, but...but it was so damn *old* looking.

"First things first..." He paused. "I'm required to inform you that you are no longer of the rank Star Sergeant. The spaceborne forces, now that we can integrate them with the official Alliance military, will be folded into the standard military organizational system. Due to your age and lack of battlefield experience, and the abundance of qualified NCOs, you will be made a Corporal again without any negative repercussions on your record." He tapped a few buttons on the laptop. "This won't change your backpay, but when you are recycled back into the service after—"

"Excuse me, sir, but..." I coughed. "What was that?"

He looked at me. "When your leave is over, Corporal Zhao."

I blinked. I blinked again. A ringing filled my ears. "I—I..." I put my hands over my face, breathed in, then breathed out. Losing a pay grade? Didn't even register as an issue. Hell, after what happened on the Forge, I wasn't sure I deserved anything above Private. But...

I slid my hands off my face and asked the man. "Sir, respectfully, how would I go about, uh, mustering out? Retiring? I've served my term, I thought—"

He held up his hand, silencing me. I shut up, clenching my jaw—hard enough to make my teeth ache. It was what I needed to keep myself from sobbing in his office. Or beating the guy to death with a chair as he explained it.

It.

It being the thing that I would hate more than anything save Omar Kaufman.

It being...the Emergency Acts of 2022.

"The Emergency Acts of 2022, implemented by the USA and adopted by the Alliance, state that, in a time of emergency—civil insurrection, global unrest, catastrophic climate change or impending extinction events—the Chinese American Alliance is within its right to conscript anyone deemed of acceptable age, mental and physical health. While the state of emergency lasts, the state of conscription persists and the citizens conscripted under said act are compelled by law to perform their state mandated service." He tapped his fingers on the desk. "Or, to put it in English, you're lucky to be getting leave at all, Corporal."

I sank into my chair and listened numbly as he started to move onto the rest of the checking-out process. He asked me my name, parents, date of birth—"just checking our records"—serial number, rank—"procedure, have to follow procedure"—and then moved onto a question that actually required a bit of thought.

"Do you have a legal guardian that you will be remanded to for the duration of your leave?" he asked. "Or would you prefer to be put in the custody of one of the Alliance's state orphanages?"

Sarah and I had discussed me going to her mother's place after I finished checking out. As a guest. It hadn't occurred to me that I'd need to visit there as a legal ward...after all, I had killed people for the state. You'd think that would mean you count as an adult. Legally. Right? Nope. Apparently, when the Emergency Acts gave the senate and the President powers to decide who was "of age" to be thrown into a uniform, it didn't give them the power to decide that those people were adults. Or...

Or, to think more like Jillian, it totally did give them that power and they just preferred their teenage soldiers to be defanged completely while in civilian life.

The bureaucrat kept looking at me, waiting for an answer.

"Mary Cayer." I said, feeling a weird, sinking feeling. The kind of feeling that comes when you take a leap and you're not sure if you are going to reach what you've pushed towards or be left flailing in the middle of the corridor to the sound of your friends mocking you.

"Mary Cayer..." he said, frowning.

I gave the extra details that Sarah had told me over the years and during our conversation yesterday.

"Ah, she applied to be your legal guardian last night," he said, checking his desktop computer for confirmation. "Very well, you are logged as being a ward of Mary and George Cayer. Your backpay, all rated at E-5, not E-4, will be forwarded to a private account for your own use. Report to the Quebec International Airport for recall on the first of next month." He stood up, holding his hand out to me. I stood as well, taking the hand by reflex. He shook.

"Enjoy your leave."

He let me go and gestured me to the door. I opened it and found myself in the main building of the base, a huge chamber that held even more troopers, most of them waiting for their chance to board a VTOL. They were sitting in a few dozen rows, lined up along the floor and snaking around terminals for VTOL loading, their gear by their feet and their uniforms creating a sea of conformity. I didn't see Jillian.

I walked towards the exit, which was large and obvious, and walked outside. An auto-bus terminal sat next to the highway that ran along the base. Huge buses, the same kind that had been pioneered in China before the Slump, big enough that smaller cars could drive underneath their rectangular bodies, picked up troops and drove off to who knows where. The auto-bus terminal also had what looked like half a dozen charging stations for mobile electronics. I had turned in my PPR and my

G.I.S.S.S. in orbit, so all I had on down here was my skinclothes. That still included a phone built into the sleeve, but I didn't dial for Sarah just yet.

I just stood there.

My emotions felt as if they had done a hundred-and-eighty-degree turns one too many times. Jealousy at the other soldiers and their belonging. Their happiness at being part of something larger. That...that moment when I had felt like I had been a part of that too.

Fear. The intense, clinging, stinking fear that comes when you know you are not immortal.

Pain. Separation.

Elation at being welcomed back in.

Horror at being dragged, screaming, back in.

"Dru!"

I spun around and saw Jillian stepping out of the exit. Her eyes were streaked with red, her cheeks glimmering and wet. That was almost as shocking as being told I was still drafted, seeing hardass Jillian crying. She stepped closer and in the moments between a blink, she managed to completely wipe her face off with her hands and looked like she had never sniffled in her whole life.

"Hey, you walked right past me," she said, putting her hand on my shoulder, practically shoving me towards the auto-bus terminal. "So, I've radically altered my whole life course in a few seconds. Got a bit of temporal whiplash."

"Yeah. That...whiplash...a bitch..." I said, vaguely, rubbing my neck, as if the joke had become real.

Jillian bit her lip, then forced a grin. "How about instead of spending that backpay on apartments or jobs—"

"Can't get either..." I mumbled.

"We blow it on thirty days in Neo-Vegas? Thirty days of binge drinking, gambling, whores—"

"Can't do any of that…"

Jillian stepped around and looked me in the eyes. "Dru. Come on. Focus here."

I looked into her eyes, shaking my head. "I need to call Sarah."

Jillian closed her eyes. "Dru, you're going to kill her."

I stepped past her, ignoring her as I tapped my wrist. The cloth of my skinclothes shimmered, quantum dot projectors flicking on and showing the holographic display and interface for the phone service. I started to tap in area codes. Jillian grabbed my wrist, the hologram fuzzing around her fingers like ghosts.

"Dru," she said. "Dru, if you go to Sarah, you're going to spend thirty days with her, then go back into the meat grinder. Surviving it once was a miracle. Surviving it twice, with a definite one hundred percent chance of going into space again, is going to take the intervention of pretty much every single deity we both do and do not worship. Thirty days with that hanging over your head…" She trailed off.

I looked at Jillian, frowning. "It's worth it," I said, my voice holding the steel that got me through the hell of Basic. Squash the feelings, all of them, and find the one you want. Use it. Use that steel. "Besides, it isn't going to be thirty days of moping. It is going to be thirty days of you and Sarah and me working to find a way out of this."

Jillian laughed, her fingers releasing my wrist.

I sighed quietly and finished tapping out Sarah's number. "We've broken regs before. We'll find a way out of this. We will survive. We will spend our money responsibly—"

"Damn!" Jillian snapped her fingers.

"—and we will figure this out." I tapped the last number and my collars buzzed with a ringtone. A few short seconds later, Sarah picked up and I tapped the speaker on so that Jillian could listen in.

"Hey, Sarah," I said, feeling a strange mixture of confidence and terror. Like I was going into combat again. "Are you still in San Jose? Because...my friend and I need a ride." I grinned. "And we have some sneakiness to get up to."

"Ooh, sneakiness. That's my third favorite kind of ness." Sarah said. "Can you take an auto-bus to the city? Mom doesn't want to risk the highway again."

"Sure." I said, nodding. "See you soon, Sarah-Bear."

"See you soon, Snoogums."

I tapped the phone off.

Jillian mimed vomiting.

www.ingramcontent.com/pod-product-compliance
Lightning Source LLC
Chambersburg PA
CBHW032120180726
48284CB00002B/632